TWELVE MILE BANK

a novel by
nicholas harvey

Printed in the United States of America

First Printing, 2017
First Revision 2019

ISBN-13: 978-0-692-99046-9

Mermaid illustration by Tracie Cotta
Cover photography and design by author

This is a work of fiction. Names, characters, businesses, places, events and incidents are either the products of the author's imagination or used in a fictitious manner unless noted otherwise. Any resemblance to actual persons, living or dead, or actual events is purely coincidental. Except Jen and her Greenhouse Restaurant, you can't make up Jen.
The Twelve Mile Bank exists as described but the two pinnacles are fictional. The dive sites and wrecks described around Cayman, except the U-1026, all exist and are as fantastic as described. The German submarine designated U-1026 was planned but never constructed.

For Cheryl, my mermaid.

Chapter 1
Caribbean Sea, 1945

The night was dimly lit by the sliver of a moon low in the sky, barely visible in the gathering cloud. The day had started with calm seas but the wind had picked up from the south throwing up a swell that was worsening as the evening wore on. The U-boat rocked and rolled as a young submariner, Andreas Jaeger, stepped from the deck of the sail boat tied alongside the steel decking of the Type VIIC/41 submarine. He glanced back and caught a final nod from his Captain.

The deck of the sailboat was packed with forty one sailors, the majority of the full complement of forty five men they'd left Wilhelmshaven with several months ago. Off the east coast of America they'd lost one man overboard in heavy seas. To each of them it seemed that was a lifetime ago. Forty one tired, dirty, hungry men watched Andreas struggle across the decking in the growing winds and rising swell. Sweat glistened from the brow of each man in the muggy warm air of the Caribbean, a far cry from the chill of the early spring days they'd left behind in northern Europe.

The Captain loudly barked an order in German to be heard over the wind and several men untied the lines holding the sailboat to the submarine. The seas quickly pulled the smaller boat away. The sailing vessel was a seventy foot Kauri yacht, a beautiful pleasure craft owned by a French national of German descent who lived on Grand Cayman, the island a dozen or so miles to the east of where they currently floated.

Andreas climbed the conning tower and with a last survey of the seas and a glance at the sailboat hardly visible now a hundred yards away, he lowered himself down the narrow ladder into the U-boat and closed the hatch above him, dogging it tight.

U-1026 was built in 1943 in the dockyards of Blohm & Voss in Hamburg. She was finally commissioned and launched in early 1944, 12 months ago, and this was only her third patrol of the war. A war that was rapidly drawing to a close. The coded messages from command naturally gave no indication of this but every other radio broadcast they picked up from France, America, and now through the Caribbean told a different story. They all knew defeat for the Reich was only a matter of time.

Andreas dropped into the control room where the remaining two members of the crew were waiting. Lars and Wilhelm looked pensive and anxious but clearly relieved to see Andreas and finally proceed with the task at hand.

"Okay, here we go" Andreas tried to sound confident. "Is the boat sealed?"

"Yes, we have a seal" Lars replied, scanning a panel of lights.

"Good. To the engine room Lars and be ready". Lars nodded and hurried aft to the electric motor room.

Andreas stepped out of the control room to the tiny radio room and put on a headset and pinged the sonar. "Thirty one metres… good, we're still over it, start blowing the ballast tanks Willy, slowly now, slowly," he ordered, returning to the control room.

Wilhelm wiped the sweat from his face and started cranking the ballast tank handles, moving along them systematically to lower the boat evenly. The U-boat was still rocking in the surface waves but became more stable the further she sank towards the bottom. The caged bulbs of the interior lights cast odd shaped shadows around the control room, silhouetting the myriad of pipes, handles and wheels that littered the cramped walls and ceiling. Often the alternative red lights were used to keep the men's eyes adapted to the dark night sky, ready to focus through the periscope or dash up the narrow ladder to the observation deck upon surfacing. Seconds could make the difference between spotting an enemy ship waiting to pounce or being seen first and blown to pieces before they could submerge to safety. But no one was spotting them tonight.

U-1026 was taking a one way trip down.

Chapter 2
Grand Cayman, 2017

A thirty foot RIB boat speeds across the azure blue waters off Grand Cayman's Seven Mile Beach. It's another glorious day in the Caribbean and the young woman at the helm deftly cruises the boat up to a buoy bobbing in the ocean. With the efficiency of two people having performed the task repeatedly, AJ positions the boat perfectly. Her deck hand Thomas hooks the tie line floating below the surface with a gaff and ties it off on a cleat on the front of the boat. The sign on the side of the centre console reads 'Mermaid Divers'.

The rigid-inflatable boat was the kind used by the Seal teams and SAS soldiers. Designed for the toughest marine environments, the hard hulled craft had the upper constructed of flexible, inflatable tubes. Lightweight, incredibly buoyant and known for speed and maneuverability in rough seas they are the choice for rescue as well as military applications. Driven by twin Yamaha two hundred and fifty horsepower four stroke outboards, the vessel had more power than they could ever need in the coastal waters.

The RIB boats were not cheap and wouldn't normally be affordable or the first choice for a dive operation. It was purely by chance when AJ was looking to buy her boat this one came up at auction. A formerly wealthy young stock investor was indicted in America for insider trading and all his assets were seized, including a condo on Seven Mile Beach, a Mercedes and the RIB boat in the marina. She snapped it up at one third of its value, added benches and tank holders along the sides and now had the fastest dive boat on the island.

Annabelle Jayne Bailey stood five feet and four inches tall... if she stretched, tippy toed and lifted her chin up a little too high. A tomboy in her youth she was a dynamic centre forward for her school football team and cared a lot more about her sports than her studies. She made decent grades but not the straight A stuff her barrister mother and CEO father were hoping for.

AJ's life completely changed on a rare family holiday to the Cayman Islands when she was sixteen. Her father Bob hired Pearl Divers to take the three of them SCUBA diving and it was game over for AJ, she was hooked. She fell instantly in love with the freedom of gliding through the open water and the ability to soar in three dimensions. It felt like another world, completely detached from the clumsy two dimensional land topside. The colours, the abundant life, the majestic swaying of the fans and soft corals, it all mesmerized her and she couldn't get enough of it.

She negotiated a deal with her father that if she got A's in her O-Levels he'd pay for her SCUBA certification. She just scraped through with some A-minuses in the mix but he'd agreed on A's and stuck to his end of the deal. The south coast of England was a far cry from the crystal clear, balmy waters of Grand Cayman but AJ didn't care. Cocooned in layers of neoprene and anchored down with a steel tank and heavy weights to counteract the buoyancy of the thick wetsuit, she lumbered around on shore but felt the same abundant freedom once submerged.

Great visibility off the Sussex coast was fifteen feet on a perfect, calm day, yet she was fearless. She soon passed her Open Water Certification and was taking trips with the local dive shop to more interesting locations along the coast and over to the Isle Of Wight. She was fascinated by the wrecks which littered the coast line, especially the ships and submarines that were victims of the Second World War.

She laboured through the two years of A-Levels to keep her parents appeased and continuing to fund her diving exploits, but she couldn't find any enthusiasm for university and avoided her mum and dad's pressing over her continued education. She visited a few universities and sent letters to a few more but it was really for show as she had no intention of going to any of them. She had the full court press going on her diving education, racking up dives at every opportunity and was halfway through her instructor training when her father finally sat her down and insisted she share her future intentions with him.

AJ had a strong streak of rebelliousness in her but it was always dampened by her underlying love for her parents. She couldn't lie to him and came clean that she had no intention of heading into further schooling and furthermore planned to grab an overseas divemaster gig as soon as she was done with her A-Level exams. Robert Bailey was not as shocked as she thought he'd be. He shook his head but couldn't hide a slight grin. He commanded respect and got his way in the toughest corporate board room but his daughter melted the man and he adored her free spirit and sense of adventure. Her mother was not so easy.

Beryl Bailey didn't take shit from anyone. As a barrister she handled mainly high profile corporate cases, making her living in a predominantly male dominated world of cut throat business. She dressed confidently, she walked confidently and she asserted herself confidently. Beryl liked to hear the facts, discuss both sides in a concise manner and then make a decision, all wrapped up in a neat bundle, handled, put to bed. She wasn't a cold woman, she was a loving and caring mother and she and Bob, after some rough years early on in their marriage, had found an even balance between their take charge personalities. She liked to have a plan and she liked everyone to stick to that plan. AJ was definitely not sticking to the plan.

Six customers on the boat began bustling about preparing their dive gear, eager to splash in and enjoy the warm waters. Thomas, a light brown skinned local with a heavy Caymanian lilt to his English, which to the unfamiliar sounded Jamaican, busied himself helping the customers into their dive gear, checking air tanks were turned on and masks were defogged. AJ dropped the ladder over the back between the outboards and pulled her lightweight wetsuit up, wriggling into the snug, flexible neoprene. The divers would back roll over the sides for entry but use the ladder to return to the boat.

"Welcome to Neptune's Wall everyone, this will be our first dive this morning". For a petite girl she had a firm, assertive voice, a trait she inherited from her mother, and everyone had eyes on her while she gave her briefing.

"This is a sloping reef down to around a hundred feet and then it drops off sheer down to almost a thousand, a little deeper than PADI likes us to go! We'll stay around that hundred foot mark please".

The crowd chuckled nervously, enjoying a touch of humour. Most recreational divers visiting the Caymans dive only a few times a year so it's always a little nerve wracking leaping off a boat and dropping down the equivalent of a ten story building, especially when a mistake can take you into the abyss. AJ was skilled at making people feel at ease and coaching them through each step, one of the reasons her client base was predominantly return customers.

AJ wore her blonde hair short, cropped at her neck with flashes of brilliant purple highlights. She had several piercings in each ear. Her muscles were toned from working the boat all day, schlepping dive tanks around at thirty five pounds apiece, and her skin was a very un-English tanned brown. But her most striking features were her half sleeve tattoos on both upper arms. Her left depicted a vibrant reef with brightly coloured fish and her right a more sinister scene of a ship wreck with sharks and a vintage style deep sea diver in copper helmet and bulky dive suit.

Her mother was horrified when she saw the tattoos, her father sighed and hugged his little girl. She was twenty two, living in Florida at the time, and he rarely saw her so why be mad when he did? Beryl finally came around to some level of acceptance, AJ promising she was fully decorated with no intention of getting more. Her mother cornered her one day and in an uncharacteristically bumbling style asked if Annabelle was interested in other women. AJ laughed and swore she was not a lesbian. The idea actually appealed to her that people might be unsure, she felt it gave her an edge somehow, knocked some people off balance a bit. For a girl that grew up thin on self-assuredness it felt good to sense she may have the upper hand sometimes.

"Bottom time around twenty five minutes and I'll have you back to the boat. Everyone's on computers so if you've got air remaining you're welcome to cruise a little longer just please keep the mooring in sight and back on the boat with no less than thirty five bar, that's five hundred psi. Top of the reef here is around sixty to seventy feet so watch your no deco time carefully and make sure you get a full three minute safety stop in. Any questions?"

She scanned the group and with no takers she continued. "Great, keep your eyes peeled for turtles, eels and smalls on the reef. This is a good spot for sharks and rays as well out over the drop off so scan the open blue water from time to time. Pool's open, let's dive!"

With that she stepped aside so Thomas could start helping the customers finish gearing up and back roll over the side of the RIB boat into the ocean. AJ quickly slid her gear on and was in the water and descending before all her customers were in.

It was a chamber of commerce day above and below the water, blue skies, eighty six degrees, light breeze and flat calm up top and crystal clear, no current below. AJ loved her job.

She descended down to the top of the reef around sixty five feet and her group gathered near her where the mooring line was fixed. The sunshine easily penetrated the crystal clear waters and saturated the colourful reef in radiant light. Vibrant blue, green, purple and orange corals painted a perfect backdrop for the myriads of fish busying themselves around the reef.

AJ had always been impressed how the Caymanian government strictly regulated the diving industry in the islands waters and created a mooring system for the boats to tie off to. By drilling and bolting to rock or dead parts of the reef the mooring lines were well anchored and ran to the surface with a buoy to mark the spot. Using a tie line, about thirty feet long that came off the buoy, the boat captains had a secure tether. Rotating the buoys regularly gave each reef some peace and quiet undisturbed by divers, enhancing healthy growth. Anchoring a boat directly on any of the reefs was strictly forbidden. As a protected marine park, the waters surrounding the islands had 'no touch, no take' rules, further promoting the perfect natural environment for the reefs to continue to flourish.

AJ, along with most professionals in the diving industry, did all they could to help coral preservation. With the oceans progressively warming, along with pollution and over fishing, a fifth of the world's reefs have already been lost. Coral grows at less than an inch a year in the best conditions and branchy corals at a maximum of three to four inches a year, so a diver can inadvertently cause decades of damage. A boat scraping the reef or dragging an anchor can set it back hundreds, even thousands of years of growth.

Once she'd got an okay sign from each of her group, AJ gently finned towards the wall where the reef sloped easily down to a sheer drop into the pitch black abyss. It was an unnerving sight at how vast the ocean suddenly seemed and how small and insignificant each human felt.

AJ unhooked a stainless steel carabiner she carried clipped to her buoyancy compensator, or BCD as they're known, and softly tapped it against her air tank. Pointing ahead and down a little deeper she got the group's attention to see a Hawksbill turtle taking bites from an orange sponge. The divers moved in closer and several pulled out cameras and filmed the young turtle having his breakfast.

AJ levelled off at the hundred foot mark and started along the edge of the reef with the drop off on her right. The group peeled away from the turtle, who didn't seem to care that he had an audience, and fell in line behind her. Further along she tapped again and pointed off into the deep blue of the open water and made a hand signal like pulling the trigger of a gun. A small school of silvery Ocean Triggers were sweeping in for a look at the edge of the reef, their larger top and bottom fins giving them a distinctly ethereal appearance.

As the Triggers turned in a long arc back out to open water a movement was sensed more than seen from deeper below. It caught AJ's attention and she stayed absolutely still and let her eyes adjust to the darker water below. There it was again, a slight movement of something larger but barely detectable. She held up both hands to signal everyone to hold still. Her divers tried to follow her line of sight, puzzled as to what to expect.

With an almost lethargic sway a shadow emerged from the depths. It appeared to move effortlessly, the casual ease of a creature lulling the world into a sense that it couldn't be bothered to mess with you. The Hammerhead shark was about seven feet long. Because light refracts through water at a greater angle than through air, everything underwater appears bigger. To AJ's group this appeared to be a ten foot monster.

All but two of the group froze motionless, mesmerized by the prehistoric looking creature casually swimming towards them. The teenage son of an investment banker from Milwaukee flailed around trying to get his GoPro camera fired up and pointed in the right direction. In his haste he fumbled it and watched it drop down the wall, past the approaching Hammerhead which ignored it completely, continuing into the depths. Unseen, somewhere around two hundred and fifty feet the plastic housing imploded as the water pressure became too much for it to stand.

A middle aged woman from San Diego was fighting the urge to bolt, she edged backwards up the reef away from the shark that appeared, in her mind, to be heading straight for her. Her husband was so transfixed and excited by the Hammerhead he was completely unaware that his wife was terrified and about to make the potentially fatal mistake of shooting to the surface.

AJ scanned the group. As rare and exciting as it was to see a Hammerhead, especially on the west side, she knew there might be trouble. Not from the shark. He was unconcerned by the divers, to him they were noisy, clumsy things covered in inedible materials. Beyond mild curiosity he wanted no part of them.

She spotted the woman backing away, the look of terror

in her eyes and the rapid streams of bubbles from her regulator as she gasped for breath. AJ smoothly kicked towards her and covered the ground between them rapidly. She gently took the woman's arm and pulled her attention away from the shark just as the Hammerhead glided by and turned back out to sea. The woman immediately calmed and her breathing settled down. Her husband, who was also her dive buddy in the rules of recreational SCUBA diving, finally looked around and was surprised to see her thirty feet above him.

The group were all excited and signaling to each other, babbling in diver's sign language. AJ rapped her carabiner on her tank to get their attention and then tapped two fingers on her wrist mounted dive computer, the signal asking them their air pressure levels. Two of them gave her the okay sign, meaning they still had more than half their tank remaining. The rest, including the lady she'd helped, signaled they were under fifteen hundred psi which was the divemaster's cue for turning back towards the boat at a shallower depth.

AJ chuckled a little. One shark sighting and the group sucked down about ten minutes worth of air in thirty seconds. That was normal. You don't get used to being around carnivorous sharks by sitting at a desk in a downtown high-rise.

Back on the boat the group stowed their gear back in the custom racks along each side and once everyone was set Thomas untied from the buoy and AJ eased the RIB boat away. She headed closer in to the shoreline where they'd do their second dive on a shallower reef after a surface interval.

They motored for a few minutes before Thomas tied the boat off to the next dive site buoy and the group relaxed and chatted excitedly about their shark encounter. AJ and Thomas worked their way around the boat and switched the customers gear over to a fresh tank, chatting with them as they went

The GoPro kid stopped AJ and asked, "How long do we have to stay out of the water AJ?"

She sat down next to him and glanced at her dive computer, "An hour should be enough, we've already been up about twenty minutes."

"Why is it we have to stay up so long? I know you taught us this in the class stuff but I don't remember, it's kinda confusing."

AJ smiled and patiently explained. "Yeah, it's a bunch of physiological stuff. The key thing to remember is the deeper you dive the more pressure you're surrounded by so your regulator delivers more compressed air to compensate, allowing you to still breathe easily. Air, as you know, is a mixture of oxygen that we need, and nitrogen that we don't. Your body has to deal with all that extra nitrogen it's not used to getting, which it does by dissolving it into your tissues and dissipating it. When we come up we have to let our bodies get rid of that excess nitrogen before we can dive again."

"What if we just stay down there, what happens?"

"If we get overloaded with nitrogen it makes us sick and if we come up too fast the nitrogen can expand to form bubbles in our bloodstream and tissues and we get the 'bends'. That's really bad. Your computer gives you all this information. Keep watching your 'no deco' time which is how long you have until you've got too much nitrogen in your system, and never ascend too quickly. Remember the rule?"

The kid was excited to remember something from his certification class, "Never go up faster than the bubbles from your regulator!"

"You got it."

He was on a roll now, "And if we go too deep we go crazy right?"

She laughed, "You get nitrogen narcosis which sends

you a bit crazy yes! Some people get really happy, some get really wigged out but either way you start making bad mistakes and losing your ability to make good decisions."

"How deep before you go crazy?"

"Varies, depends on a lot of things but the rule is don't go below a hundred and thirty. In Cayman we try and stay above a hundred feet to be safe."

They spent the hour or so topside 'off gassing', basking in the Cayman sunshine. Thomas kept the group in fits of laughter with his island tales while they snacked on fruit AJ passed around.

Chapter 3
Caribbean Sea, 1945

On the surface where it could draw in fresh air and exhaust the fumes, the submarine ran on a pair of diesel engines. Outside, the noise of the motors was dampened by the surrounding water, but inside the steel pressure hull the racket was deafening. Below the surface it ran on electric motors powered by a huge array of batteries and the boat was silent except for the creaking and droning of the metal resisting the ever increasing water pressure as they descended.

Andreas called out the depth every five metres. When the gauge read twenty five he turned to Wilhelm.

"Willy, easy now, level off at thirty".

Wilhelm frantically spun the series of handles controlling the ballast tanks to slow the boat's descent. The two men nervously glanced at each other. The hull quietly creaked and groaned. Andreas checked the depth gauge again which read twenty nine. Wilhelm spun the handles some more.

"Steady, steady, thirty metres…" Andreas read off. The boat continued to slowly drop further away from the surface, further away from fresh air, further away from their shipmates.

"Thirty one metres." Andreas braced himself, holding onto the bulkhead in the control room but still they continued down silently. "Thirty two metres… scheisse… be ready Willy, if we've missed somehow we'll have to come back up to twenty metres and circle until we find it".

Wilhelm wiped his sweaty face, the air in the boat was

hot and humid, he glanced at Andreas. "We couldn't be that far off, could we? It's five and half kilometres long and more than a kilometre wide, surely we haven't drifted that far?"

Andreas shook his head. "Thirty four metres".

The U-boat suddenly jarred and a loud grating sound shuddered through the hull, both men staggered a little before regaining their balance. He grinned at Wilhelm and waited silently to see if the submarine had settled securely. The big boat creaked and crunched a few more times, slowly listing to starboard and bow down by a few degrees. Finally it became completely silent and the two men relaxed. Andreas pressed the intercom. "Lars, shut the motors down and hurry back to the control room, lock each bulkhead on your way".

He waited for a confirmation from Lars then headed forward and began closing each bulkhead from the torpedo room back to the control room, securing the front of the sub.

Lars shut down the controls for the electric motors on the switchboard. He looked around him, doing a mental check that all was correct before he left. Satisfied, he stepped through the first bulkhead and dogged the hatch behind him by spinning the latch wheel until tight.

He was now in the engine room with the two big supercharged diesel engines on either side of the gangway. Packed down one side were wooden crates stacked three high leaving only a narrow walkway through the already cramped compartment. Each wooden box had a German swastika painted on the side and top. Lars paused a beat, giving the boxes a last look before proceeding through the next bulkhead and locking it behind him.

The three sailors reunited in the middle of the boat after taking extra care tightening the bulkhead doors either side of the control room. These two bulkheads were the only internal ones truly designed to withstand the water pressure at anything below about twenty feet. As they now rested at thirty four metres, which is one hundred and eleven feet and change, they were relying on these two to keep the rest of the submarine dry.

Andreas pulled what looked like three light brown life vests from a cabinet and handed them out. The three men had only used these emergency escape Draeger rebreathers in training back at the deep pool in Gotenhafen. They all looked at them nervously, it was one thing trying them out in a training pool, quite another now their lives depended on them.

The device worked by the sailor breathing through a hose from a 'lung' that was supplemented from a small oxygen cylinder attached to the vest. Their exhaled gas passed through a primitive carbon scrubber that removed some of the carbon dioxide. The amount of oxygen topping off the system was controlled by turning a knob once the air tasted stale. The Draeger was basic but quite effective for a short time, however, it did not last long at depth before the small oxygen cylinder depleted.

They donned the vests and climbed the ladder into the conning tower. No part of a submarine could be described as roomy but the conning tower was an especially confined space. Designed to hold two people maximum during a submerged attack, the three were wedged in and closing the hatch to the control room proved quite a task.

"Ready?" Andreas tentatively asked the other two, to which they both nodded reluctantly. "Remember, breathe easy and don't panic, we have to be completely flooded before we can open the hatch".

Again they nodded without a word.

"Raft?" Andreas asked, looking at Wilhelm who fumbled behind his back retrieving a deflated canvas and rubber raft. Andreas nodded to his shipmate and cautioned,

"Don't drop that Willy, we may be floating for a while before they pick us up and that storm was getting closer".

Wilhelm tightened his grip on the dinghy.

Andreas reached up to the hatch in the roof of the conning tower and with much effort started turning the hatch wheel. After a half turn of the wheel water hissed through the tiny gap at an alarming pressure, shredding the grey paint from anything it hit. The water began filling the base of the tower and covering their shoes almost immediately. As the pressure in the tiny room sky rocketed their ears dulled and they felt a spiking pain in their foreheads. They pinched their noses and blew pressure back through their sinuses to try and equalize but it felt like they couldn't keep up and their heads throbbed. The noise was deafening. Water jetting in and ricocheting off the walls of the tower mixed with air being compressed and trying to escape through the same tiny gap in the hatch made for a terrifying clash of sounds.

The tepid water was rising up past their waists and they fought with everything they had not to panic, none of them wanting the shame of breaking in front of their shipmates. As the water level came up to their chests they all put the breathing hoses in their mouths and at once felt the restriction of breathing through the contraption. And then the only light in the tower exploded and everything went black.

Somebody grabbed Andreas' arm and clamped him so tight he thought they'd break it. Something slapped Lars in the face and he jumped just as the water reached his face and he instinctively stretched up on his toes to get his nose and mouth clear, gasping at the hose to deliver more air. He pushed back at whatever had hit him and felt the palm of his hand shoving another man's face and knocking his hose away. Andreas scrambled to grab his hose and get it back in his mouth, gulping a slug of sea water which made him choke and cough into the mouthpiece before finally getting some air.

As the sea water covered their ears the raucous sound became muffled which helped calm each man enough to resist a full panic. The compartment finally filled, pushing all the air out and equalizing them to the ocean. Complete silence fell upon the boat.

Andreas realized he was holding his breath. He took a big gulp of air and heard the other two do the same as all three managed to regulate their breaths through the Draeger. Andreas reached up again and spun the latch wheel, which turned freely until it stopped. He tip toed up and pushed on the hatch which slowly raised up and open. They remained in complete darkness.

Chapter 4
Grand Cayman, 2017

Annabelle hadn't cared for her name when she was young. It sounded rather stuck up and old fashioned. Some kids would tease her, and for a young girl who wasn't overburdened with confidence, it was enough to make her even more self-conscious. When she started playing football and other sports her friends started calling her AJ as it fit her tomboy personality and she loved it. From then on it stuck with everyone except her mother. Beryl adored the name she'd given her only child and abhorred the acronym used instead. She absolutely refused to use it or even recognize it and it became a race when labelling anything of her daughter's to see who could mark it first and claim a small victory.

As she matured, AJ came around to appreciating her full name and actually liked the traditional nature, especially once she moved abroad. But by then she was known by everyone as AJ and there was no going back. That was fine with her too.

Thomas circled the boat checking tank valves and helping the divers into their gear for the second dive. AJ stood at the bow, zipped her wetsuit back up and began her briefing.

"Our second dive site is a favourite of mine, the Doc Poulson wreck. A former cable laying ship, it's about seventy feet long and sits upright in fifty five feet of water. The wreck is named after a local doctor who set up the first hyperbaric chamber here on Grand and was donated and sank as an artificial reef in 1981. We'll spend some time exploring the wreck, it's safe and easy to penetrate as much of the decking has corroded away. Then I'll take us over to the surrounding reef which is around forty feet on top. We'll finish up back at the wreck at forty minutes or so and feel free to stay up to an hour if you have air and no deco time remaining."

Thomas gave her the okay sign that everyone was geared up and ready so she grabbed her tank and BCD, nimbly slipping into it as though it weighed nothing.

"This is a great spot for pictures and video." She glanced at the boy from Milwaukee and grinned. "If you didn't donate your GoPro to King Neptune of course... Pool's open folks, I'll meet you at the top of the wreck".

The divers back rolled over the side of the boat one by one and splashed into the clear water. Once they were all in AJ sat on the side of the boat and slipped her fins on, she glanced up at Thomas. He looked like a puppy dog watching his owner heading out the front door without him.

She chuckled. "This will be you in few weeks Thomas, better get that book work done this weekend". Thomas grinned and promised, "Don't worry Boss, I'm on it."

With that she pulled her mask down, put her regulator in her mouth and back rolled over the side.

Thomas Bodden was local born and raised and a rare sight for a Caymanian to be working in the dive industry on the island. He had his boat captain's license and was working with AJ on training for his divemaster certification so he could lead dives. It would make him the one and only Caymanian divemaster on the entire island.

The locals had made their living from the ocean since the islands were settled in the sixteen hundreds, but as fisherman, and the idea of going under the waves by choice was inconceivable to them. Because of this the dive boats were all manned and operated by foreign nationals, who needless to say were more than happy to live and work in paradise.

The Boddens were one of the first permanent settlers of the Caymans in the sixteen hundreds and his father was indeed a fisherman. As far back as Thomas could remember his father left the house before sunrise and wouldn't return until he'd caught enough fish to sell at the market. Occasionally that would be midday, but often he wouldn't be home until sunset.

Originally named Las Tortugas by Columbus in 1503 because of the abundance of turtles, they appeared on the Turin Map of 1523 as Los Lagartos, meaning alligators or large lizards, also present on the islands. By 1530 a derivative of the Carib word for marine crocodile, Caymanes, became the name that stuck.

The crocodiles were killed off centuries ago but the turtles kept European mariners coming back to the three islands that make up the Caymans. It would be a stopping point to fill up with fresh water and stock up on turtle meat before making the journey back across the Atlantic.

By the early nineteen hundreds the turtle population had been decimated and soon international bans stopped the taking of turtles for their meat and shells.

Thomas' grandfather had caught turtles as well as fish to put food on the family table but both his sons grew up in a time when it was illegal to do so. The two boys were put to work on the fishing boat at a young age and their education became a secondary pursuit. Thomas' uncle Herbert, the elder of the two brothers, took over their father's boat, which was little more than a wooden skiff and a small outboard motor. Thomas' father, Jeremiah, built his own by hand and saved up until he could buy a used motor to strap to the stern.

From a young age Thomas would spend the day on the water with his father, but not at the cost of his schooling. His father was determined that Thomas would get a full education but on weekends and holidays he fished for snapper, hogfish, and occasionally tuna, as his family had done for centuries.

Today their fishing boats were a little bigger and at least one day a week they'd head miles offshore in the deep waters fishing for tuna and mahi-mahi for the restaurants on the island.

A school of Horse eyed jacks made wide circles over the wreck as AJ descended through them to the wheelhouse encrusted with corals. The large cable winding reels mounted forward of the structure had beautiful bright orange sponges growing from it at strange angles. Ahead of that towards the bow the decking had rotted away to reveal the hold below. After getting the group's attention, AJ glided down below the deck of the sunken vessel into the hold.

Moving rearwards through a wide opening in the bulkhead she gently finned her way into the centre of the ship. This section under the cabin and wheelhouse grew dimmer the farther they moved from the holes in the decking. A large grouper stared back at her from a dark corner. He considered bolting, his eyes darting about looking for escape routes but decided to edge back deeper into the shadows.

Through another doorway she entered the larger rear hold faintly lit from the large hatch to the rear deck. AJ turned on the small flashlight she carried in her BCD and the bright LEDs illuminated the back corners of the hold. A five foot barracuda glinted in the light's rays, his shiny silver scales sparkling as he moved towards the divers. His mouth was slightly open revealing multiple rows of needle sharp teeth, perfect for tearing flesh from bones and ripping prey apart. AJ held a hand out to the group so they stopped and all watched anxiously. The big fish eased past AJ and with barely a noticeable movement of his fins or tail glided out the hatch opening and was gone.

After circling the hold AJ followed up through the opening and led the group aft to the rudder and props buried in the sand behind the ship. The stern curved steeply down and forward creating an almost cave like feel underneath and AJ again shone her light around to see if anyone was home. Sure enough the resident green moray eel peered back her, his mouth opening and closing menacingly displaying another fine set of teeth.

Once the group had all seen his head on the port side, AJ moved around starboard and shone her light on his tail that could just be seen on the other side of the rudder. He was at least six feet long. A couple of the divers nervously moved in for a closer camera shot and the eel obliged by coming further out of his hole to meet them. Morays actually have terrible eyesight and rely mainly on smell and movement so he was coming out to get a better sense of whether the intrusion was worth a nibble. Deciding it wasn't he shrunk back under the ship and the divers moved on behind AJ towards the reef.

The rest of the dive was relaxed, they explored the reef and enjoyed the thousands of critters going about their day in and around the corals and sea fans. From the Poulson it was a short boat ride back to the West Bay dock area where AJ docked and kept her boat. She motored in and pulled up to a dock that was a simple jetty reaching out about fifty feet clear of the ironshore that lined much of the Cayman coast.

West bay dock itself was a public jetty used by most of the dive operators running from the north end of Seven Mile Beach. Just beyond that was a newer, smaller jetty on a small parcel of land which was the one AJ used.

Thomas jumped to the dock as she pulled up and he quickly tied the boat off front and rear to cleats on the dock. Once secured they both helped the customers off the boat and passed them their gear and personal belongings. AJ thanked everyone and reminded them the boat leaves at 8am on Sunday morning.

A shiny thirty foot Newton dive boat was moored on the other side of the jetty and a large man in his early sixties with a scruffy grey beard and a dirty cap stepped from the boat to the dock. The logo on the hull of the boat was Pearl Divers.

AJ looked up and saw the man. "Hi Reg, are your other two due in yet?"

Reg Moore slapped Thomas on the back as the lad hustled by with a hose to wash down the boat and smiled at AJ. He had a deep tan, his skin wrinkled and scarred from years of manual labouring in the hot sun but when he spoke he had a warm, low tone tinged with a London accent.

"Nah, you're good for at least thirty minutes. Going back out?"

"Not today, I promised Thomas we'd sort out his uncle's boat this afternoon. I'll be off the dock in a few."

Reg was a former British Navy diver, a hard hat guy and a veteran of the Falklands conflict. Tough as nails, he was the son of a factory worker, raised on the blue collar streets of East London. The Navy had saved him from ending up in Wandsworth prison like so many he knew in his youth. Reg retired out of the Navy at forty five and wandered his way through the Caribbean for a few years before settling in Cayman. Starting with an old boat that could carry six divers which he kept running with a lot of nursing, bailing twine and duct tape, he grew the business to three Newton dive boats running seven days a week with forty eight customers per trip at capacity. He ran two of the boats for the regular recreational customers on the west side off Seven Mile Beach or trips to the North Wall but the third boat he preferred to charter to groups for advanced or technical dives. Sometimes trips out to the

Twelve Mile Bank or even a run to Little Cayman or The Brac, the two sister islands seventy five and ninety miles towards Cuba.

It had been Reg's first boat that AJ's Dad had chartered twelve years before that started AJ's passion for diving. She'd stayed in touch with Reg via the internet from that day and he loved to hear of her adventures as she expanded her diving education back in England. It was Reg that suggested she get her feet wet as a divemaster in Florida and he'd helped her get her first gig there. Once he felt she had enough experience under her belt he offered her a spot on his expanding crew in Cayman and sponsored her work permit.

She was a natural and Reg was like an uncle to her. Pretty soon she was one of his lead instructors and divemasters, so when he bought his third boat he put her in charge of it. Reg also kept up with Bob Bailey and the two men chatted often and conspired occasionally, always with her best interests at heart.

After five years at Pearl Divers, Reg sensed AJ was getting itchy feet to do more. Divemasters in the islands make almost enough to survive at subsistence level, savings were not really an option, so Reg and Bob put a business proposal together. They'd buy AJ a boat and Reg would help get her started with some customers, in high season he was turning away people even with three boats. The rest was up to her.

AJ jumped at the opportunity, Mermaid Divers was formed and she never looked back.

AJ helped Thomas unload all the empty dive tanks from the boat to the dock and Thomas ferried them to AJ's van in the car park while AJ took the boat out to its mooring. No one kept their boats tied to the docks. They were allowed to put a mooring in the shallow sandy areas just offshore where each night the boats could be tied up.

AJ paddled back in the kayak she had left tied to her

mooring buoy that morning which she then stowed in Reg's building by the dock. Each day they had to take the dive tanks over to Island Air who filled dive tanks for just about every operation on the island. A few resorts that were hotels, dive shops, and operators all in one had their own compressors, but for most it was easier to use the fill service than to buy, maintain and often repair your own compressor.

With her fifteen passenger van loaded with tanks in the rack she'd built in the back, they set off for Island Air located in the commercial section of George Town near the airport.

Chapter 5
Caribbean Sea, 1945

Andreas fumbled for the ladder and the other two men sensed what he was doing and squeezed as much out of the way as they could in the cramped conning tower. He found the rungs and began climbing, reaching up through the hatch opening he hauled himself on to the top of the conning tower. He'd spent more hours than he could remember at this very spot, scanning the horizon for potential targets, tankers, freighters, anything of size and value worth spending a torpedo on. But never while the U-boat was thirty four metres below the surface.

He'd hoped that sliver of moon he'd admired earlier in the evening would be lighting the sky and filtering a touch of brightness through the ocean to him now but it was not to be. He couldn't make out a thing, it was pitch black all around him. He couldn't actually tell which way was up, only logic suggested that above where he stood was the surface. Lars clambered up through the hatch and the two men steadied each other and clung to the rim of the sheet metal surrounding the conning tower. They waited for Wilhelm to join them for what seemed like forever.

Wilhelm had calmed his breathing and finally felt comfortable with the Draeger. He sensed one of his shipmates push past and ascend the ladder and was happy to let the others go before him. The second sailor bumped him as he too went up the ladder so Willy knew it was his turn. He told himself it was time to go but he didn't move. His mind felt heavy and he tried to clear his thoughts but was confused. "Am I supposed to go somewhere? No, I'm fine, I can just sit here, really, I'm fine".

His thoughts were slow and it seemed like he'd forget what he was thinking mid thought and have to start over. He shook his head. "Damn it, what am I doing?"

Something deep down kept urging him to act but his body had no interest in moving. "Am I under water? Why am I underwater? I can't breathe down here... how am I breathing?"

He reached up and felt the tube and mouthpiece. "What's this?" He pulled the mouthpiece away and sea water immediately flooded his throat, making him choke and he spat out violently. He was jolted back to the present and his brain went into overdrive for a moment. "I need air!"

He jammed the mouthpiece back in and dragged a big breathe mixed with warm salty water, the air was rank and stale and gave him no relief. "The valve!"

He grabbed for the knob on the end of the oxygen cylinder and cranked it open, fresh air quickly replaced the carbon dioxide rich gas he had been sucking on and his head cleared instantly. He cursed himself for forgetting to open the oxygen valve and finally reached for the ladder. He felt a hand grab his shirt and he half climbed and was half pulled out of the conning tower.

Andreas still had hold of Wilhelm's shirt with one hand and grabbed Lars' arm with the other. He shoved them upwards in the darkness, hoping he was at least starting them in the right direction. He bent his knees and pushed off the decking as hard as he could, praying to God he was heading towards the surface behind his shipmates. In sodden clothing he felt he was barely moving through the water. He pulled as hard as he could with his arms but tried not to panic or flail around in case he sent himself off course. It seemed like he'd been swimming forever and he still had no idea if he was heading up or across. The rebreather didn't exhale bubbles so he couldn't follow those, regardless it was ink black so he couldn't see the bubbles if there were any. He kicked and pulled further. Surely he'd gone a hundred metres by now, they were thirty four metres down, something wasn't right.

Andreas stopped swimming. He put his right hand on top of his head and slid it forward like he was making a visor over his forehead. With his other hand he pulled the mouthpiece aside and exhaled out the corner of his mouth so the bubbles exhausted into the water. He felt nothing with his right hand. If he was upright in the water the bubbles should have tickled his hand.

"Scheisse!" He moved his right hand down to his nose and exhaled again. He felt the bubbles roll over the very outside of his hand, he'd been swimming up at about forty five degrees. He righted himself so the bubbles were running up his face, secured the mouthpiece again and gently began to swim up.

After a few kicks he could tell that breathing through the Draeger was becoming easier, a sure sign the pressure was lessening. In a few moments he broke the surface and felt a warm blast of wind hit his face.

The next thing that hit his face was a huge churning wave and he quickly realized he'd surfaced in a violent storm. That approaching weather had arrived, the wind howled and rain was lashing down, mixing with the sea water whipped off the crests of the broiling surf. Andreas fumbled for the inflator on the vest as the surge dunked him back under the waves. He bit hard on the Draeger mouthpiece to stop it being pulled from his mouth and took a lungful of air in before he surfaced again. He pulled the mouthpiece away and blew hard into the inflator tube of the vest, as he tried for a second time he was once again swept under and jammed the mouthpiece back in. He surfaced spluttering and gasping. This was exhausting.

He reluctantly settled for one breath into the inflator each time so he could be prepared to submerge as he was hit with the next wave. Slowly the vest was getting inflated and becoming more buoyant so his dunking lessened and soon he was bobbing on top of the water.

As a wave picked him up he tried to scan all around him. Between the rain, the spray and the cloud cover he was still in near complete blackout.

"Where was the sailboat to pick them up?"

He figured it could be a stone's throw from him and they'd never see him. He screamed as loud as he could. "Lars! Wilhelm!"

He could barely hear himself over the storm, not a chance they could hear him. He rode up and down in the waves trying to keep his face directed away from the wind that brought the rain and spray. He turned the oxygen supply off and capped the breathing tube. If he could manage without it he'd save it in case he really needed it again.

Andreas wondered what time it was. He was certain his watch had stopped when they flooded the conning tower but he had no way of knowing as he couldn't see it in the darkness. The rain was relentless. It felt like he'd been in the water for hours and he was beginning to get chilled. The water was only a little under eighty degrees Fahrenheit but the rain was quite a bit cooler. Both were well below the temperature of the human body and would drop his core temperature down and cause hypothermia given enough time.

He had no idea which direction he was drifting in. Without the stars or the sun to reference he had no way to know. Even the normal current directions would most likely have been turned around by the storm. The storm was coming from the south so he was probably being pushed north with the weather front. They were due west of Grand Cayman so maybe heading for Cuba? That was a long way away, he'd never make it that far, he'd be dead long before that.

An even bigger wave picked Andreas up and shoved him down into the trough, his vest struggling to keep him on the surface. As he popped back up he was slammed in the back of the head by something firm and rubbery.

He screamed out in shock and surprise before being grabbed by two pairs of hands and dragged upwards into the dinghy.

"Andreas! We thought you'd drowned you crazy bastard!" Lars slapped him on the chest in delight.

Chapter 6
Grand Cayman, 2017

Thomas slid the wheelhouse door open to his uncle's fishing boat. It was an old wooden boat built in the late sixties and had seen plenty of time on the ocean. About thirty five feet long with a worn out diesel, long overdue for an overhaul, she didn't have great speed but that didn't matter to the fish Herbert reliably caught from her.

The wheelhouse was nothing more than a small hut in the stern and smelled strongly of tobacco, dead fish and diesel. There were steps down below that led to a cabin that smelled worse and had boat parts, fishing gear and other crap scattered everywhere. He may have been a great fisherman but Herbert was not big on a clean work environment.

"Oh my God." AJ covered her nose and mouth as she followed Thomas into the confined space of the cabin. "How about I start in the wheelhouse," She offered sheepishly and swiftly retreated up the steps.

Herbert had worked the fishing boats his whole life. He'd also smoked and drank rather heavily since his early teen years. The two conspired to catch up with him in his mid-forties and a year shy of his fiftieth birthday his liver succumbed.

His funeral, which in Cayman tradition would be an enthusiastic affair, was to be held in a few days time. Thomas' father had intended to sort through the boat himself but the thought of rummaging through his dead brother's belongings proved too distressing for him and he'd asked his son to handle it.

Herbert had a son of his own, but no one had seen him in twenty years. The boy was born to a Jamaican woman that Herbert had met in a bar in West Bay. After a torrid fling that lasted six days, he didn't see her again until she arrived back on Cayman two years later with a toddler in her arms. Based solely on her word the child was his, they lived together and tried to make things work but between his drinking and her infidelities it was an unhappy arrangement for everyone. She returned to Jamaica and that was the last anyone ever heard from mother or son.

The boat was willed to Jeremiah who already had his own, newer fishing vessel so he was happy to sell it to another local fisherman who was keen to buy it. All that was needed was Herbert's possessions to be removed and the man would take the boat, to which end AJ and Thomas now found themselves, wishing they had hazmat suits.

The boat was in the harbor off the North Sound, tied off to a wide walkway. They started making four piles on the walkway; junk, personal effects that family may want, fishing related stuff that went with the sale, and a final stack for 'I don't know' that needed help or research to identify. The first pile was by far the largest.

Herbert had owned this boat for about fifteen years and Thomas was pleased to note that he'd not been throwing his rubbish and cigarette packets overboard like so many unfortunately do. Bad news was he apparently didn't take them off the boat either and now his nephew was having to move fifteen years of two packs a day from the cabin to the dock. He thought that was disgusting until he started on the food wrappers, fast food bags and empty booze bottles. It appeared cheap whisky was his beverage of choice.

AJ removed a fair sampling of similar items from the

wheelhouse before setting about the various tangled up lengths of fishing line, odd leaders, a mix of rusty hooks and a few lures. She threw anything that looked useless in the junk pile and the few serviceable items went with the gear they'd return to the boat.

The wheelhouse was thin on electronics. There was a VHF radio that she turned on and was amazed when it came to life. A floating bracket style compass was mounted on top of the control panel which also housed a battered depth gauge. Fuel gauge was on empty but when they checked the filler on the tank they could see it was at least half full. There were rpm and temperature gauges but after discussing it they decided against tempting fate and firing the motor to check them. No radar, no GPS.

The local fishermen were renowned for piloting around the island without navigational aids of any sort. With the treacherous shallow reefs that were famous for bringing ships to grief and the speed at which a squall could blanket the island, this was no mean feat. Many of them still took their wooden skiffs with cheap old outboards miles offshore if they thought the fish were running.

Rummaging under the control panel AJ happened to glance up and noticed something wedged between the nests of wires from the gauges. She carefully pulled out the rolled up paper to discover it was a navigational chart of Grand Cayman and about twenty five miles of open ocean around it. She spread it out across the shelf in the back of the wheelhouse. The map was old and torn at the edges and a large coffee stain had managed to penetrate the waterproof coating, blurring out much of the eastern section. The chart was the marine navigation type that had lines marking significant depth levels and notations of hazards. In faded red marker pen there were various markings and notes that AJ had a hard time reading, the letters were small and the handwriting looked like that of a child.

"Hey Thomas, come and look at this". She'd seen and indeed owned a navigational map similar to this but the notations caught her attention and now she was intrigued. Thomas came up the steps from the cabin with a box of empty plastic oil bottles which he set down and peered over AJ's shoulder.

"What did you find?"

"What do you reckon these notes mean? I can't even read the writing," She pointed to one of the red markings.

Thomas studied it more closely for a few moments and then smiled. "It's the sweet spots, man, his secret honey holes where he had good luck catching the fish." He pointed to the lettering. "Uncle Herbert, he could barely read and write, that's his chicken scratch for the type of fish he caught there. That one I believe is grouper."

He pointed at another. "That one's tuna." His finger slid over the chart to another marking. "And that one's mahi."

Thomas looked over the chart and shook his head. "My Pap will want this for sure."

AJ was surprised "Surely brothers would have shared their information and helped each other?"

"All the fisherman guard the spots with their lives and they're crazy competitive and secretive about it, even families don't tell each other." Thomas looked again at the chart and pointed to an elongated area straight west of Seven Mile Beach marked Cayman Bank. The depth lines around the area showed it sloped quickly away through five hundred feet to over six thousand feet but the top of it was at around eighty to a hundred and twenty.

"This chart calls this the Cayman Bank but it's what we always called Twelve Mile Bank, see he didn't mark much there, it's great fishing but everybody knows about it. You've seen this, you always see the fishing boats when you go out there with Reg."

AJ mused over the chart, "It's amazing to think the Cayman Islands are the peaks of a huge mountain range." She ran her finger along the mainly submerged ridgeline, from Cuba in the East to Belize in the west.

She pointed to the depth rings that plummeted to over twenty five thousand feet to the south of the islands, part of the trench that paralleled the ridge across the Caribbean.

"Over here the Cayman Trench is growing where the tectonic plates are pulling apart."

Sliding her finger back to the island chain, "To think, that by some miracle, these fault blocks have been pushed upward by the moving plates until they barely broke the surface and formed the islands."

Thomas smiled and tapped his finger on Twelve Mile Bank. "And this, what'd you call that now, fault block? Right here, didn't quite make it to the top!"

AJ chuckled. "Yup, that's why they refer to it sometimes as the Cayman's fourth island. It may well be an island one day though. The other three were under water millions of years ago. That's why they're covered in ironshore. Ironshore is limestone rock which is just dead coral from when they were below water. As the coral grew taller and the water level dropped when the ice caps froze, they broke the surface and became islands."

Thomas gave her a puzzled look. "How'd you know all this stuff? I'm born and lived here my whole life and never knew this!"

She smiled. "I googled it!"

He laughed loudly in his infectious way which made her crack up as well. A thought dawned on him and he stopped laughing. "Wait now, the ice caps are melting these days, ain't that right?"

"Yup, so right now we're on a path to losing Grand and Little Cayman to the sea and only the bluffs on Brac will be left."

Thomas looked at AJ in a panic. "When's this gonna happen?!"

"Depends who you believe, could be as soon as forty or fifty years. More likely it's over a hundred years away but that's not very long if you think about it. Your children will probably witness this island going under water."

"That's a horrible thing to think about!" Thomas shook his head in disbelief.

AJ tried to make it sound better. "One day we'll start heading the other way again and the ice caps will freeze and then the Caymans will be back and the fourth island could well be a real island. When that happens there'll be hills on Grand!"

"Me and all my kin'll be long gone and buried under the dirt by then." He mumbled despondently.

AJ's curious mind had spotted something else, she slid her finger from the Bank just slightly north where a much smaller pinnacle appeared to rise out of the depths to around four hundred feet. There was a red line through the number four hundred and in Herbert's jittery writing was the number one hundred and twenty. "Now what do we have here," she puzzled, "Your Uncle liked this spot apparently."

Thomas took a closer look as AJ continued. "That's weird, can't imagine the chart is wrong, but I'm guessing it's pretty old. Once you clear the wall off Cayman, the Bank is the only place shallow enough to have a reef on any chart I've seen,"

AJ traced the line on the map defining the six thousand foot mark, it made an oval around the island and Cayman Bank.

"Everything else runs down to six thousand feet, or

more to the south where it drops into the trench. The ten miles between Grand and the edge of the Bank is around a thousand feet all the way. There's a couple of these smaller peaks that are four to six hundred feet down but I've never seen or heard of anything shallower."

Thomas turned and picked the box back up to add it to the rubbish pile on the dock. "Best we keep this map aside, my Pap will definitely want to see it."

AJ rolled the chart back up. "Thomas, would you mind if I took some measurements off this first? I'd like to locate that pinnacle if I can."

"Sure thing, but what are you so interested for? You don't fish, anyway, who knows how long ago he was marking this, good spots they come and go, fish don't stay in one place you know," he chuckled.

She gave him a friendly shove as he headed back down to the cabin, "If it's actually a hundred and twenty feet, we're diving it, silly. Besides, Reg and I have been looking for something out here. I told you my Grandfather sailed these waters in the war didn't I?"

Thomas stuck his head back out the cabin. "Yeah, I remember you talking about him, he used to tell you the war stories of patrolling out here and all, right?"

She smiled, nodding and thought of her Grandfather. He died early in the year the Baileys first went on holiday to Cayman. AJ was devastated she couldn't tell him about her new love of diving and have him tell her his stories for the hundredth time now she'd been in the waters he'd patrolled.

AJ could listen to Grandad Bailey tell stories forever. Some old folks drone on about the way it used to be and every relative runs a mile avoiding getting cornered by Grandad and his war stories. But not Grandad Bailey. He had an easy way about him that made everyone feel comfortable in his presence, he spoke softly but not too quietly, he used his hands and expressions but wasn't overly theatrical or dramatic, the man had a subtle charm about him.

He was seventeen when the war broke out in Europe and he signed up right away, lying that he was eighteen. At the time you could still choose which branch you preferred and he went for the Navy. His father had told him the horror stories from the first war of Army guys in the trenches being cannon fodder and figured he wouldn't end up flying planes as they'd dig a little deeper and catch his age. He began by serving on patrol boats off the southern coast of England, picking up downed flyers and chasing around after reports of German U-boats before being transferred to a similar boat based out of Jamaica in the Caribbean in 1943. There he spent the rest of the war until VE Day on May 8th 1945.

AJ missed him terribly.

Chapter 7
Bournemouth, 1997

Grandad Bailey sat in his recliner in a dimly lit sitting room of a simple brick post war terraced home. A fire was crackling away and the man looked content admiring his eight year old granddaughter, perched legs crossed on the sofa across from him. He leaned in a little bit and grinned at her.

"What story are you looking to hear young madam?"

The young girl's face lights up and she bounces up and down as she replies. "The submarine Grandad, tell me about the submarine!"

He leaned back and took a slow sip from his tea cup, relishing these moments when the girl still wanted to hear his old tales.

"Alright then, I think I can remember that one still."
He shuffled in his chair, getting himself settled and comfortable before he began. He had a heavy London accent but his voice was smooth, his words clear, his mind still sharp and these memories were the backbone of his existence, the years that shaped his world and the man he became.

"We was based in Jamaica, an American base at Goat Island, place was run by the Yanks but there was a mixed bag of all sorts there. We were on an MTB, a Motor Torpedo Boat, only thirteen of us ran it, ours was an early one but it was really fast and we would patrol all around Jamaica. It was a small boat but we could reach as far as Haiti to the east, Cuba to the north and the Caymans to the west. Main job was looking for U-boats.

Tricky ole Germans started sending their subs into the Caribbean in forty two, called it Operation Neuland, of course we didn't know that then but after the war I read about it.

I used to like going over to Cayman as we'd pull in there and top up with fuel. We could just about make it out and back from Goat, but not if we had to run around chasing the Hun. Anyway, Cayman was a quiet little place but it was gorgeous, beautiful sandy beaches, we'd get to go ashore for a bit in the town there. The locals would cook us up some fish or turtle. Back in those days they'd catch and eat the turtles, sell the shells and all that.

Most of the time the waters were calm around the islands but every once in a while a storm would stir up and our little boat would be a bugger in the open sea. That weren't no fun then I can tell you. Sixty Seven, that was our boat number, MTB-67. She could fly across the water when it was calm or just a bit of a swell but she was too small once the seas got big, we had to go a lot slower and boy did it beat us up. We'd head straight for the nearest port as soon as we could.

So this all happened right at the end of the war in early '45. We all read the papers and listened to the wireless and all they talked about was the war was nearly over. I hadn't been back to England in nearly two years and I was ready to go home. We was on a patrol doing a lap around the Caymans and we headed for George Town, the little town on Grand, to get some petrol before we headed back. We'd come around the two sister islands, Little and Brac already.

Weather had been great, it was April I think, and it was clear and nice but not quite as humid like it got in the summer. We'd report in over the radio each day and tell them if we'd seen anything and they'd tell us what the weather was supposed to be. Well, that day they says we better watch it cos there's a big storm coming for us from the south. It was still a lovely day as far as the eye could see so we figured we'd take a wide swing around Grand that afternoon and then pull into George Town and dock until the storm passes.

The MTB's had a bridge up on top, as I say they weren't a big boat so you weren't up in a crow's nest or nothing so you couldn't see really far, but on a smooth day with binoculars you could see a bit. So I'm on the bridge with the Captain and my mate George, he was a Londoner like me, and we were the look outs. We're looking through binoculars and scanning the seas all around us as we trundle along. Next minute George starts barking and getting excited over his side, says he sees a U-boat! Me and the Cap rush over to the starboard side where George is looking and sure enough way off out there, probably half a mile or more, there's a bloody submarine on the surface.

Captain gives the order to get after 'em at full speed, ready the torpedo tubes and prepare to attack. You've never seen thirteen men move so fast, blokes running everywhere, manning the deck guns and getting the torpedoes ready to fire. On an MTB our torpedo launchers are these bloody great big steel tubes bolted to the decks on either side. Quite a sight I tell you when you launch them things. Torpedoes come zippin' out the deck tubes and make a big old splash into the water, take off at a hell of rate, you could see 'em just below the surface leaving a wake behind 'em. But not that day. The U-boat starts submerging as soon as we turned and down she went. By the time we'd swung about and started after her she was disappearing under and we were still too far away.

My heart was beating outta my chest I tell you, all the running about we'd done down there in the islands I'd never actually seen a German submarine. And now those buggers were underneath us somewhere! All we could see around us was water knowing somewhere down there is a boat full of Germans ready to take a shot at us. Of course, we knew we weren't worth shooting at for them but still, just knowing they was under there was giving me the willies.

Cap takes us over to where he figured they dived and we threw a few depth charges down there for good measure but we knew we didn't stand a chance, they could have gone anywhere. We ran around for a while pinging our sonar at 'em but couldn't find 'em.

By now it's pushing on late afternoon and the clouds are rolling in and starting to get darker, winds are picking up and we head straight for George Town before that storm catches us.

Normally you see the local fishermen coming back in towards the end of the day as you get closer to shore but not this day. Words out about the storm and they all headed home already to secure their boats. These storms can turn into hurricanes down there and believe you me, you don't want to be near the water in a hurricane. That's why I always remembered the sail boat.

Big one, probably nearly as big as us and we were seventy feet long. He's heading out as we're heading in, made no sense. Cap, he flashes some signals at him but he never even acknowledged us. He was a ways off port side and we would have to turn back out to sea to chase him down so we kept heading for George Town. Cap tried hailing him on the radio but nothing. Boat didn't fly a flag of any sort, which you were supposed to fly your National flag so you didn't get shot at by mistake. Whoever he was he was heading for trouble in that storm.

By the time we get tied up and the sun's going down it's raining cats and dogs and the winds whipping up pretty good. We leave a couple of unlucky blokes watching the Sixty Seven and the rest of us find some grub in town and have us a pint or two. We were all still jabbering and excited about seeing that damn U-boat.

Storm was a big one, not quite a hurricane but it blew hard all night and most of the next day. We spent one more night in George Town harbor before the Cap said we better head home. I can tell you we was extra watchful on the binoculars all the way to Goat Island, knowing there was a Jerry sub out there somewhere. 'Course at this time we had no idea we didn't have to worry about him."

Chapter 8
Grand Cayman, 2017

AJ helped Thomas heave the last of the rubbish from his uncle's boat into the skip at the marina. They'd sorted out anything recyclable and put that in the blue bins. Thomas thanked her profusely for helping and putting up with the foul smell and mess. It had taken them all afternoon to sort through everything and they were both ready for a shower and some clean clothes.

She told him he was welcome and headed for the van with the navigational chart under her arm which she promised to return to him over the weekend.

Her cell phone rang and she answered it as she climbed in the van. "Hey Reg, what are you up to?"

Reg was never big on flowery salutations and small talk so as always got right to the point. "Are you coming tonight?"

"Planned to, why you need a bouncer?" She grinned and could hear him chuckling on the other end of the phone.

"I think we'll be fine, but we need to talk." His voice turned more serious and that got AJ's attention. "What's up, everything okay?"

"I have a charter starting Sunday, booked me for a week, real secretive lot out of Argentina. They're paying top dollar, didn't even flinch when I gave them the rate. They booked a month back and I didn't think a whole lot of it until this afternoon. This guy Art Renfro, I know him from the old salvage and treasure hunting days, a real piece of work this bloke. He showed up at the dock, says he's working with these guys. Apparently they have a research and salvage boat all kitted out with side scan sonar coming in, they're just using me as a ferry back and forth. Guess where they're hunting?"

AJ looked at the chart she'd placed on the passenger seat and felt a lump in her throat. How could anyone know about this already? Her mind was racing. "Uh, shit Reg, where?" she stammered.

"Twelve Mile Bank... Why, what were you thinking? You sound like someone just shot your dog. We know there's nothing but an old barge out there, we've dived every inch of it."

AJ recovered and realized she was being paranoid. "Of course, it's just interesting timing, I may have found something today cleaning out Herbert Bodden's boat. I'll show you tonight, we may want to have a little boat ride tomorrow if you're off?"

"Yeah, just one boat running tomorrow, but we'll take your rig, it's cheaper and faster." That would normally be about as much conversation you could get out of Reg on the phone but he continued on.

"I just wanted to give you a heads up on these guys, they're a serious bunch with some high tech gear. This bloke I know isn't the type that plays nice either, he's had his share of trouble over the years. If I'd known he was involved I wouldn't have taken the gig but I can't renege now.

Point being, they're putting a lot of money and effort behind finding something out there and I'm guessing it's the same thing we've been looking for. Difference being, if they find her she won't be an historical site or preserved or probably even declared to the Cayman government. They'll cut it apart, take anything of value then kick her over the side to cover their tracks."

AJ knew by law any wrecks found in Cayman waters had to be declared to the Receiver of Wrecks at the Port Authority of the Cayman Islands, which then went through a series of legalities and procedures to establish ownership of the vessel and its contents. This could take a long time, especially in the case of an old wreck, even if its statute of limitation had expired.

If the salvager eventually gained the rights to the wreck they then had to split any and all value of the wreck with the Cayman government. For marine archeology researchers and explorers this wasn't an issue as their goal was to preserve and study what they found. But for some treasure hunters and salvagers this simply meant less profit for them. If the wreck contained a cargo of value they could salvage quickly then they may well be keen to grab and go before anyone knows any different. If this meant destroying an historical site or disturbing a war grave they didn't let their consciences, if they had one, get in the way.

AJ and Reg agreed to chat more that night and she was relieved to step through her apartment door and head straight for the shower.

She rented a small guest house over the garage of a vacation home owned by an American couple who came down to the island five or six times year. The couple in their fifties lived and worked in Atlanta, Georgia and gave AJ a great deal on rent in exchange for keeping an eye on the property and some free diving when they were on island.

The five bedroom house was on the north end of Seven Mile Beach on Boggy Sand Road nestled amongst a row of similar multi-million dollar homes. As she dried off from her shower and gazed across the garden to an amazing view of the Caribbean Sea lapping against the sands of one of the most acclaimed and famous beaches in the world, she once again marveled at the blessed life she was leading.

At twenty eight it occurred to her she probably should be worried she wasn't married and having children yet, but couldn't bring herself to fret over it. She was also lucky that neither of her parents pressured her in that direction.

Contrary to the alternative look AJ evolved she had always been conservative when it came to dating. She was shy and unsure of herself in most ways but her mother had installed in her the value of love, sexuality and relationships which she was careful to maintain. In school she'd been a late bloomer, she was a pretty girl with long blond hair but still a tomboy into her teens. Secretly she already saw herself with tattoos and an edgier look but neither her school nor her parents would ever have allowed it.

She didn't start dating until she was in sixth form, her first boyfriend was her only boyfriend all through sixth form and two years of A-Levels. He was a year older than her, left for university as she was in her final year and things were already fizzling out by the time she decided to head to Florida.

AJ found she really preferred the company of older, more mature men, or women for that matter, but was attracted to neither of them sexually. Finding maturity in the younger crowd was proving quite a challenge but she was in no hurry to be in a relationship, pursuing diving and travelling the world held more appeal and a lot less drama.

The Florida Keys was a wild new scene altogether, the guys loved her English accent but in the main she found them brash and rather childish. She was amazed how many of the divemasters and instructors smoked cigarettes when your lungs were sort of important for SCUBA diving. There was also a lot of other things being smoked and consumed which she had never seen in her sheltered little school tucked away in rural Sussex. She wanted no part of that either.

AJ wasn't a prude and really didn't have a problem with recreational drugs but she hated the feeling of being out of control. The handful of times she'd gotten drunk in school she didn't find particularly enjoyable, the next morning was definitely not fun and she hated the thought of being 'the drunk girl at the party'.

During her second year in the Keys she met a guy from Oregon who was working as a contract computer programmer and living in Islamorada. He was a nice departure from the crazy dive industry scene, he was easy going and pleasant to be around and a keen diver and outdoorsman. They took trips to dive the underwater caves in northern Florida, ride mountain bikes all over the Keys, and explore the mangroves and more obscure dive spots.

AJ's move to Cayman two years later randomly coincided with him receiving a job offer in Silicon Valley, California. They talked at length about continuing the relationship long distance but the closer the time came the more they realized that this probably wasn't the final relationship for either of them so why drag it through a prolonged demise.

Since she'd been on the island she'd discovered the dive worker scene was only a slightly slower version of the Keys and very migratory. Most of the younger divemasters spent no more than two years at any one place before moving on to the next exotic location and adventure.

She had dated occasionally and sporadically over the past seven years but there'd been only two men she felt were worth her time and invited into her bed.

Jason had been working for Reg for a few years when AJ arrived. When Pearl Divers expanded to two Newtons he was put in charge of the second one. Five years older than AJ he'd burnt out on the bar scene and was more interested in what he could build for a stable future. It took a year before he finally persuaded her to have dinner with him as a date and she was very tentative and careful starting something with a co-worker. He was originally from England but had been raised in Australia where his family still lived near Cairns. His love of diving was formed on the Great Barrier Reef and he had a passion for coral conservation, having witnessed the loss of so much of it back home.

Cayman allows foreign workers to hold work permits for seven continuous years as long as they're sponsored by a local company, but after seven you have to leave the island for at least a year before you can get a permit again.

Jason's permit ran out and he was forced to return home to Australia. While back there his father was diagnosed with cancer and he needed to step in and help with the family business. His father was in remission but the business was expanding and doing so well a year passed by and Jason resigned himself to staying there. He asked AJ to come and join him but by now she had completely fallen in love with Cayman and couldn't see leaving. She also felt she owed Reg some loyalty and he was depending on her more and more.

Number two was a mistake. When it seems too good to be true, sometimes that's exactly what it is. François was an athletic, good looking professional wind surfer with a French accent, a disarming smile, and captivating blue eyes. Within three weeks he told her she was the only woman who'd truly stolen his heart. After three months she discovered there were at least two more true loves he was juggling.

AJ was devastated. For the first time she'd really let her guard down and allowed herself to believe the words because she wanted them to be true. After she got over the initial heartache and embarrassment she was just mad at herself for not being more cautious. He came knocking on her door about two months later full of apologies but before he could explain how he'd changed she split his lip with a right hook that surprised them both.

She felt much better watching him leave.

AJ pushed the door open to the Fox and Hare Pub and strolled up to the bar and found Reg on his regular stool. The place was half full and on a small corner stage a full figured woman in her fifties with an ample chest and a voice to match was strumming a guitar while belting out an edgy version of the Rolling Stones' Wild Horses.

Reg's wife Pearl ran everything behind the scenes at Pearl Divers from bookings and schedules, to accounting and orders. Reg ran everything to do with the boats and the diving. Pearl would dive occasionally, mainly when she wanted to spear some lionfish for dinner, but her passion was music and she had a regular gig on Friday nights at the Fox and Hare.

Pearl had a gritty rock n roll voice singing covers of Melissa Etheridge, Bonnie Raitt and Sass Jordan, with some Janis Joplin mixed in. The place would have been a smoky little dive bar but in today's tobacco free world it was just a dive bar. Tucked away in West Bay it filled up with ex-pat locals, a few Caymanians and the occasional tourist or two who stumbled across the place. The bar itself was a hefty oak wood structure lined with bar stools and a resin top over maps of England and the Cayman Islands. The place was strewn with pictures and memorabilia from the homeland with the authentic feel of an old English pub brought over by the owners when they emigrated.

Reg loved to hear Pearl sing. He couldn't wait for Friday nights and would sit quietly at the bar, sipping his neat bourbon and hung on every note she played and every line she sang. The bear of a man was completely besotted with his woman and often a tear would roll down his cheek as she crooned a sadder song. Between sets she'd sit next to him and they'd chat about the old days in London or the day they just had on the boat. It didn't matter, what she wanted to talk about he wanted to hear and vice versa.

Regulars would stop by and join them or tell her she was great as usual, Reg would always thank them. He could be mistaken for a harmless, sappy fool to an unfamiliar customer a few drinks into the evening, but one thing would always stir up the bear.

Pearl was good so critics were few but God help any complainers in the crowd. Reg was known to drag people outside and fix their poor musical taste by pinning them to the wall by the throat. Most were apologizing profusely before he got them that far.

The bartender slid a bottle of Strongbow cider across the bar before she had a chance to order. AJ held the bottle up in thanks before telling Reg cheers and taking a swig.

Pearl finished her song, announced she was taking a short break and after the applause died down she put up her guitar and joined them at the bar. AJ gave her a big hug as Reg pulled a stool over for her.

"Wonderful as always Pearl, sorry I missed most of your first set, I ran a little late helping Thomas with his uncle's boat" AJ apologized.

"That's fine dear, don't worry, glad you could make it, I'm sure you had somewhere better to be than listening to this old woman scratching out some ancient tunes."

AJ laughed. "There will never be somewhere I'd rather be than listening to you Pearl."

Reg leaned in and kissed his wife on the forehead and gave her a wink. She already knew there was no place he'd rather be.

He leaned back and quizzed AJ. "So what's this big secret you didn't want to tell me over the phone? You found something on Herbert's boat? I'd hate to think what you found on that pile of floating fire wood, that thing was a mess any time I saw it."

"Bloody hell that thing reeked, we damn near filled the big skip at the marina. Ninety percent of what we carted off was complete rubbish."

She felt a little stupid leaning in close and whispering all clandestine like but there was no telling who might overhear. "What I did find though was Herbert's navigational chart with his favourite spots marked on it. Most of it was standard stuff, the Bank and all that, but you know those two little pinnacles just off the Bank? The ones that are about four hundred and six hundred feet down?"

"Yeah, I know 'em, but they're way too deep, there's no reef down there, not enough light so don't know why that would be good fishing, no reason for the big stuff to be there."

"Exactly, but look at this." AJ opened a picture on her phone she'd taken of the chart and held it up for Reg and Pearl to see. "Herbert scratched out the four hundred foot mark and wrote one twenty there instead, Thomas says that chicken scratch next to it says tuna."

AJ closed the picture quickly as though a drone maybe hovering over them capturing everything on film and then felt silly again. "I can't imagine the marine surveyors got it wrong but Herbert seemed to be catching fish there so maybe they did."

Reg nodded. "You know these waters have been mapped over hundreds of years and different sections were surveyed at different times, not necessarily all at the same time. If those pinnacles were done early on with basic sonar it's possible they made a mistake. Now they use a combination of side scan sonar and multibeam sonar to determine the shape and depth of the sea floor and GPS to pin point the location. If poor ole' Herbert's correct it's just a matter of time until it gets surveyed again and they amend the charts."

AJ smiled at him. "Worth a look?"

He grinned back. "Bloody right it is, we've looked everywhere else, damn thing has to be somewhere!"

Chapter 9
Caribbean Sea, 1945

There was no way to steer or propel the dinghy. They were completely at the will of the ocean and the winds, which took them south east as best they could figure. As an expert navigator this frustrated the hell out of Andreas for the first three days. Now, a week adrift he'd accepted the fact that they would either hit land or another vessel eventually. The question was whether they'd be alive or corpses when this happened.

Between the tract of the sun and using the stars on the clear nights, he was confident they'd gone to the south of Grand Cayman and were heading roughly towards Jamaica. Without the charts he was going from memory but was also fairly confident if they missed Jamaica there was only the string of eastern Caribbean islands from Puerto Rico to Trinidad and Tobago to stop them drifting into the Atlantic Ocean.

He wasn't sure why that troubled him as at the rate they were moving they'd be long dead before that problem even became a problem. But time was something the three men had an abundance of so Andreas chewed over these dilemmas at length.

The raft was supposed to hold four people but it was clear to them that the designer had used four very small people to get his dimensions. The three men were touching each other at all times, there was no escaping it. The dinghy was made of rubber and canvas so every movement created a reactionary movement in the raft whether it was the men fidgeting or a wave rolling under them. It made sleep for any period of time impossible.

Wilhelm still couldn't believe he'd hung on to the deflated raft when he was struggling out of the conning tower and then all the way to the surface. More of a surprise was that he and Lars surfaced right next to each other and not only managed to stay together in the storm but inflate the dinghy enough for it to float them.

The final miracle was literally bumping into Andreas in the huge swells hours after they'd all surfaced. The fact that the storm and winds had blown them all in the same direction made sense but it was still a million to one shot in almost zero visibility to land right on him. He could have been a dozen feet in either direction and they never would have seen each other.

The three men now agreed they had probably used up every piece of good luck and fortune they'd had in reserve as the last seven days had been rather bleak.

The fresh water from the storm was heavily mixed with seawater splashing in the boat and had been undrinkable. They'd bailed it out after the seas calmed and hoped for another, milder rain so they could gather some drinking water in the dinghy and wash their rapidly burning skin. The sea water helped cool them a little, especially after dark when the sun didn't evaporate it straight off their skin making them feel even hotter, but now the burns were worsening and the salt was becoming too painful.

It finally rained early afternoon on the fourth day and it felt like Christmas to the three submariners. Refreshed and optimistic again they had chatted the rest of the day about everything from families to post war plans to their favourite actresses. The rain water that gathered in the dinghy evaporated completely by sunset and they wished they'd forced more down before it had all gone. Three days further on and not a drop more precipitation had fallen.

Without food for a week and water for nearly four days again the men were suffering and the optimism was slowly being seared out of them by the relentless sun.

Andreas was the most even keeled of the group, his mood swings were relatively small. As an officer and a man with a mathematical brain he had established the odds in his mind early on and hadn't seen much to change that. It was going to rain at least once a week in the Caribbean Sea at this time of year and could rain as much as four or five times. So far it hadn't been much in their favour, no point getting too excited over one shower.

Wilhelm was the opposite. He was ecstatic when it rained and contemplating the least painful way to end the misery two days later. Andreas and Lars felt they were using up a lot of energy trying to keep Willy from doing something crazy and talking him off the proverbial ledge. Earlier that morning he'd gotten really melancholy and suggested they all hold each other's heads under water. Lars lost it and threatened to strangle him and afterward he and Andreas would enjoy a good meal gnawing on dead Willy. Things had calmed down since then and the boat was mainly silent.

Andreas attempted to raise their spirits. "So boys, what will you spend your share on when we get out of this mess, huh? A house in the mountains? Maybe on a beach in the islands?" He waved his hand across the horizon as though he was presenting the grand prize in a drawing.

Wilhelm looked at him as though he was mad but Lars chuckled and enthused. "I would choose the mountain lodge, it would be in Bavaria were I will ski all winter and climb the peaks all summer. I will have a beautiful fräulein waiting for me when I return home every day." He leaned back and smiled, imagining a lovely girl greeting him at the door.

"You two are fucking crazy." Wilhelm snapped. "We're going to be dead out here and the rest of those bastards on the crew will have all the mountain homes and girls and beaches and shit, we'll have our eyes pecked out by fucking seagulls!"

Andreas had had enough. "Damn it Willy, you survived the escape from the boat at thirty four metres, you survived the storm, you're surviving now, you can't just give up man, there's still a chance, stop being such a pessimistic shithead!"

The dinghy returned to silence again and the three men drifted on in the sweltering sun.

Chapter 10
Grand Cayman, 2017

The stillness and calm of the dawn added to AJ's anticipation of the day that lay ahead. The west side was dead flat with nothing but a gentle ripple brushing up the beach and the only breeze was a soft touch grazing her cheek. Perfect.

The RIB boat was loaded with six dive tanks, enough for the two of them to do three dives each, an unlikely scenario but AJ wanted to be prepared. They could do with a third person to stay with the boat while they both dived as there was nothing to moor to in the open water but Thomas had to start work every day at six. The lad cherished his Saturday mornings when he could sleep in, she didn't have the heart to ruin that.

Saturday was the most popular day for flights to and from the island so AJ worked the boat six days a week and took Saturday off. To run the seventh day she'd have to employ one more person just to get each of them a single day off which didn't make financial sense to her. In high season they ran morning and afternoon trips, often did a couple of night dives each week as well as pool work for diver training courses she taught. She felt they earned and deserved one free day a week.

Reg was always up early regardless of the day. He had enough employees to rotate people during the week and run one or two of his boats on Saturdays. He still was at the dock at six thirty seven days a week. Too many years in the Navy being rousted at dawn or earlier, his mental alarm clock woke him around five every day and he was not one for laying around hitting snooze buttons.

They pulled away from the dock just as Reg's crew were rolling in and he gave them a quick wave as AJ eased the throttles forward on the powerful twin Yamaha two fifty horsepower four stroke outboards. Once she cleared the shallower water she nodded at Reg to hang on and opened up the throttles. The boat shot across the water coming up on plane and the motors purred effortlessly as she levelled out around thirty knots.

From the navigation chart she'd done her best to pinpoint the spot but it was a fairly small scale map so at best she figured their search area was probably a couple of miles square. In the open ocean, looking for something on top of the water in that large of an area would be a challenge. Searching for something underwater with no visual reference was going to be even harder. Fortunately AJ had the benefit of the marine GPS on the RIB boat. It had the nautical maps built in, including depth profiles, so she was aiming them right at the pinnacle.

How Herbert would find his honey hole God only knows. He had no GPS and worked from the same chart and co-ordinates they had, but obviously he did so she felt optimistic they could do the same with the tools she had.

The more the sun came up the surf and winds picked up to a light chop. She was still able to comfortably run at twenty knots but it beat the hell out of them to run much faster. The wind and motor noise was loud but Reg leaned on the centre console frame next to her and they could hear each other behind the screen.

"It's a beautiful morning to be out here." Reg scanned the horizon. Behind them the island could no longer be seen.

"Perfect, should be good vis." AJ was beaming, she felt giddy like a kid waking up on their birthday morning.

Reg added, "I'll splash first if we find something, you'll

just have to float with the boat and keep an eye on my bubbles."

"Sure, no problem." AJ was keen to be the one in the water but she knew arguing with Reg was useless. He was over protective with her and he wasn't about to budge, he wanted to check things out in case the current was too strong or some other unforeseen peril awaited.

Reg and Pearl had never had children of their own. He travelled so much with the Navy they thought it best to wait a while and by the time they said to hell with it they found they couldn't. Turned out Reg was the problem, which was not easy for him to accept, and he felt incredibly guilty he couldn't provide his wife a child. They talked about adopting but Pearl was the one that said no. Reg was still gone so much and she was scared how she'd feel about raising someone else's child when times became difficult.

They'd come to terms with it over time and if anything, it brought them closer together. They'd both enjoyed AJ when she first came to the island with her family and it meant a lot to them that she kept in touch. But once she landed on the island to stay they grew closer and closer until now she felt like family to them. If not the child they'd never had then certainly a niece, and the trust Bob and Beryl put in them to watch their little girl sealed the deal.

They were about forty minutes from the dock and AJ could see the destination approaching on the GPS screen. The depth finder had been reading over a thousand feet for the past thirty five minutes and continued to do so. She eased back on the throttles and zoomed in the GPS screen for better clarity as they got closer.

According to the screen they were a mere five hundred feet from the pinnacle, yet the depth was still at eleven hundred. She slowed even more and almost coasted in the direction of the target on the screen. She made a small correction with the left motor as the boat drifted to the south slightly. "There's a little current out here."

Reg nodded in agreement. The depth suddenly started ramping up showing a shallower ocean floor beneath them, it quickly came up to seven hundred and kept moving. They both huddled closer over the gauges and she made another small adjustment as again they were being pushed to the south. The depth gauge read six fifty and then fell away again to over seven hundred as they went past the target on the GPS.

"We've run over it," Reg noted.

"Yep, I'll swing around from the east and make another pass." AJ whipped the boat around in a tight circle and lined up another approach from the opposite side. She made sure she was slightly north this time to allow for the drift.

The depth shallowed rapidly again as they approached the pinnacle and they watched carefully as it passed through six hundred and hit five thirty before going deeper again.

"This pinnacle is like a small column of rock in the middle of nowhere! The thing's tiny!" AJ couldn't believe it. "I don't think there's room on this thing to rest a rowing boat."

Reg agreed. AJ swung around for another pass and carefully lined up from the west.

They went through the same process and cautiously edged over the pinnacle a step further north than before. This time the depth started ramping shallower sooner and with a gentler slope, getting them both excited again. It kept sloping up through five hundred feet and took another fifty feet across the surface to see four fifty and still kept getting shallower. Finally, she thought, we've found something.

At four hundred and six feet the depth starting falling away again and Reg slapped the side of the console. "Damn it."

"Let me see if I can get on the top of this ridge, it seems like it's a spine running north south so I'll approach from the south and run against the current, it might keep getting shallower to the north." She again spun the boat around but this time approached perpendicular from how she'd done it before. It took a little jogging back and forth to find the top of the ridge but then she was able to track it as planned.

The ridge indeed shallowed in that direction and she reached the four hundred foot mark again pretty quickly. That depth stayed steady for a while and peaked at Three hundred and ninety one before dropping off once more into the depths.

AJ couldn't believe it. "I'm really sorry Reg, I dragged you all the way out here for nothing, I really thought I may have stumbled across something."

She felt incredibly dejected and a little embarrassed to have got her hopes up. Reg rested his hand on her shoulder and smiled. "Wasn't a waste of my morning love, got to spend a few hours out on the water with my second favourite gal, time well spent in my book."

AJ gave him the best smile she could muster and aimed the RIB boat back towards Grand Cayman, pushing the throttles forward and resetting the GPS for West Bay Dock. Reg stayed next to her and thought carefully for a few minutes before speaking again.

"Old Herbert liked his booze you know, there's no telling where he actually was when he wrote on that chart. Obviously, not where he thought he was. Most likely he was over the Bank and got confused."

Reg knew how much it meant to AJ to find this wreck but they'd hunted for it for nearly seven years now and come up dry. This lead was the first new hope in a long time and he hated to see her disillusioned again but he'd finally come to terms with the fact that they were on a goose chase.

"You know that thing was most likely on Twelve Mile Bank and one of the many hurricanes over all these years blew it off the side? It's the only thing that makes any sense. I wish there was another answer but it'll take side sonar to find it sitting at a thousand feet down."

AJ nodded in agreement. "You're probably right Reg, I hate to give up on it but we've certainly given it a good effort."

A thought suddenly crossed her mind. "So those guys chartering with you may well find it if that's what they're doing this week?"

His head dropped. "I'm afraid so. It'll take 'em a while to scan the top of the Bank and we know it's not there, but if they expand their search they may well find it. I doubt they have the means to get to it down there though."

AJ shook her head. "If they know what's in there they'll spend whatever it takes to get to it."

Reg had no argument for that.

Art Renfro was a Canadian national who'd grown up in various countries around the world that his father, a diplomat for the Canadian government, was posted to. Once he hit his teens he became more unsettled by the migratory life and the endless stream of new schools, new languages and new people.

By seventeen, they were living in Germany and he was getting into serious trouble which the German police had little patience for. Finally, in exasperation his father sent him to an American military academy in Alabama where he was systematically pushed, pulled and beaten into line.

He was taught to shoot, stab, disarm, survive and also how to dive. A list of skills he would put to good use down the road. He was not a big man, around five foot nine, but by the time the academy was done with him he was lean and strong, and what he lacked in brute size, he made up for in agility and ruthlessness.

After leaving school Art bounced around a series of hard

labour jobs in the oil fields of Alberta, Canada which eventually got him onboard with a crew that was assigned to another oil field gig in Houston, Texas. While he was there he heard about the big bucks the divers made on the rigs in the gulf so he signed up for his hard hat training.

Kicked off the first rig job he got for getting drunk and fighting, he was back hunting for work in Houston with no work permit and running out of money. As luck would have it he ran across a guy named Dale Carter running a marine salvage company and he was looking for divers.

Carter's group was a rough crowd, they ran hard, drinking and womanizing, and worked twice as hard. If they had a dispute they stepped out back and bare knuckle brawled until only one man was standing. Art loved it.

Most of the work was dragging commercial ships off the rocks or cutting them apart where they lay stranded. Occasionally they'd recover cargo from a stricken ship that went down or raise sunken vessels and tow them to shore.

After six years with this outfit Art had earned his way up to being the senior diver and pretty much ran things for Carter. They all made good money but the man in charge was raking it in and the men were becoming more and more disgruntled as they were taking all the risks and he was getting truly rich.

They were working a job recovering barrels of motor oil from a freighter that went down off the coast of Belize after losing its motor during a storm. The wreck was sitting upright in two hundred and forty feet of water so they were diving mixed gas fed through an umbilical from the surface. High tech dangerous diving.

Art persuaded Carter he needed to come down and take a look as there were issues getting the barrels released from the wreck. Two hours later the crew helped Art back on the surface boat and pulled up the other umbilical with no diver attached. The body of Dale Carter was never found.

Renfro Salvage Services was formed with Carter's old crew and equipment and Art picked up the contracts the former boss had already lined up. He paid the guys a percentage from net profits on every job they did which gave them incentive to work hard and get the job done at the lowest cost possible. It was amazing how many corners they were willing to cut and rules they were willing to break when it meant more money in their pockets.

Art Renfro now stood on Reg Moore's dock wondering where his old acquaintance and the tattooed young lady in her RIB boat had gone at such an early hour.

Chapter 11
Bounemouth, 1997

Grandad Bailey took a long easy drink from his tea cup and set it carefully back down on the table beside his chair. AJ was still sitting cross legged, hanging on her Grandfather's every word. She'd heard this story several times but still soaked it up as though it were the first.

Most stories grow with each repeat telling but Grandad stayed true to his memory each time. Sometimes he'd go into more detail here and there or expand on a side story about the islands or the Navy. Sometimes he'd recall more about his ship mates, but he never embellished, never strayed from the truth as he remembered it.

Arthur Bailey always felt a story should stand on its own merits, if it wasn't interesting then so be it. The man avoided lies his whole life, preferred the company of those who felt the same, and steered clear of those that didn't.

"It was about two weeks later when we set out again on the same patrol, from Jamaica we'd go towards Cuba, sweep around the two sister islands and then stop in Grand for petrol before heading home to Goat. US Navy had a small station on Grand and they'd supply us with the fuel and water we needed.

Weather was back to nice again, seas were pretty calm and as I recall it was an uneventful patrol for the most part. I know there's a few people on the little islands these days, airports and what have you, but back then there was only a handful of people so we never went ashore there. Occasionally we'd spend the night off one of the islands if we didn't want to press on through the night and we'd anchor in a bay. It would take us another half a day for the run across to Grand and we'd take a wide swing around the west side see if we could stumble across anything interesting.

We were all remembering that U-boat sighting so were keen on the binoculars, none of us fancied getting popped off by a torpedo but we'd surely like to take a crack at him. Needless to say he was nowhere to be seen so we made our way to George Town in the late afternoon.

Back in those days it was mainly local fishermen and wealthy retired people in nice houses, none of the big hotels and shops like these days, I've seen pictures of the place now, buildings all along the beachfront, shame really.

Anyway, we left George Town the next morning and motored out towards Goat, usually took us a long day so we set off just after sunrise to get going. From George Town we'd turn around the south side of Grand, past the East End. We'd stay well off the shoreline as the reefs were shallow and dangerous along the south.

The East End was where the famous wreck of the Ten Sails happened, quite the story I tell you. This flotilla of ten British ships leaves Jamaica back in the late seventeen hundreds heading home to England. So, crazy as it sounds they would sail west from Jamaica, plumb opposite direction to England. Then, cut north around the Caymans and the northwest tip of Cuba, before turning east between Cuba and Florida to pick up the trade winds they needed to cross the Atlantic.

Well they thought they'd cleared Grand Cayman, island is really low, barely above sea level and hard to see across the water, especially in the dark. So they started heading more to the north in the night and boom, straight into the reefs off East End! All ten of them hit the reefs one after another, not easy turning big 'ole sail boats around so they either hit the reef or each other and the bloody lot foundered right there. Incredible. Amazingly many of the sailors made it ashore with help from the locals.

So once past East End we'd be heading south east in open water for Jamaica, pretty boring most of the time, we'd be scanning for the Jerrys with the binoculars and we'd take shifts on watch 'cos it was hell on the eyes looking through the binoc's all day. We'd do a couple of hours and then get to rest or do something else on the boat for a while, only thirteen of us so everyone ended up doing a bit of everything. Those MTB boats were made for shoreline type patrols where you'd be close to land and home every night so it was not really designed for going out on two or three day patrols.

Anyway, we'd gone a few hours and next minute one of the lads on watch starts yelling he can see something off the port side in the water. I was cleaning the deck gun at the time and I ran over to the rail but couldn't see what he was getting excited about. We'd see dolphins sometimes and even saw a whale out there once so figured that's what it was. But Cap he turns us over that way and says there's definitely something out there in the water and it's floating on the water so it's not a whale or nothing. He tells us to man the battle stations just in case so we all rush about and man the guns and I'm supposed to be on the bridge with the Captain during attacks so I run up there.

Once I got up there I could see what they were talking about and as we closed in on it we could see it was a dinghy just bobbing on the water. We're probably a hundred miles from land now and this dinghy is just drifting in the open ocean. We gets to it and see there's blokes in this dinghy! This thing looks like it's pretty beaten up, sun's all faded the canvas on it and there's three poor buggers curled up inside this thing.

We got alongside and we've got no idea who this lot are so a couple of the guys are covering them with rifles and we get a rope ladder over the side to the dinghy and Cap sent one of the lads down to tie on the dinghy. There's definitely three of them and they haven't stirred a bit, bloody eerie I tell you, just us out here in the middle of nowhere stumbling across this dinghy full of what looks like dead sailors.

Well, then one of them moves a bit and the lads about jump over the rails ready to shoot the poor bugger and Cap's yelling at them to hold fire! Our lad in the dinghy leaps about halfway back up the ladder he was so scared out of his wits!

He gets back down there and sure enough the one is still alive, barely mind you, but the other two are both dead as doornails. We get a rope tied around the live one and haul him up the side like a sack of potatoes, he's groaning and mumbling stuff we can't understand all the way. We get him laid out on the deck and he's in a bad way, he's wearing a dirty white vest, grey pants and no shoes, every bit of exposed skin is sun burnt so bad it's blistering. His lips are all cracked and bloody so we try and get some water down him but he gurgles and chokes most of it back up. We get some rags wetted down and try and cool him off but it's eighty something degrees out so there's no escaping the heat.

We spent the whole war hating these blokes, the Germans, but now we've got one laid in front of us. He's terrified and just a young lad like the rest of us. He's damn near dead and all we want to do is try and save him, hour earlier we would have done everything we could to try and kill the bugger! Strange ole world innit?

Couple of the lads didn't quite feel the same way, one of them said kick him back overboard and let the sharks have him, but Cap says he might have information and we need to keep him alive. He can't say much this Jerry but he's trying to talk, all in German of course and none of us speak a word of it. Cap asks him over and over.

'U-Boat? Are you from a U-Boat?' Finally in his delirious state he mumbles. 'Yes, U-Boat, das unterseeboot'.

That was the Jerry word for submarine, we did know that much. We hauled the other poor fellas up and wrapped them in some old sheets and tied the dinghy on the deck. Cap gets everyone back on station and heading for Goat as fast as we can and we take the live one down below. It's tight quarters down there but he's more comfortable on a bunk than lying on deck in the sun.

We don't have a medic onboard so Cap tells me to stay with him and do what I can to keep him alive. Well, I've had some basic field medic training, your regular patch 'em up type stuff but they didn't cover anything about treating dehydrated, starving, near dead Germans.

Pretty soon he stops mumbling so much and I get little bits of water down him. I keep talking to him, telling him he's alright now and we'll take care of him. Of course I'm doubting he understands a word but hopefully I sound friendly enough and it's some comfort. At one point he takes hold of my arm when I was switching the wet rags on his forehead, so weak he can barely grip hold of me. I have to lean close to even hear what he's trying to say but I can just catch it.

'Ich heiße Andreas... my name.... Andreas'."

Chapter 12
Grand Cayman, 2017

Reg took a careful sip of his coffee from his travel mug as the thirty six foot Newton dive boat bounced across the gently rolling waves. Built in Louisiana, Newtons are the most popular dive boats and the thirty six was the perfect size for most dive operations. Custom built for the industry and delivered kitted out with forty dive tank racks, rinse tanks, preparation tables and benches down each side. The deck space in the back was wide and open to cater to a large group and the swim step ran the width of the boat with two swing down ladders to move the people in and out of the water quickly.

Forty tank capacity meant two dive tanks for sixteen customers, two or three divemasters and a few spares. Today Reg carried only a few tanks that would stay unused and three customers.

Renfro joined Reg on the bridge, leaving his two goons down on the deck smoking and telling crude stories about their unsavoury adventures the night before. Reg tensed as he heard Renfro climb the ladder to the bridge.

"Nice boat you have here Moore, got yourself quite the cushy number running fat tourists around oohing and aahing at the fishies," The man liked to put people on edge and lived for confrontation. "Don't you miss working for a living, doing some real diving? Can't beat gas axing steel at three hundred feet in frigid water with zero vis man, that's real diving."

As in the first time they'd crossed paths fifteen years

earlier, Renfro immediately got Reg's hackles up. He'd taken over Dale Carter's operation about a year before that first meeting and Reg was working for a treasure hunting outfit called Davis Historical Salvage, or DHS for short. Reg's group was working off the coast of the Florida Keys down near Big Pine Key. DHS specialized in researching missing ships from the sixteen and seventeen hundreds and trying to locate where they may have gone down. Those old wooden ships rotted away long before SCUBA was invented so all that was left was anything metal which usually meant cannons, braces and hardware from the ship itself and coins and precious metals. Much of the wealth being shipped back from the New World was lost in those dangerous days of sailing from continent to continent and reports of the wrecks were often sketchy, unclear and inaccurate.

DHS would study all the information they could dig up about a wreck, take their best estimate at where it might be and then spend months, sometimes years scouring the sea floor using modern search technology. They only had to hit pay dirt once every five or six years to make it worthwhile with the treasure they'd haul in.

DHS did it by the book. When they found a wreck they'd immediately report the find, claim the wreck, and wait out the process with the local government before going any further. This presented quite a security problem at the wreck site. Although they tried to operate stealthily and not advertise what they were looking for and definitely not where, others in the industry all watched each other like hawks. It had been known for one group to give up a search for a lost ship having exhausted their investor's money for the project and another bunch to swoop in and keep looking where the former had left off. Several treasures had been recovered this way so it was a competitive business and poaching key people from someone else's operation was rife.

The wreck they were hunting was the San Felippo, a Spanish galleon on its way from Honduras back to the homeland loaded with gold. The historical records had it foundering on the reef in a storm further north near Marathon but DHS had found a personal account from one of the few survivors that described the coastline and it didn't match.

They were using state-of-the-art magnetometers to pick up anything metallic in eighty feet of water outside of the shallow reef. Their theory was the ship struck the reef but got clear before sinking in the deeper water. After five weeks of systematic searching they found it.

Reg was one of the divers in the water and they brought up a cannon for carbon dating and a couple of handfuls of coins that were encrusted together. They quickly registered the find, claimed the wreck, and began the wait for the bureaucrats to clear them to begin bringing what was left of the ship and its contents topside.

Renfro Salvage Services was working further north on recovering some cargo that had dislodged off the deck of a freighter and lay in deeper water, but had been spotted snooping around the lower keys. Some of Renfro's crew got friendly with one of the DHS guys in a bar in Big Pine and they had a big old time getting drunk and telling stories. They all left the bar and next minute they weren't so friendly anymore and started beating the hell out of him in the corner of the car park. With a knife to his throat he told them everything they wanted to know about the San Felippo.

Embarrassed and scared the man didn't say a word to his employers who were still waiting for the all clear to work the wreck. They had someone on watch from shore twenty four seven and they were diving the site every day as they laid out a grid map of markers and lines in preparation for excavating the site.

One day they splashed in to discover the site had been worked over in one section and a lot of the treasure had been hauled. DHS brought in the authorities but of course there was no evidence left at eighty feet and no one had seen a boat come or go.

They suspected Renfro, so Reg and some of his men drove north along Highway 1 to Marathon Key marina to speak with him at the dock when they came in. Reg had never met Renfro but knew his reputation so he was careful to confront him in a public area with witnesses around to hopefully avoid any violence.

Naturally Renfro denied any knowledge and told Reg in his smug way that he was flattered they thought he could pull off such a daring and stealthy raid. With zero proof there was nothing Reg or DHS could do but at least he felt he'd served notice that they knew who was behind it. All they could do was watch the market and warn all their buyers and dealers that any precious coins and gold antiquities hitting the market were potentially from the stolen cache.

From then on DHS, with permission from the Looe Key National Marine Sanctuary, put a mooring in at the site and had a guard there overnight. Two nights later the night watch heard a boat approaching but never saw it. The boat was running blacked out with no lights on, an illegal practice in itself. The guard called it in but once again there was nothing to be done, the offending boat was long gone.

DHS got their permission and excavated the site over the following few months without further trouble but Reg ran into Renfro a few more times in Big Pine. He'd be snooping around the marina when they came in for the day, clearly trying to see what loot they were hauling in. Reg asked him if he could help him in some way and Renfro just smirked and told him he was simply wandering around a public marina seeing what loot was left on the San Felippo. The man had balls that's for sure.

About a year later the man they'd beaten left DHS after a dispute with other crew members who'd become fed up with his drinking habits. One of them told Reg the man had confessed to him one night about the confrontation with Renfro's men, the crew had kept it quiet to save the man's job at the time.

Reg ignored Renfro's baiting as they motored on towards the Bank. "So what is it your clients are looking for down here Renfro?"

"You know these waters, what's down here worth looking for?"

Reg knew he was getting that arrogant smirk although he couldn't see the man's face as he stood at the top of the ladder behind him. "Everything I know about has been dived already and picked clean, at diveable depths at least, guess you might find something new in the deeper stuff."

Reg was fishing but really didn't expect this cagey thief to give up anything.

"It doesn't matter, shallow, deep, we've got the gear to find it. Of course if you know something and point us in the right direction it would save a shit load of time and I can make it worth your while."

Reg glanced over his shoulder and indeed the man had the conceited look he'd pictured. "Tough to guide you to something when I don't know what you're looking for Renfro."

Renfro laughed. "My client prefers to keep it quiet, just in case someone tries to poach it from them, you know how that goes, don't you Reg?"

It took everything Reg had not to wheel around and throw the guy off the bridge but he kept his cool with a few deep breaths. "So how come you're working for someone else anyway? Who is this guy?" He hoped redirecting the conversation might stop this arsehole jabbing at him and he was getting more curious the more Renfro avoided giving him straight answers.

"The rest of my crew are working a job in Mexico off the Yucatan Peninsula, this guy insisted I help him and by insisted I mean he's paying me a shitload of money. He's a wealthy guy from Argentina, owns a winery. Nice set-up, latest side scan sonar, magnetometer, all the latest gear. He's staying on the boat out here, there it is." Renfro pointed at the horizon where they could just make out the silhouette of a large boat, Reg reckoned it had to be at least a hundred and twenty feet long.

"So why do you need me?" He queried.

Renfro laughed again. "I enjoy your company Reg, because we're old friends, besides I didn't want to stay out here with this lot, me and the boys prefer the action in town."

Reg believed the part about them wanting to live it up on the island but they both knew they were not friends and never would be. There was another reason Renfro had chartered Reg's boat and not one of the thirty others, between fishing charters and dive operators, he could have picked. He just wasn't sure what that reason was.

Thomas was at the helm of the RIB boat while AJ checked over and prepared their clients gear. She often traded with him to keep his boat skills fresh and let him know they worked together and she considered him more than just an employee. AJ admired Thomas' work ethic and the fact he was not only keen to make something of himself, but he chose to do it on island. So many young Caymanians were eager to seek out the exciting world of shopping malls, frenetic night life and bustling cities. Ironically, many of that world were just as enthusiastic to live on a beautiful Caribbean island with the tranquility away from the chaos of a modern metropolis. Contentment is an elusive state of mind.

The couple from San Diego were back on the boat along with a family of four, the Campbells, who were starting their week of morning dives with AJ. Reg had taught the parents to dive around ten years back and AJ had certified the son and daughter as each had become old enough. As with many of AJ's customers they returned each year and dived with her exclusively.

It had rained early in the morning before sunrise but now, as they cruised west to their first dive site, it was clear blue skies and calm seas. To the south in the distance they could see George Town harbour and lined up in deeper water were five cruise ships, the mammoth floating hotels that leapfrogged from one island to the next.

Mr. Campbell caught AJ staring at the big ships. "Do the islanders and residents really want those things here? I suppose they're worth a ton of money to the island, but boy they cause some chaos the mornings a bunch of them dock."

AJ shook her head and smiled. "Depends on your perspective, which mainly depends on your business interests. They bring a lot of income to some of the local shops and businesses. The ones that cater to the cruise shippers, but the average spend on island is only about a hundred dollars per passenger. Spread that amongst all the businesses fighting for those dollars and most are just scraping by while a few of the bigger concerns do very well."

"Man, the traffic in town these mornings and all the people flooding the streets drives me crazy. George Town has such a cool little area by the water in the middle of town, we love it when it's quieter, so relaxing, but we won't go anywhere near it when the ships are in."

AJ agreed. "For all of us outside the day tourist trade it

means total lockdown of traffic in town and swarms of people hitting the beaches they bus them to. We just try to stay clear."

Stepping up on her soapbox, AJ continued, getting more animated. "Here's what I struggle with. As an island, Cayman uses diesel generators to create electricity, a desalination plant for fresh water and a land fill to dispose of rubbish. All our recycling has to be shipped off island to Florida to get processed. Think of the massive impact on the island's limited resources two million passengers a year has. To me that's not worth the income in the long run. I have nothing against cruise ships or the people that choose to go on holiday that way, I just think there's a sensible limit to what a small island can accommodate. One or two of the smaller ones a day, like they are in low season, seems reasonable to me."

"Cayman government probably doesn't share that view I'm guessing?"

AJ laughed. "No, no they don't, they're making out pretty well on cruise ship docking fees."

AJ refused to take cruise shipper reservations for diving as too often they would cancel at the last minute, hungover, decided to do a Jeep tour instead, had to go to Hard Rock Café, dive operators had heard it all. She couldn't understand why you'd travel halfway around the world to a beautiful island to spend two hours getting drunk in an overpriced chain restaurant you can find in your nearest city anywhere. But to each their own.

AJ had Thomas pull up to the buoy at a dive site called Trinity Caves and she used the gaff to hook the line and tie them in. For a nineteen year old she was pleased to see Thomas was calm and comfortable at the controls of the boat and took the passengers comfort into consideration. Most lads his age would be enjoying the power of the boat too much at the expense of throwing the paying customers around. AJ thought about how much trust she had in the young Caymanian. He had never let her down and always went out of his way to be helpful, efficient and learn the business. He was responsible.

She made a big decision at that moment, she would burden Thomas Bodden with a secret she had only ever shared with one other person. She just needed to find the right moment.

Trinity Caves was a beautiful coral face that dropped from around fifty feet over the edge to the depths. The wall was rugged and full of nooks and crannies and swim throughs big enough for divers to negotiate without touching if they were careful. AJ always made a point of only taking divers she felt were suitably skilled in controlling their buoyancy through places like this.

Part of what she enjoyed about teaching and coaching divers was seeing them learn and perfect the skills of controlling buoyancy. It takes practice to master balancing the volume of air in the BCD and your body against the mass trying to make you sink. This constantly has to be adjusted with depth as the surrounding pressure compresses the air and makes it less effective at keeping you buoyant. Calm and experienced divers manage this well and seem to hover in the water regardless of the depth. Inexperienced or anxious divers struggle more with consistently controlling buoyancy and tend to accidently bump into things. AJ referred to it as Zen diving when you become so relaxed and at ease that most of your buoyancy control is done with subtly managing the air in your lungs and leaving the BCD alone.

Today's group were all competent recreational divers and she felt confident taking them through the tighter confines of the wall. She led them into a tunnel that was well lit from both ends but sheltered enough inside that no coral could grow. She rolled a little to her left and spotted the antennae of a lobster reaching out to sense what creature was swimming through his house. AJ shone her light towards him and made a couple of circles with the beam to show those behind where to look.

As she exited the tunnel she turned right into a large crevice between two vertical sides of coral that led back to the wall itself and open water. But it didn't. Ahead, the crevice narrowed until the two sides came together and blocked the way. She paused for a moment, confused, before realizing where she was and saw the next tunnel in the left side. She finned gently forward and ducked into the short tunnel that led to a second crevice which indeed brought her out on the main wall at ninety feet. Damn, she thought, I've dived Trinity a hundred times but I got lost there for a moment. None of the customers even knew she'd hesitated but she still felt a little embarrassed. It reminded her how easy it is to make a mistake in the vast, complex landscape of the ocean.

She almost blew the regulator out of her mouth as the epiphany hit her, what if Herbert made a similar, simple mistake?

Reg sat in the captain's chair on the bridge reading a book. He'd been tied alongside the Explorador de los Océanos for over an hour since watching Renfro and his goons go aboard. Occasionally a deckhand would glance over at him but otherwise no one had said a word.

A voice boomed down from the ship above, "Señor Moore, forgive my rudeness at not introducing myself sooner."

Reg looked up to see a handsome, slender man with grey hair down to his shoulders, dressed in a tropical weight button down shirt and slacks. The man smiled.

"I am Carlos Costa, welcome to my research ship." He beckoned Reg to join him.

The ship was indeed one hundred and twenty eight feet

long and was kitted out as a serious ocean going research and salvage vessel. A large A-frame and crane was mounted on the stern and a twenty eight foot RIB boat tender, similar to AJ's, hung from davits off the port side. Reg recognized the long travel case on the deck as the kind for carrying side scan sonar equipment.

Costa shook Reg's hand and led him through a survey room full of computer equipment and monitors down some stairs to a luxuriously furnished lounge. He spoke perfect English with a thick Latin accent.

"As you can see we have a well-appointed ship, she was originally built for the Argentinian Navy in the seventies and I was fortunate to acquire her about ten years ago. They made some cut backs to save money which was lucky for me."

He offered Reg a seat on one of the settees and stepped over to a bar in the corner of the room. "Can I offer you a drink? We have some exquisite wines you may enjoy." Costa pulled the stopper from a bottle of vintage Malbec and held it for Reg to see.

"I'm on the clock so no thanks, another time."

"My apologies Mr. Moore, of course, you must sail back later today, can I get you anything else? A Perrier perhaps?" He poured a wine for himself and Reg politely declined. "I'm fine really."

Sitting on a bar stool the man continued. "You have crossed paths with the Argentinian Navy I understand Mr. Moore, an unfortunate set of circumstances, I hope you don't hold against myself or my ship."

Reg waved his hand as though it was nothing. "Water under the bridge, The Falklands was a long time ago." He glanced around the room. "I guess it's possible this ship was there though huh? I hope it doesn't mind me aboard."

Costa found this quite amusing. "I assure you my ship

welcomes you!" He took a sip of the wine and switched to a more serious note. "I'm told you are the man that knows these waters the best Mr. Moore, I hope I can persuade you to share some of this knowledge with me."

Reg thought a moment before responding, what is this bloke about? He's clearly dumping a ton of money into whatever project he's here for, could be something really interesting. But he hires a thug like Renfro to work for him which means he's either been misled and made a bad choice or he's up to something illicit and needed the kind of help that doesn't mind getting his hands dirty. He didn't seem like a sucker who would be duped into anything, shit he'd researched the guy he was hiring to be a glorified tour guide. Reg's navy record didn't spring up on google, someone did some digging.

"I have no idea what you're looking for Mr. Costa, so it's rather hard to know if I'm of any use to you or not."

"Please, call me Carlos, and of course you make a good point, one cannot hit a target one cannot see. Let me ask you this Mr. Moore, you have dived the Bank here many times correct?"

"Reg is fine, and yeah, I've pretty much covered the whole thing over the years."

"Have you ever found a wreck or traces of a wreck?"

"Sure, there's a flat barge that was dumped here years ago, otherwise no, I don't know of any other wreck here. It would have been one hell of a piece of luck or coincidence, or I don't know what you'd call it, for a ship to go down in this vast body of water right on top of the only strip of coral that happens to not quite reach the surface instead of heading down to a thousand feet plus... be a bit odd don't you think?"

Costa grinned. "Indeed Reg, that would be as you say, quite odd." He paused and looked Reg squarely in the eyes. "Unless it was intended."

Bollocks, Reg thought, he knows. He tried to remain unfazed and give nothing away with his expression but as Pearl often pointed out to him, poker was not his game.

AJ sat between the Campbell kids with a Caribbean Fish Identification book opened on her lap. The daughter, Ashley, excitedly described a fish she'd seen. "It was really small and it was black and white and had a long willowy tail and swam around in little circles, it was soooo cute!"

AJ flipped through the pages until she found the fish in question. "Here, is this the little guy you found?"

Ashley bounced in her seat and pointed at the picture on the page. "That's him! See, he's the cutest thing ever!"

Her mum peaked over and looked, smiling at her daughter. "Beautiful, that's a juvenile spotted drum isn't it AJ?"

"Yup, that little fellow will live under that coral head probably his whole life, once they find a spot they like they stay there unless something else runs them off."

She points to the other side of the page. "That's what he looks like when he grows up, his body grows into that long tail fin so the bigger his body gets the smaller his tail gets."

AJ turned to the son, Kelby. "So what critter caught your eye down there Kelby?"

The boy was a year older than his sister and typically tried to act more mature and one up his sister. "Aah, I knew most everything I saw, I've seen 'em all before."

His sister rolled her eyes. AJ flicked through some more pages stopping at a picture of a strange flat fish, white with blue markings and both eyes on top of his body. She showed the picture to the boy. "Did you see one of these? We passed over him in the sand at the end of the dive before our safety stop."

"I did see it, but it had more green coloured spots than that picture. That's a ray of some sort isn't it?"

"It's actually a Peacock Flounder but you find them in the sand like rays and often they'll wiggle down in the sand to hide. They can actually change colours and will tint their body markings to better camouflage themselves."

She points to the eyes in the picture. "See how both his eyes are on what is really one side of his body. They start life looking like a regular fish just laid on its side but then one of its eyes moves around over time to the other side so they're both on top like that."

AJ leaves the book with the kids who eagerly thumb through the pages and pick out the various creatures they'd seen. She addressed the group. "How about Aquarium for the second dive? My very first dive was at Aquarium and I love this site as much today as I did then."

With the groups approval she freed the boat from the mooring and joined Thomas at the helm as he gently motored south towards the next dive. She spoke quietly, "Fancy doing a little exploring this afternoon Thomas?"

"Sure thing man, what you got in mind?" He beamed, eager for an adventure.

"I'll explain on the way out, three or four tanks will be enough and we should have enough fuel from this morning as we haven't gone far."

Thomas' enthusiasm combined with his Caymanian lilt always made AJ smile. "Alright then, we'll have some adventure this afternoon!"

AJ's cell phone rang from under the console, she grabbed it and answered. "Mermaid Divers this is AJ."

Reg's voice was quiet and the line scratchy and unclear. "Hey it's me."

"Hi Reg, what's up?"

"I'm just leaving the Bank, they've got one helluva research ship out here, I met the owner, an Argie with pots of money by the look of it. He says he'll tell me more about what they're looking for tomorrow, but I'm pretty sure we know what it is."

AJ was disappointed although this was not unexpected news. "Are they searching the Bank?"

"Yeah, but he already knows there's nothing on top, they'll search the deep stuff around it next. They've got all the right gear."

"Keep 'em looking at the Bank as long as you can, I have another idea. I think Herbert was mistaken, but not how we thought, I'll know more by tonight." AJ hears a voice in the background over the phone and Reg hurriedly whispers. "Gotta go" and hung up.

Renfro stepped down onto the Newton and grinned at Reg. "Let's go Reg, we can head back, these guys want to do some more scanning, we're just in the way."

Reg climbed the ladder to the bridge and started the motor while Renfro, without prompting, freed the rear line first and then went to the front and untied the front line. Reg put the boat in reverse and carefully edged away from the Explorador de los Océanos. It dawned on him that he was alone with Renfro. "Just us going back?"

Renfro looked up with a smirk. "Yup, just you and me old pal, the boys are staying out here to help."

Not exactly Reg's version of an ideal situation, alone with this arsehole across a large stretch of open water. For a moment he felt a little paranoid but shook it off as he thought it through. What would be their incentive to cause him or his boat any harm at this stage? He couldn't think of any unless they really believed he knew something concrete and needed persuasion to discuss it with them. Costa seemed smart enough to try prying any information with money before he resorted to violent means. People tend to notice when bodies stack up or go missing and it gets much harder to cover their tracks, especially on a sleepy little island.

He just hoped Renfro would stay on deck so he didn't have to deal with him for forty five minutes back to the island. He brought the boat up on plane and ran her as hard as he dare without being abusive but the tanks in the racks banged and rattled as they landed off each wave. He set his GPS for West Bay dock and settled in for a bouncy ride back.

His plan worked for forty minutes. The waves smoothed more and more as they closed on the island and when he slowed a little as they approached the outer wall and the water depth went from five hundred feet to eighty, Renfro scaled the ladder and parked himself on the bridge.

"Have a nice chat with Costa did you Reg?"

Reg fought the urge to look at the man. He knew he'd have the same smarmy expression and Reg would have a hard time staying calm. "Seems like a nice bloke. Can't say I'm much the wiser about what you lot are up to though."

"Oh I think you know Reg, I think you and your little girlfriend know quite a bit."

Reg clenched his jaw and took three deep breaths. He knew he shouldn't bite on the hook but damn this guy could push buttons. He kept his voice calm.

"Perhaps I could be more helpful if you weren't so cloak and dagger about all this. You're obviously looking for a particular wreck so tell me what it is and I'll tell you if I know anything."

"You will huh? So if I say we're looking for a galleon from the Spanish Treasure Fleet that sank on the Bank you'd tell me where it is?!" Renfro sneered and laughed.

"I said I'd tell you if I know anything, and I can tell you that I know nothing and have seen nothing that would lead me to think a Spanish galleon wreck is on the Bank." He felt sure that's not what they were looking for and he was being tested or messed with but if he played along maybe Renfro would slip and give up something. "Is that what you're looking for?"

"I'm always happy to find Spanish gold, but no, that's not what Costa is after. Something more recent than that. Ring any bells Moore? Something from the war perhaps, huh?"

Renfro leaned over the console so Reg couldn't escape his gaze and his tone became sterner and more menacing. "So Reg Moore, Bank expert, seen any evidence of a wartime wreck out there? If you know something I suggest you take some of the Argentine's money for it, that'll be the pleasant way for this to go down, much better for you. This would be a great time to tell me."

Reg eased the throttles back as they approached his dock and stood to watch for swimmers and snorkelers in the water. As Renfro became more agitated and aggressive somehow it made Reg become calmer and clearer headed.

"That old fuel barge was probably built around the forties, I'll take you right to it tomorrow. How much is that worth to you?"

He didn't look at Renfro as he busied himself docking the boat but he knew he was seething.

"That's damn funny Moore, apparently you think I'm just fucking around out here on your pretty little island, is that what you think?"

Renfro was holding on to the roof framework of the bridge which if he gripped any tighter he'd snap the aluminium tubing in half. Reg gave no response to his question and continued neatly parking against the dock.

"Let me ask you this Moore, Pearl know you're off sailing around the islands with that hot little tattooed chick? Huh? She probably wouldn't like it too much if she knew you and little purple hair were hunting wrecks and getting it on out there. You know with my high moral standards and all I may be forced to clear my conscience and tell her all about it!" Renfro was practically spitting the words out.

One of the Pearl Divers crew tied the boat off on the dock cleats and Reg shut the motor down. He yelled in the direction of their little storage and office hut. "Pearl! Are you up there?!"

Pearl stepped out of the hut and Reg waved her down to the dock as he descended the ladder leaving Renfro steaming on the bridge. As he stepped onto the dock Pearl walked up and gave him a peck on the cheek. Reg was as cool as a cucumber.

"Hey hon, this bloke I just ferried in wants to talk to you," He pointed to Renfro on the bridge. "I'll grab the kayak and take the boat out." With that he strode up the dock leaving Pearl suspiciously eyeing Renfro while politely asking how she could help.

Renfro climbed down and exited the boat, clenching his teeth watching Reg walk away. He looked at Pearl with cold eyes.

"I might want to close the bill at the end of the week with a different credit card, if that's okay?" Without waiting for an answer he stomped off up the jetty.

Chapter 13
Bournemouth, 1997

Beryl Bailey handed AJ a glass of Ribena. The eight year old hadn't moved from the settee across from her Grandad in over an hour and after a few gulps she set the glass down, ready to get back to the story.

"Annabelle, you mustn't bother Grandad all afternoon, he probably has a football game he'd like to watch."

Arthur put his freshly refilled tea cup down. "Nonsense Beryl, Tottenham don't play until later anyway, me and AJ are just trading stories about some of the old days, ain't we squirt?"

AJ nodded at her mother who smiled at them both.

"Alright then, just warning you though, she'll keep you here all afternoon Grandad."

"That would be fine with me Beryl." He grinned at his daughter-in-law and winked at AJ. Beryl chuckled and walked to the door. Nana Lily was peeking through the doorway and the two women looked back in the room as AJ fidgeted anxiously, impatiently waiting.

Arthur and Lily had met during the war when he was stationed at Portsmouth Royal Dockyard on the south coast, near where she grew up in Cowes on the Isle of Wight. Arthur and some shipmates took the ferry over the Solent to the Isle one weekend on leave. While there they dropped in for lunch to a small tea shop that happened to be owned by Lily's family.

Arthur was besotted with the pretty young girl working there but was much too embarrassed to ask her out in front of his mates. Later in the afternoon he made an excuse to slip away from them for five minutes and ran back through town to the little shop. It was three o'clock and she was just turning the closed sign on the door when he arrived out of breath and insisted she unlock the door again.

She couldn't believe this handsome young soldier was going to all this trouble to speak to her and he couldn't believe this beautiful girl was giving him the time of day. After some negotiation her mother reluctantly gave permission for Arthur to take Lily to the cinema that night.

All the men had return tickets on the ferry that evening so Arthur told his mates to go ahead, he was staying and would catch the ferry back tomorrow. He had nowhere to stay and about enough money for cinema tickets, a new ferry ticket and hopefully a soda or two.

The movie was Citizen Kane. He watched some of it but mostly he looked at Lily. This girl was the sweetest, prettiest creature he'd ever seen, he felt his whole world change in that one evening. Fifty seven years later, as he noticed her in the doorway, he felt exactly the same way.

"I'm ready Grandad, his name is Andreas, that's where we were up to. On the boat heading back to Jamaica, you were in charge of Andreas."

The two women chuckled and left them alone.

"Right you are my dear, right you are…"

Arthur could not be happier in this moment, with his adored wife close by and his precious granddaughter in front of him eager to hear his tales. Relieved his mind was still sharp enough to recall these memories from a time and a world gone by, he carried on with the tale.

"So this fella, Andreas, he's still in bad shape. He keeps curling up and clutching his stomach and groaning and I feel terrible 'cos I've no idea what I'm supposed to do for him.

Seems like when I get some water in him a few minutes later he's doubled over in pain again. I'm guessing his insides are pretty messed up from dehydration but I'm at a loss how to fix him. At least I could dab a bit of this burn ointment we have on his skin where it's all blistered and raw, gotta be painful as hell for the pour bloke.

It's hot as hell down in the boat too, he's out of the sun but it's sweaty and damp down in the bunks, we didn't have air conditioning or anything fancy like that so it's pretty miserable. Of course he's off a sub and those things were always hot and sweaty, especially when they was submerged. No circulation whatsoever and the electric motors producing a lot of heat, the air getting staler the longer they're down there. I don't think I could ever go down in one of those things, called 'em iron coffins. Right name for 'em I reckon.

I keep talking to him and tell him my name and so on and every once in a while he sorta comes around and he talks some more. Start with he kept mumbling in German and I've got no idea what he's trying to say, but then out of the blue he looks up at me and says, 'thank you Arthur'. My first thought was bloody hell I hope he wasn't compos mentis enough to hear the lads talking about kicking him overboard!

Next he says 'my stomach, something bad, my stomach is much hurting'. His English is pretty good but he's still mumbling a lot and he's got this heavy Jerry accent so it's hard to catch everything but at least we can talk a bit.

I ask him about his submarine 'cos I'm thinking maybe it's the one we saw two weeks ago. He says they were off Grand Cayman the night of the big storm and I tell him we chased after him that evening. What a coincidence eh? Same boat we saw weeks before and we run across this bloke floating in a raft in the middle of the ocean two weeks later.

He tells me they'd been in the dinghy since that night of

the storm so no wonder he's in a bad way. Another day and he'd be dead like his mates. So now I'm really curious, there's no way we hit him so who sunk their submarine?

'Nein, we turned back right under you, we heard your motors over our heads and then the depth charges, we were long away by then' and he's grinning like a fox when he says that!

'So who sunk you then'?

'Nein, nein, niemand, no-one, nobody sink us, we leave the boot'.

Of course this makes no sense so I'm figuring he's delirious again and I'm putting another wet towel on his forehead and calming him down. He was getting excited which couldn't be good for him.

'The sail boot, the sail boot was gone. Wilhelm and Lars, we get to the top and there's no boot? We don't know where is the sail boot'?

I tell him we saw a sail boat that night heading right for the storm, we tried to stop them but they were hell bent on sailing right into it.

'Ya, ya, the sail boot must pick us up but it is gone, we come up in the storm and it is gone'.

The more he talks the more confused I'm getting 'cos nothing seems to make any sense. I ask him about the rest of the crew, if him and his two mates ended up in the dinghy then where's the rest of them?

'In the sail boot, they wait on the top in the sail boot. The Kapitänleutnant and all the crew'.

So I'm wondering where did they all go then? That was two weeks before and I hadn't heard anything about a bunch of Jerry's showing up in a sail boat. Of course Andreas had no idea at all, he seemed as muddled about it as I was. I told him I didn't know how they could have made it in that storm which got him more upset.

His stomach was cramping and hurting real bad again so I tried to calm him down a bit and stopped asking him questions. Despite the pain he was more coherent now and clearly worried about his shipmates so he kept asking me.

'No-one has seen the sail boot? This can't be... they must have been blown from the course in the storm'.

I tell him I don't know but nothing has been reported I've heard about, I even ran up top and asked the Cap in case he knew something but none of us did.

He'd been coming around and he's sitting up now and talking quite a bit but the stomach pain attacks are getting closer together and he's burning up like he had a bad fever. I keep the wet cloths on him but it doesn't seem to help much. He was all stressed out about his shipmates which wasn't helping anything either.

I asked him what boat he was on and he said it was U-1026 so I asked him again where the sub was and why they were leaving it. He got really nervous when I asked and said he needed to know where the others were.

He was getting worked up again and then he had a really bad stomach cramp and starts dry heaving 'cos there's nothing in his stomach to come up. He's shaking from the fever and curls up clutching his belly, it was awful. He stares up at me and I can see he's terrified, his eyes are all big and full of pain and fear. He grabs me and starts babbling in German again and I'm telling him just to lie still and rest but I think he was sure he was dying. Then he starts in English again.

'They're dead, they're all dead, you think they're all gone? The sail boot? If they're all dead there's no-one left, no-one who knows, someone has to know. My family, can you tell my family'?

I tried to reassure him, 'you can tell them Andreas,

you've got to stay strong, you'll see your family again. This war is nearly over, you'll make it and you can go home to 'em.'

He's getting delirious again and he's begging me to tell his wife and his family about what happened to him, poor bloke. So I says of course I'll tell them, I'll find them and tell 'em whatever you want.

Then he says 'you have to get it to them, I'll tell you but you promise you'll get it to them'?

I'm sure he's out of mind now but he makes me promise so what can I do? I tell him I promise although I've no idea what I'm agreeing to. Then he tells me.

'The boot, it's on the bottom, we rested it safe on the bottom. You have to find the boot'.

So all the waters around there are at least a thousand feet deep and most of it is much deeper than that so I'm thinking they scuttled this U-boat in the shallower stuff just off Grand but he says no. He tells me the sub is miles off shore but it's only thirty odd metres down, which I checked later is about a hundred and twenty feet. The next bit really surprised me, he tells me, 'the three of us take the boot to thirty four metres and set it down there and then we swim out to the top, to the surface!'

According to my little German friend, Andreas, they parked a bloody great big submarine at over a hundred foot down in the middle of an ocean that's much deeper than that and then swam out of it to meet their shipmates at the surface who were there when they went down but disappeared somewhere in the storm never to be seen again.

I know he was the enemy, but I liked this bloke. He was just a lad doing his duty like we all were, he just happened to be on the wrong side of things. I guess if I was born in Germany I would have been in his shoes and probably wouldn't know any different. I clearly remember really hoping this little bloke wasn't dying, but I was convinced about one thing; he was off his rocker and had no idea what he was babbling about, 'cos none of that seemed possible to me."

Chapter 14
Grand Cayman, 2017

AJ made sure her customers had all their gear off the boat and were happily on their way at the dock. The Campbells were back tomorrow but the couple from San Diego headed home the next day so these were their last dives this trip. It took a few minutes extra to wrap up their paperwork and say goodbye. They gave AJ a generous cash tip which she split with Thomas back on the boat, their standard arrangement was to split all tips.

They cast off the dock and AJ was bristling with anticipation to get back out there and see if her theory was correct. She turned on the marine GPS and set the target she wanted as she eased across the shallows. Thomas finished putting the dock bumpers away, neatly rolling up the lines and stowing them and joined AJ at the console. "So Boss, where are we heading on this adventure?"

AJ chuckled. "Well Thomas, first of all there's a story I have to tell you and then we'll get to the where we're going part."

"I like a good story now, don't be leaving anything out!"

AJ thought for a moment quite how much detail she should go into and decided the abbreviated version was probably all that was needed.

"So, I've talked about my Grandad before and how he patrolled these waters in World War Two, right?"

Thomas nodded as he grabbed a water from the cooler

and tossed it to AJ. He rummaged around and came up with a soda for himself.

"Well, on one of those patrols they spotted a German U-boat and chased it around but never caught it…"

Thomas about sprays soda all over the boat. "You mean a U-boat like the submarine?!"

"Yup, just like a submarine. A big storm was brewing so they headed for port and didn't think anything more about it. So a few weeks later they're patrolling again and they run across this raft floating in the middle of the ocean. Inside this raft is three German submariners, two of them are dead and one is barely alive."

Thomas' jaw is hung open as he soaks up this tale in amazement. He can't believe this all happened out here in the waters off his sleepy little island.

"They haul them aboard and my Grandad is left to tend to the one that was still alive. They wanted to try and keep him that way and get him back to the naval base in Jamaica. Maybe he'd be able to tell them stuff to help the war effort. This poor fellows name is Andreas Jaeger and my Grandad does his best to make him comfortable and they take a shine to each other on the trip back."

They reach where the wall drops away and AJ opens the motors up and the RIB boat planes out and skips across the gentle swell. She shouts over the noise of the wind and the motors to continue.

"Well it's hours to Jamaica and Andreas isn't doing well, he's feverish and delirious and he starts telling Grandad all kinds of things. He says they were the U-boat he saw two weeks before and him and the other two in the raft had ditched this U-boat in a hundred and twenty feet of water way off shore from Grand. They'd come up in the middle of the storm and the boat that was supposed to pick them up had gotten lost so the three ended up in the little dinghy. Two weeks on the open water with no food and only rain water and by some miracle Grandad's patrol ends up running into them. Too late for the others but lucky for Andreas. Well, not really, but maybe lucky for us."

AJ pauses to drink some water and Thomas mumbles, still stunned in amazement.

"This is some kinda tale you're telling me, I ain't never heard nothing like this before."

"Well, you gotta promise me Thomas you won't tell this to a single soul, the part coming up is a secret that's been kept for a very long time."

"Ain't nobody gonna believe me if I did tell 'em! But I swear, I won't tell a soul."

"So, the only place that matches the depth and description Andreas told Grandad is Twelve Mile Bank. But, as you know, we've covered every square inch of it over the years and there's no sign of a submarine there. Reg, who's the only other person who knows about this, believes it was on the Bank and slid over the edge so now it's somewhere around the base of the Bank at five hundred to a thousand feet down.

Something has always told me that's not where it is so when we found your uncle's chart with the pinnacle marked at one twenty instead of four hundred I thought we'd unlocked the secret."

"I was wondering why you were getting so excited over that old map! Is that where we're going?"

AJ smiled and shook her head.

"Nope, Reg and I went out there yesterday, that pinnacle is right at four hundred feet where it's supposed to be. What I'm hoping is your uncle got his pinnacles confused. There's another one less than a mile from the first and it's closer to the Bank, charts have it deeper at six hundred feet, that's where we're heading."

Thomas looks a little confused. "But if that one is deeper why we going there?"

"Like I say, my theory is your uncle thought he was on the shallower one when in fact he was on the deeper one. That's all it is, a theory, we may just be having a nice afternoon on the water. But if he was catching fish on that pinnacle it means there's a reason the fish like being there and that normally means there's smaller fish there and the smaller fish like a reef and there's no reef growing at six hundred feet. Hence my theory."

She took a deep breath. She wasn't sure whether it sounded better or worse when it was all spelled out and spoken to someone else. But Thomas was buying in.

"That's a great theory right there! We'll find a submarine this afternoon for sure!"

Costa stood on the rear deck of the Explorador de los Océanos looking at a line running from the crane into the water as the ship ambled slowly along. He dialed his cell phone. "Renfro? We're about done on the top of the Bank, any luck with Moore?"

Renfro stepped onto the balcony of a luxurious hotel room on Seven Mile Beach overlooking the smooth pale yellow sand and beautiful blue water. With just a towel wrapped around his waist he glances back over his shoulder into the room as he closes the French door behind him. Inside a slender young lady rolls gracefully off the bed and walks naked across the bedroom into the bathroom.

"That son of a bitch knows something but he's not talking. He's a tough old bastard but he'll cave under the right pressure."

Costa pauses and thinks a moment. "Do nothing yet, we

will likely find it ourselves in the next few days, no reason to complicate matters."

He was far from being above using whatever means necessary to achieve what he wanted but Carlos Costa was good at avoiding preventable scrutiny. Curiously he enquired. "Where do you think this man has his pressure points Mr. Renfro?"

Art Renfro grinned at the very thought of being able to inflict pain directly or indirectly on Reg Moore. "The women. His wife, or even better that hot little tattooed number he treats like a daughter. Either one will bring him to his knees."

Even the Argentinian, who had caused much pain and suffering over the years, was amazed at the ruthlessness of Renfro and his thirst for inflicting misery, the kind of thirst that Costa had known too well before.

Carlos Costa was born in Mendoza, Argentina in 1957, the only living son of Garcia and Renata Costa. Their first child died in infancy six years earlier and they had given up on the hope of having children when Renata became pregnant again.

Garcia had spent the prior eleven years building a lucrative wine business in the foothills of the Andes and from birth Carlos was trained and educated to succeed his father. At forty one, Garcia felt an urgency to prepare his son for the future both in business and in life. The Costa's lived well and by twelve Carlos would be home tutored in the mornings and spend the afternoons with his father in the winery.

On weekends Garcia took his boy to the mountains, hunting in summer and skiing in winter, the two became inseparable and young Carlos idealized his father. By age twenty two he was completely immersed in the running of the winery which was not only distributing wine throughout Argentina but exporting throughout Latin America and beginning to find markets in North America.

In 1979 on a cool August Sunday morning, Garcia took Renata for a drive around the vineyard as they often did together. At the top of the hillside they parked the car and stood beholding the view across the slopes of vines and enjoying the refreshing crisp air of the morning.

Neither heard the man approach from behind and Garcia was confused and shocked by the muffled report and his wife crumpling to the ground with her hand still holding his. He then felt the muzzle of the silenced pistol rest against the back of his head and all became clear. The last thing the man formerly known as SS Officer Kurt Neinstadt heard was the word 'Gerechtigkeit' before he joined his wife on the ground dead.

The Israeli Special Forces operative snapped a photo of the bodies to go in his account of the execution along with a note that the message 'justice' was delivered before the sentence was carried out.

Carlos was devastated, but he was not completely surprised. A year earlier his father had sat him down one afternoon in his home office overlooking the vineyard, poured them both a glass of vintage Malbec, and told him the whole story.

He explained how he was born Kurt Neinstadt in Hallstatt, Austria, a small town in the northern mountains. Enamored with Hitler's policies to reestablish Germany and the central European countries to the dominant power it once was prior to the Great War, he followed his countryman to Berlin and joined the Nazi party.

At the outbreak of war in 1939 Neinstadt was assigned to the department responsible for Jewish affairs within the Schutzstaffel, or SS, under the infamous Lieutenant Colonel Adolf Eichmann. In 1941 Hitler's Jewish policy changed from emigration to extermination and Eichmann and his group began herding the Jewish population into their newly formed concentration camps.

As a powerful high ranking officer in the SS, Neinstadt attended many Nazi party functions which were renowned for their indulgences and grandeur. It was at one of these events in Berlin that he met the seventeen year old daughter of the owner of an iron works in Frankfurt. He was twenty seven and decided this pretty young girl from a solid German family was the perfect arm candy for a man of his standing and future mother to pure blooded Aryan children.

He married Freda the following year and was surprised to find himself quite in love with the girl by the time the war came to an end a year later in 1945. Like Eichmann and many of their Nazi counterparts, they fled the country as the Reich crumbled and the Allies marched towards Berlin. Unlike most of his fellow officers he chose to escape with his wife rather than abandoning his family to whatever fate befell them.

They made their way to Austria and on to Spain where the network, later named the Ratline, was forming. In 1946 the Labour Party led by Juan Perón took over government in Argentina and openly denounced the Nuremberg Trials of Nazi war criminals. This opened the doors for former Nazis to make their way to South America, assume new identities and new lives. The so called Ratline was complete, a clandestine network of sympathizers and zealots with deep reaching connections throughout the European community, even the Vatican was suspected of involvement.

Kurt and Freda Neinstadt were reborn as Garcia and Renata Costa arriving in Argentina on a Government owned freighter used for exporting sugar. Before leaving Germany Kurt had managed to exchange Reichsmarks for gold and landed in his new country with enough wealth to buy some land and start a business. He chose Mendoza for its proximity to the Chilean border should further relocation be necessary, and closeness to the mountains which he missed from his youth.

In 1960 Adolf Eichmann, who'd adopted a new life as the foreman at a Mercedes Benz factory under the name Ricardo Klement, was snatched and smuggled to Israel by their Intelligence Service. He stood trial, was sentenced to death for war crimes and hanged two years later.

The Costas contemplated running when the news broke but the thought of fleeing again with their infant son and leaving the winery behind was too much. They gambled that if they hadn't been grabbed by now then they were probably safe. It took another nineteen years for them to lose that wager.

After his parents deaths Carlos continued to run and grow the business but his anger and hatred towards the Jews, passed down in his family, was deep seated and bourgeoning. He was also smart enough to realize that he'd been spared from execution for now, but they knew where he lived. Any obvious or advertised anti-Semitic actions by him could mean the same fate as his parents, so he was careful. He hid the donations he made through layers of dummy off-shore corporations and always remained at least an intermediary away from any illegal activities. Through these covert means, the blood of many Jewish business men, financiers and politicians were on his hands.

Ever since that day in the office with his father, where the man had put faith in his son to accept, understand and embrace his beliefs and secrets, Carlos Costa had an obsession. Kurt Neinstadt had put an elaborate scheme in motion back in 1945. Now to complete that plan his son would need money, a ship and a lot of research.

"Well, let's see what we find ourselves with the Explorador, we also have our man in place tomorrow do we not?"

Renfro shook his head, disappointed, but Costa was paying the bills so his fun would have to wait. "We do."

"Alright, have Moore bring you out again in the morning." He walked back across the deck heading towards the stateroom. "I trust your accommodations there are acceptable?"

Renfro turned around and surveyed his room through the French doors, the girl was back in the bedroom, she'd tidied her hair and put on a skimpy black bikini. "The room and the… accompaniments are exceptional, thank you."

Costa chuckled, "Have a good day Mr Renfro," and hung up the phone.

Renfro stepped back into his room and checked out his escort who appeared ready to leave. He dropped the towel from around his waist. "We're not done, you can take that back off."

AJ had the stereo cranking out some State Radio rock reggae tunes and the motors humming. The RIB boat was a fun craft, built to ride out any weather and more than enough power to make the twelve mile run in short order.

Checking the GPS she made a small course adjustment and motored for a few more minutes before backing down the throttles and hitting pause on the music. "Okay, we're getting close, now we start trolling around and watching the depth, see what we find."

Thomas joined her at the helm and studied the gauges. Pretty soon they were right on top of the pinnacle according to the GPS but the depth gauge hadn't moved off eleven hundred feet. After she was sure they'd gone well beyond where the GPS thought it was she backtracked parallel to the first path but about fifty yards to the north. Still nothing.

"Where the hell has that pinnacle gone?" Thomas tapped the digital depth gauge like it was an old analogue type that sometimes sticks. The read out was changing as they moved but only by five or six feet which had as much to do with riding the swell as changes in the sea floor.

AJ moved another fifty yards north and made a return pass with the same result. "One more try further north and we'll move to the south and do the same."

Still no change in depth on the third attempt so she turned the boat ninety degrees, ran two hundred yards south and turned ninety again to begin another parallel run.

"Something's gotta be wrong with the satellites, those GPS are normally money aren't they?"

AJ concentrated on making a straight run. "Yup." She was using the GPS to judge how far she was away from the original target where it located the pinnacle, and the compass to run straight on the heading.

After three runs to the south they'd covered a hundred and fifty yards square around the GPS location, the pinnacle wasn't there. Thomas looked across the open ocean all around them. "Man, how does a whole rock pinnacle disappear Boss? This is terrible! What we do now?"

AJ smiled calmly at Thomas. "It doesn't. This is actually great news. And what we do now is start a broader search pattern."

Thomas threw his hands in the air in confusion. "How on the Lord's great earth is this good news?!"

"Because if it's not where the GPS thinks it is, it means it's not where the charts have it, 'cos that's what the GPS used to put it here. If the charts have it wrong, it strongly suggests the chart hasn't been updated in years with better technology and they may be wrong about other things too... like the depth."

Thomas beams from ear to ear. "You're pretty damn smart Boss!"

"Having a theory doesn't make me smart Thomas, but if we do find it somewhere else and I'm right, I will feel a little bit clever."

"So how are we gonna search this whole big ocean?" He looked around at all the endless water around them. "There's a lotta places it could be and we only know it's not here where it's supposed to be."

AJ had been thinking about this and trying to decide the best way to do it. The GPS and compass were her only guide but they didn't steer the boat, they just told her which way she had steered the boat. It was up to her to make the maneuvers which was incredibly hard in open water with no physical references, not even land on the horizon.

She strained her eyes in all directions. Something caught her eye way out to the south of them, she grabbed her binoculars from under the console and trained them on the horizon. "Bugger."

"What do you see?" Thomas questioned as she handed him the binoculars so he could take a look for himself.

Pointing, she explained, "That's the salvage guy's boat, the people Reg has been chartered to run back and forth to the Bank. They're running side scan sonar looking for the same thing we're after."

"That's a nice boat!" Thomas exclaimed as he returned the binoculars to the console. "They looking for the sub too? How'd they know about it?"

"That's a good question, a really good question, but Reg is sure they do. That's the Bank over there they're running on. What we don't need is for them to see us and what we're up to.

We're much lower in the water so hopefully we're not as easy to spot as they are."

AJ was really bothered by the thought she'd be seen and raise their suspicions but she shook it off as best she could. There was nothing she could do except abandon her search, which got them no closer to an answer, or carry on and hope they'd find the pinnacle... and it's shallower than advertised... and it's got a submarine sitting on it... and the salvagers don't see her over here. When she stacked all the 'what if's' in her head the getting spotted part seemed a lot less significant.

"Spiral search pattern. That's how we'll search. We start about two hundred yards off the GPS target and make a circle around it. Then we move fifty yards further out and make another circle. We keep going in wider circles until we find the pinnacle or we bump into Grand Cayman ten miles away!"

"Alright then, that's what we'll do!" Thomas agreed.

The GPS had a feature where she could lock the screen and it would trace the boats movement as a line on the screen. She put the GPS's idea of where the pinnacle was dead centre and lined the boat up directly two hundred yards south. From there she began a long, slow circle trying to make a smooth arc at an even distance from the centre. Thomas watched the depth carefully, looking for it to get shallower.

It was a tedious task. As she made the next circle another fifty yards out AJ was able to speed the boat up a little as she was making a wider turn. She kept increasing the speed with each wider circle for the first few but levelled off around five knots as any faster was getting a wake going that was making the waters choppy.

It was late afternoon by the time she was seven hundred yards out and still nothing, pretty soon she'd be halfway to the Bank. She had three things starting to weigh heavily on her mind.

First problem was the boat was getting low on petrol. She knew how much she needed to get back to Grand so she had a cut-off level on the gauge she couldn't go below, but this was an imperfect science. It was a gauge measuring the level of a fluid getting slurped around in a tank as the boat rocked in the swells. Running out of petrol in open water was a bad plan and an expensive fix when you had to pay a marine tow service to drag you back home.

Second issue was the salvager's boat. As AJ made bigger circles every one took her closer to the Bank on the south side where they were operating. Fortunately they had been running side scan sonar off the edge of the Bank and had been heading away from her position. So far. Pretty soon they'd be turning around the west end and coming back towards where she was making circles and would see her for sure.

Third and most troubling problem was they hadn't found the damn pinnacle yet. The longer they went the more she questioned her whole theory. Maybe the first pinnacle was the only one, both the charts and Herbert were incorrect.

"Last lap around Thomas, that'll leave us just enough fuel to make it back." She cursed herself and her impatience to get back out here. "I should have taken the time to top off before we left, that was stupid of me."

"No matter, we come back here tomorrow if we have to". Thomas' optimism was relentless and made her feel a little better.

The next circle took about fifteen minutes and as she completed it, with yet again no real change in the depth profile, she studied the petrol gauge. Thomas took a look through the binoculars at the ship on the horizon.

"Where they at Thomas?"

"Looks like they're just turning across the west end now, they're moving pretty slow with that scanning and all."

"Damn it Thomas, I apologize if I run us out of petrol but let's give it one last lap around."

"No problem Boss, I can row us home if I have to!" Laughing, AJ moved out another fifty yards and began the arduous trudge in another circle in the middle of the ocean. She sped up just a little, wrestling the need to hurry against the necessity of saving petrol. The ship was about four miles away from them on the far end of the Bank as she approached the spot directly between the first pinnacle and the Bank.

"Wait up!"

AJ had been more concerned with the ship than with the depth and jumped, surprised when Thomas yelled. She looked at the depth reading nine hundred and fifty feet.

"That's the first time it's been less than a thousand Boss!" She swung the boat about and ran back the way they'd come but a little further west. The depth shallowed even more. She turned directly towards the Bank at west south west and within fifty yards it was reading six hundred feet. AJ held her breath and kept going. Six hundred was what the chart said just in a different spot, she could barely look. Five hundred and still getting shallower, four fifty, still going, four hundred… and it levelled there for a moment and started deeper again.

"No! Not deeper!" Thomas complained.

AJ whipped the boat around and started a parallel pass to the south, the depth began rising again until it hit three eighty and back to deeper. She turned again and throttled down to think about it a moment. She was directly between the shallow Bank and the first pinnacle so there must be a mountain spine running in this direction. They tended to be flat topped from the coral growth years ago when the water levels were lower so it's unlikely a shallower reef would be either side of the plateau they'd found. She rolled the throttles back on and aimed straight for the Bank. The depth dropped away again down to four seventy five, she kept going, five hundred, a little further, still five hundred, it had levelled but finally it began rising again.

The ocean floor was coming back towards them and rising quickly. Finally it levelled off again at one hundred and twenty eight feet. She'd been right, they'd found the elusive pinnacle.

Thomas jumped and hopped around yelping like he'd won the lottery and AJ slumped over the console, mentally exhausted.

"You found it Boss! This is amazing! Now all we do is dive down and find us a great big ole submarine!"

AJ stood up beaming from ear to ear. "Well, we'll see if there's a sub down there but at least we found the missing pinnacle! Apparently your uncle Herbert was only half crazy!"

She started looking around to gather her diving gear when it dawned on her she'd forgotten about the ship.

"Shit, where's the salvage ship at?!"

She grabbed the binoculars and quickly found the ship on the horizon. At first it appeared to have gotten smaller. Then she realized it only seemed smaller because its bow was pointed right at them, they'd turned the corner and were making their way back along the north side of the Bank. Anyone on the bridge could see them bobbing on the water about three miles straight ahead.

"Damn it, we gotta go!" AJ hurriedly recorded their location in the GPS, swung the boat around to head directly east and opened up the throttles. Thomas hung on and looked back over his shoulder at the salvager's ship in the distance. "They're a long way out there Boss, good chance they're not seeing anything."

AJ wasn't convinced but all she could do was hope. She glanced at the gauges, "Maybe... now we gotta pray we don't run out of petrol.."

On the bridge of the Explorador de los Océanos Costas held the powerful binoculars to his eyes and watched the RIB boat hurriedly head away from him.

Letting the binoculars down to hang from the strap around his neck he noted the compass heading from his ship to AJ's boat skipping across the waves towards Grand Cayman.

Once AJ felt she was out of sight of the ship she backed the motors way down and went into fuel conserve. There was a sweet spot where the boat was up on plane but at the lowest rpm's to keep it there that should be the most efficient.

As they coasted to the dock on idle she heard one of the motors cough. She shut them down as they bumped alongside where Reg and Pearl were waiting to tie them off. Thomas hopped up on the dock. "I'll get us filled up Boss."

"Thanks Thomas, I'll grab the kayak in a minute, I need to chat with Reg first."

AJ walked with Reg and Pearl up the dock to the hut. Reg grabbed three Strongbows from the fridge, popped the tops and handed them out. "Well?"

AJ held her bottle up so all three could clink them together. "We found the second pinnacle. It's not where it says on the chart, it's in line with the first one and the Bank. And it's got a section that's around a hundred and thirty feet!"

Pearl gave AJ a big hug and Reg smiled and shook his head. "Well stone the crows, ole Herbert was right about part of it, he just didn't know where the hell he was. Did you splash in?"

The smile left AJ's face. The more she thought about it the more she could feel her own optimism talking herself into having not been seen, but in the back of her mind she knew different.

"No, we had to jet out of there, that salvage lot..."

"Costa, I met him this morning, Carlos Costa," Reg added.

"Okay, so Costa was doing a lap of the Bank, presumably side scan sonar off the edges. To start he was going away from us but just as we found the pinnacle he made it around the end and turned back towards us. He was maybe three miles away and we're a low profile but I'm not convinced we weren't spotted."

Reg thought for a moment. "At that distance there's no way he could tell exactly where you were, he'd just have a heading. If he looked at the charts it would look like you're on the first pinnacle, right?"

AJ shrugged her shoulders. "I guess, unless he matched it with his radar. A ship that size must have radar and we would have shown up on that."

"It does, I saw the array radar antenna." Reg nodded in agreement. "But unless he took the time to line everything up and figure distances odds are he placed you on the pinnacle on the chart."

Pearl was taking all this in, Renfro terrified her and she didn't like the sound of this Costa character either so her anxiety was building. She considered herself easy going and tended not to sweat the small stuff but she was pretty convinced this wasn't small stuff. She tentatively asked. "So, what's the plan now?"

AJ pondered. "We need to get Costa and Renfro off our tail so we can dive it. We found Herbert's pinnacle but that doesn't mean there's a wreck on it."

Reg was excited and impressed that she'd figured out a theory and proven it, but he too was wary of the salvagers. He knew what Renfro was capable of and Costa hired him for a reason, he was sure it wasn't as his public relations rep.

"You're right, it doesn't mean it's down there but it certainly matches the story. If Herbert, who knew these waters as well as anyone could get confused, I bet a bunch of German submariners sure as hell could. Who knows what their chart looked like in 1945 but it probably had the Bank on it so I'm sure that's what they intended to land on. Could have got confused in the storm and stumbled on the pinnacle by mistake I suppose."

He stared out across the water. "We have to dive the site asap but they can't see us do it."

AJ blurted out. "Night dive it! We could go out again tonight and do it!"

Pearl was not impressed by this idea. "Good God AJ, you're crazier than this old buzzard," She prodded Reg. "And how are you going to stay hidden, you have to have your lights on and Costa's ship is out there all night!"

AJ agreed that wouldn't work. The idea of diving blind in the dark in the open ocean on an unknown site gave her the chills now she thought about it. But somehow they had to get back out there.

Reg settled it. "Alright, we know what we need to do we just need a window of time to do it. I'll see what I can find out tomorrow, maybe I can figure out their movements."

AJ reluctantly accepted that's all they could do for now. "I guess so, if we knew when they were starting a pass with their scanner heading west and away from the pinnacle, that would buy us enough time to do a dive."

She thought about how long she'd need. At a hundred and twenty to thirty feet she'd only have around twenty minutes to stay out of deco. If she could see the bottom well enough from around eighty feet, which she should be able to, she could survey from there and just go down deeper if she saw something. That would get her at least half an hour.

"How fast would they go pulling the scanner along Reg?"

"Usually around three knots, you have to run pretty slow to get a good image. It's a ton of information being sent up."

AJ started crunching numbers in her head. "On a three mile run down the side of the Bank that would give us about fifty minutes or so. I figure a thirty minute dive plus time to get there from a mile or two further away where we can't be seen, plus time to get out after… that's doable but we'd have to know exactly when they turn west."

This girl often impressed Reg with her quick mind and inventiveness, not to mention she was braver than most of the hard hat guys back in the day. "I'll see what I can find out in the morning, maybe they'll have me stick around tomorrow. Are you booked for just the morning?"

"Yeah, I've got the Campbell family back on and a new guy who just booked a few days ago, I'll keep the afternoon clear so I can be out there and ready by one thirty."

Pearl looked at the two of them scheming and planning like they were organizing a family picnic. She was with Reg in the Keys when he worked for DHS on the San Felippo job, she could remember well the saga surrounding Renfro and his men. "You two need to remember who you're dealing with here, that Renfro is a ruthless piece of work, why don't you just wait for them to give up and pull out?"

AJ and Reg looked at each other and Reg put a comforting arm around his wife. "Don't worry love, I'll watch Renfro, I know too well what that bastard is like. But believe me, they won't just leave, they've invested a lot of time and effort to be here. Once we dive AJ's new pinnacle, we'll either find a sub or we won't, and then we're done either way. If it's there we file the claim with the government, if it's not... well, if it's not we've definitely looked everywhere we can and without the equipment they have we can't find it in deeper water so it'll be theirs to discover."

Pearl still looked concerned but she knew they weren't going to give up now. AJ added thoughtfully.

"You know what I can't figure out? How do they even know about the sub?"

Chapter 15
Bournemouth, 1997

"The poor bugger was sweatin' like nobody's business with the fever getting worse. Cap had us going as fast as we could in the seas and we're getting bashed and slammed around pretty good. Wasn't helping the little kraut out much either."

Arthur Bailey was clearly moved by his encounter with the enemy in such unusual circumstances. Even as he recounted the story fifty two years later he was saddened by Andreas' suffering. Or perhaps his empathy had grown with time? Memories have a way of knocking the sharp edges off experiences and recalling the more agreeable aspects. Either way, part of what made his stories so impactful and memorable to Annabelle Jayne was the sentiment with which he told them. Of course, at eight years old AJ didn't know that at the time, but in later years she realized how deeply moved her Grandad had been by his experiences and how deeply moving he'd made those moments feel to his Granddaughter.

Lily and Arthur had married in 1941, the year they met. She was not quite eighteen. The war tended to shorten courtships as the future held so much menace and uncertainty. The Navy billeted the newlyweds in a small terraced cottage in a village outside Portsmouth. The docks were a target for German bombers so they were happy to be well out of town although it made for a long bus ride for Arthur to get to his station.

They'd patrol for a couple of weeks and he'd have to stay at the naval base during that time and then he'd get a few days leave when he could be with Lily in their first home. To start with she'd take the ferry across and stay with her family on the Isle of Wight during the weeks he was away. She'd made a few friends in the village but she still felt alone and disconnected. After a while she volunteered for the Women's Land Army which was made up of housewives and single women who helped the farmers with food production for the war effort.

Lily found a purpose beyond being a Navy man's wife and felt she was at least contributing to the cause and helping her country. The experience brought her out of her shell and gave her a lot more self-confidence. Five days a week she'd work in the fields alongside women of all ages and walks of life, from girls who'd grown up on the streets, to college graduates, and even one girl who was a distant relative to the Royal Family.

The work was strenuous and many days she'd barely have the strength to fix herself dinner before collapsing into bed, still filthy from working the soil, often in the English rain and cold. Arthur was proud of his young wife's labours and was happy to see her make friends and experience more of the small world they lived in.

For Arthur, most of the war was spent waiting. They patrolled the south coast of England, mainly the stretch between Swanage and Brighton with the Isle of Wight in the middle. They never saw a German U-boat but were told daily they were out there and to be watchful. After the war they found from records that the U-boats generally stayed away from the coastline and were either east or west of where Arthur's boat patrolled. So mostly they tore up and down the coast hunting ghosts and trying to pick off German fighters with their deck guns as they fought the RAF over the English

Channel.

Often they'd be sent looking for downed pilots in the water. The majority were never found or were dead in the water from their wounds or exposure. Every once in a while they'd get to pluck a live one out of the channel and that was the most rewarding for Arthur.

He'd watch these brave men dogfight overhead in what appeared to be complete mayhem in the sky. All would be quiet and peaceful, just another pretty spring day and next moment a squadron or more from each side would meet and all hell would break loose. The way these guys maneuvered their planes in twists and turns trying to get on the enemy's tail while keep them off their own was awe inspiring. The roar from the supercharged piston engines and the rat-tat-tat of the machine guns and cannons firing completed the chaos and after a few minutes the remaining planes would separate and disappear into the clouds. All would be back to a calm spring day and the only sign anything happened would be lingering wafts of smoke in the air and perhaps a man or two dangling from a parachute, silently drifting down to the water.

Sometimes the airmen would be unscathed and grateful to be picked up but often they were not. Arthur helped pull one chap from the water on a clear day in March when the sea was still wintery cold. The medic told them he probably only survived because of the cold, thickening what was left of his blood, slowing his heart rate and numbing his nerves from the pain. The man was burnt from head to toe. His Hurricane had been hit in an oil line which sprayed hot oil all over the canopy and leaked into the cockpit. He couldn't see anything, the engine seized and the scorching oil was getting all over him. To escape he had slid his canopy open and climbed out which let more oil spray on him. The hot exhausts ignited the oil just as he pushed himself free and bailed out. The man spent the next four minutes quietly floating down with most of his flight suit burning.

Arthur could never forget that man, with no features left on his face, nubs instead of fingers and raw flesh where the skin was burnt away. The pilot begged them to shoot him and end the pain.

For most of the war Arthur was relatively sheltered from the intense violence and bloodshed of mankind slaughtering mankind. But the sight of this poor man brought it all home to him and never left his mind the rest of his life.

Lily and Arthur talked of having children right away. Most wartime newlyweds rushed to do so and were indeed encouraged to do so, but they decided to wait. Neither wanted to bring a child into a world torn apart by war across the globe. When peace came in 1945 they were finally together again as he'd been gone most of the two years he was posted in the Caribbean. Life was strange for a while as they'd both grown used to living their own lives but pretty soon they were reminded of how and why they'd fallen in love and they went about building a life for themselves. Post war England was a country financially broke from six years of supporting and funding their military so most struggled to make ends meet.

Once Arthur was released from the Navy he went to work in the shipyards where they started dismantling crippled, damaged and old ships used in the war. It was tough manual labour but it was work and he needed income, especially now they had to pay for housing as well as living expenses.

In 1949 an old friend who'd been trained as an electrician in the Navy started his own business as an electrical contractor. After six months he had more work than he could handle and offered Arthur a job. Arthur told him he didn't know the first thing about being a 'sparky' but his friend said he'd train him and a lot of the help he needed was patching walls, digging holes for wires and general maintenance work. They worked long hours rebuilding homes and businesses blown apart or damaged in the air raids but finally he had a solid income and he and Lily could buy their first home.

Robert Arthur Bailey was born the following year and again, against the way of the times in the baby boom era, they decided one child was perfect for them. Lily had been working in a local café but Arthur insisted she quit and stay home by the end of her first trimester, which she did, albeit begrudgingly at first. Once baby Robert was born there was nowhere she wanted to be, except with him at all times.

Most of Arthur's electrician work was still in the Portsmouth and Southampton area so they'd bought a tiny cottage in a village called Netley Marsh on the edge of the New Forest. It was a perfect place for a young lad to grow up with wide open spaces, the beautiful forest and a good school close by. Arthur and Lily wanted their son to have every chance they could possibly provide in a world that was rapidly evolving and developing. They'd both had a working class education which meant they'd left after O-Levels at sixteen. They intended for Robert to have better than that.

"He'd get to carrying on in German again and he'd look at me like I was supposed to understand but of course I couldn't. I'd nod like I did to try and stop him getting more worked up but eventually he'd get back to some English again.

He was frantic that I should find his submarine and get 'it' to his family which I thought he was telling me to get a bloody submarine to his wife! But then he starts talking about the gold.

'The gold, I'm the only one left, so you must get the gold and get it to meine Frau. My part, you get my part to her!'

I asked him, 'gold? Why would you have gold on a

submarine?'

He says 'from Deutschland, the gold from the SS, we were given the gold in Wilhelmshaven. We were supposed to meet a freighter off the America coast but the Kapitänleutnant, he gets the whole crew and says we don't meet the freighter. The gold is from the people of Deutschland and the SS is stealing for themselves. He says we give back to the people, we are the people and now this war is almost over the gold is for us and our families'.

I couldn't believe what he was telling me, they'd all gone AWOL and run off with the Nazi's gold! I finally began to understand what he'd been telling me. It was brilliant really. They figured they'd set the submarine down somewhere they could get back to it later when the war was over. Where that was, God only knows, but his story, as crazy as the whole thing sounded, started to make some sense at least. That's why he and his two mates were the only ones who went down in the sub and the others waited up top in the sailboat.

He tells me the sailboat was owned by this wealthy Frenchman who was hiding out the war on Grand Cayman. His Captain knew this bloke from before the war and contacted him prior to leaving Europe on their patrol. The idea was this Frenchie was going to hide the crew on Cayman Brac, one of the smaller sister islands, until the war was over. He'd get them food and water from Grand as there was not much on Brac and very few people there.

Trouble was, Andreas was now lying on a cot in a British gun boat on his way to Jamaica. His two mates were dead, the rest of his crew were missing, presumed dead and God only knew if he could make it himself."

Chapter 16
Grand Cayman, 2017

The Campbells excitedly loaded themselves on the boat and began organizing their gear with Thomas' help. AJ looked up the dock to see a tall, athletically built man in his early thirties approaching with a gear bag slung casually over his shoulder. He walked right up to the RIB boat, lifted his sunglasses perching them on top of his head and looked straight at AJ with piercing blue eyes. "AJ Bailey? Am I at the right boat?"

Not often was she speechless but this guy made quite an entrance. He was wearing board shorts, Rainbow sandals and no shirt. His chest and arms were toned and his stomach was flat with a solid six pack. He spoke with a soft Scottish lilt and had a smile that melted the ladies, including the one before him. AJ realized she was staring back, not responding and one step short of drooling in front of her new customer.

She managed to snap back into gear. "You are at the right boat, Mr. Mackenzie, please come aboard and we'll get your gear stowed. We can do the paperwork as we head out."

He stepped down onto the boat and handed Thomas his gear bag. "Please, my father is Mr. Mackenzie, I go by Mac." He nodded his thanks to Thomas before exchanging pleasantries with the Campbells as they all got sorted before casting off.

AJ wished she'd been a bit more attentive to her own appearance that morning, she had a baggy, well weathered Mermaid Divers sweatshirt over her bathing suit, her hair was a mess and as usual she wore no makeup. As her mornings consisted of dragging dive tanks around in the humid Caribbean air followed by a breezy boat ride before jumping into the ocean she always considered personal grooming a waste of time until after work. She discarded the sweatshirt.

On the ride out to the dive site AJ let Thomas drive while she wrote Mac's certification information in her log book which was required by PADI. His certification card, or 'C card' as they're known, was the basic open water cert, the first rung of the diving education ladder. She noted he did his course in 2002. "Been diving about fifteen years Mac?"

Again that disarming smile, she felt like a teenager again for a moment and mentally kicked herself in the arse. "Yeah, I did my open water course in the Red Sea a while back."

"Great place to learn, Sharm El Sheikh is amazing." She smiled at him and made herself embarrassed again. "Okay, so the usual basics I need to ask you for the paperwork, how many dives do you have and when was your last dive?"

He sat down really close to her so she could feel the soft hair of his arm brush against her shoulder. "I think I have around fifty logged but I have to say I got a bit lazy about keeping my logs when I'd sneak in a dive or two on business trips, so it should be a few more. Last dive was a few months back in Mexico."

Thomas throttled back and glided the boat towards the buoy at the dive site so AJ jumped up and grabbed the gaff to hook the line. Once they were tied off she started her briefing.

"Okay everyone, we've moored on Sand Chute which mysteriously gets its name from the fact that the sand area behind us..." She pointed towards the island side of their mooring. "...Slopes down between these huge coral heads. I love this dive. The coral towers reach up out of the sand as it slopes from around ninety feet in the flats down to a couple of hundred feet before the wall itself drops away. The Kittiwake wreck sits in the sand flats on the shore side so we can make a really cool dive taking in a lot of scenery."

She looked over at Mac. "I know the Campbells have, but have you dived the Kittiwake before Mac?"

Flashing that smile again. "I've never actually dived in Cayman, period, so no I haven't, heard a lot about the wreck and seen it in the magazines though, sounds terrific."

"It's a cool dive, maybe another day we'll go inside and explore, I think you'd like it. Today, we'll start at around a hundred feet at the base of one of the coral towers, there are some canyons and swim throughs which are fun. We'll make our way shallower by wrapping around a tower to sixty feet and then head across the flats in mid water to the wreck. We should have time to run down the port side to the stern and then return toward the bow on the upper decks before cutting back across at around thirty feet to finish the dive on top of the towers under the boat."

AJ surveyed the group for any questions but the Campbell kids were already donning their gear in excitement so she figured they were ready to go. "Alright, gear up, let's go!"

She looked at Mac. "I'll be your buddy as you're solo, we'll be back at the line around thirty minutes but I can hang a little longer if you have air and want to explore more."

She gave him the courtesy of assuming he'd be good on air consumption as he was in good shape, but she wasn't sure what to expect as fifty dives over an extended timeframe wasn't much experience.

He thanked her and as AJ got her own BCD on she couldn't help herself from glancing over at Mac as he did the same. Damn this guy's easy on the eyes she thought. He had a confidence about him in both his movements and his manner, the kind of guy that everyone wanted to hang out with, male or female.

AJ had recognized long ago that in social terms young, single people fell into two categories, the caller or the called. The callers were the ones that rang someone else to see what was going on, where to go and were always trying to be at the cool party with the cool people. The called were the ones that decided what was cool. She'd always labelled herself as a caller, which as often is the case, was a pretty inaccurate self-assessment. But Mac was definitely the called.

She once again reminded herself to focus. She noticed he definitely didn't seem like a rookie, maybe it was just the confidence but he knew his gear and was ready to go before the kids that had started before him. His BCD was a pro level piece of kit too, well-worn and used but still in good condition. She assumed he must have bought it used or borrowed it as it had way more than fifty dives on it. Hearing a splash she realized the Campbells were getting in the water so AJ let Mac follow before hurrying in behind them.

They gathered near the base of the mooring and once she got an 'okay' hand signal from each diver she led them down the coral pinnacle towards the sandy bottom. It was another perfect diving day, which was most days in Cayman, well over a hundred feet visibility and no current in the shelter of the reef.

AJ levelled off at a hundred feet just in time to see a pair of Eagle Rays majestically gliding in from deeper water and heading for the wreck. Their wingspans were at least six feet and with little effort they rippled their flat, spotted bodies to propel themselves through the water. Their faces seem to have so much expression, with a long snout and what appeared like a broad smile, which always reminded AJ of a friendly dog.

They followed the rays around the base of the coral until ahead, across the sand, they could just make out the large menacing hulk of the wreck at the edge of the visibility.

The Kittiwake was a former US Navy submarine rescue ship built at the end of the war in 1945 and sunk as an artificial reef in 2011. At two hundred and fifty one feet long it made an impressive sight resting on the sea floor and with multiple access holes cut in the upper parts of the hull and main structure it was easily and safely penetrable. For the more adventurous the lower decks were left without access holes from the sides so they remained pitch black.

AJ turned into a large opening in the coral, she switched on her dive light and flashed around the walls and ceiling revealing multiple antennae from nocturnal lobsters hiding away in the daylight hours. She glanced behind to make sure her group were following and noticed something wasn't right at the back of the line. She had three of the Campbells with her but the daughter and Mac were not and she could see movement at the entrance that appeared more frantic than it should be.

AJ u-turned and swiftly finned past the parents and son to the opening in the coral and looked around for the other two. They weren't there. She immediately looked up and saw Mac and the girl with their arms interlocked heading in a controlled ascent to the surface. Something had gone wrong with the girl's first stage on her regulator as a hard stream of bubbles was pouring from the top of her tank. She was breathing from Mac's back-up regulator, known as an octopus. The situation appeared to be in hand so she signaled for the rest of the Campbells to come back out of the swim through and they aborted the dive and ascended.

They met Mac and the girl at fifteen feet on top of the coral pinnacle where they all completed a safety stop for three minutes before making their way up to the boat.

Thomas knew something wasn't right as he'd kept an

eye on the bubbles and knew they were coming up early. He greeted them as they surfaced. "What's happening down there, you're back awful fast?"

The girl seemed completely unfazed by the potential disaster and actually excited by the drama of it all. "My regulator went wobbly and Mac here gave me his spare!"

Thomas helped her back in the boat. "Oh no miss, are you all right? You come up slow and all right?"

"Yes, yes, Mac saw it happen and he came up with me, we even did our safety stop."

The others followed onto the boat and the Campbells all fussed around their daughter. AJ made sure she was fine and then checked out her regulator. She was relieved the Campbells owned their own gear so at least it wasn't a piece of Mermaid Divers' equipment that failed but it was still unnerving to have an incident under her watch.

"Looks like it blew the o-ring to your computer transmitter, probably unwound itself a bit so wasn't seated, I should be able to fix it, I have spare o-rings."

She retrieved her toolkit from under the console and went about repairing the first stage. Glancing over at Mac she saw he was calmly switching his gear to a fresh tank ready to dive again. "Thank you for helping there Mac, that was a text book buddy breathing safe ascent, quick thinking on your part."

Mac nodded and smiled, lingering his eye contact with her until she awkwardly looked away. The Campbells profusely thanked him for helping their daughter so efficiently and AJ for fixing her regulator.

They remained on Sand Chute for the second dive just staying a little shallower and it all went without a hitch. As Thomas motored them back towards the dock Mac sat himself next to AJ and lifted his sunglasses which gave her the pleasure of being mesmerized by his bright blue eyes again.

"So what brings you to Cayman Mac?"

"Just a little holiday, get away from work for a few days."

"What line of work are you in?"

"Oh boring stuff, I rep for an auto parts company so I travel around quite a bit, I sorta live on the road really."

Oh well, she thought, there's that transitory thing, she couldn't help feeling a bit disappointed.

"I actually have a meeting with a guy here on island this week though, he's trying to get me to move here and run his import business."

She hoped her expression didn't give away her returned optimism and she chuckled to herself. She was never this way around guys, she prided herself on being level headed when it came to romance. He switched subjects. "Do you offer afternoon dives AJ?"

"We do if we have enough people wanting to go, usually like to have four divers to make it worthwhile, I have some later this week."

He nodded sympathetically. "What about unique or special dives?" She grinned at him. "Why, you find today's adventures too boring for you?"

Laughing he replied. "Definitely not, a beautiful spot and more drama than we'd like! A friend told me about a sunken island somewhere offshore that you can dive here, that's more what I meant, do you know this place?"

AJ looked at the man, for a guy with limited experience he sure seemed knowledgeable, not many people knew about the Bank. "It's called Twelve Mile Bank, we've gone out there a bit but it's a tricky site, the currents can kick pretty good, it's considered an advanced dive. Not many operators go out there as the boat ride is long relative to the sites right here on Seven

Mile Beach and it can get lumpy, tough to predict. The top of the coral heads are a hundred feet and the sand is over a hundred and twenty so you don't get much bottom time. It's also a live boat, meaning there's no buoys or anchoring out there so the boat is drifting or circling, no line to go down or come up and the currents can sweep you away. Whoever's on the boat has to carefully track the divers. Saying all that, it is a cool dive and the reef is really healthy."

Mac is listening intently. "Sounds incredible, when do we go?!"

AJ realizes he's serious and staring at her expecting a response. Well, if he only has fifty or sixty dives spread over many years then she shouldn't take him on a dive like that. But watching him today he sure seemed like an experienced diver which didn't add up. Why wouldn't he say if he'd done more? Either way she couldn't take the Campbells out there, the parents are recreational divers that aren't looking for something that challenging and the kids are too inexperienced. She took a stab at a diplomatic answer.

"Well, we'd need to fill the boat with advanced divers who'd want to go for that trip, the plan this week is to dive the west side here."

"What if I chartered the whole boat?"

She wasn't expecting that and was stumped for a moment. "Well... I can't this week as we have other people booked every day."

"But you said you were free this afternoon?"

Damn, he was persistent. For a moment the idea that he really wanted to spend more time with her made her skip a breath but she quickly dismissed it as ridiculous thinking. "Well, I didn't say I was free this afternoon, I said I didn't have the boat going out with customers."

It seemed like he'd edged even closer and leaned in

towards her, he had a mischievous grin as he asked. "What are you doing this afternoon then?"

It took a bit for her to get the message but now she was sure he was flirting with her. She was glad she'd decided not to put her sweatshirt back on despite being chilly after the dives. Though she was shy AJ knew she was a pretty girl with a good figure, she had mirrors in her house, but the male model GQ types like Mac didn't usually go for the tattoos and funky coloured hair. She was normally chased by the guys in the band or the extreme sports varieties that dug the fringe crowd look on a good looking girl. Ironically she found most of them to be shallow, self centred or too transitory… or all of the above.

"I'm afraid I have a project Thomas and I have to take care of."

He didn't miss a beat. "Honestly, I'm not the sit by the pool or on the beach type. I'd rather be doing something so I'd love to help you two with whatever it is, why don't you invite me along?"

She wasn't sure whether she was supposed to feel uncomfortable or flattered but she was going both ways. There was no way she was taking him with them this afternoon but she was rather attracted to this man and didn't want to play too hard to get. She chuckled. "Thanks for the offer but I'm afraid it's a personal project, but we should be done by six or so."

"So does that mean you're available for dinner tonight or do I get shut down on that too?" He gave her his best smoldering blue eyed look.

She missed a breath or two again and desperately tried not to appear overjoyed, despite being so. "Probably rude to turn you down on everything. But it's just a friendly dinner, nothing fancy, okay?"

"Wherever you'd like to go is fine with me."

AJ smiled. "I know a little pub."

Carlos Costa offered Reg some coffee which he gladly accepted. Reg had managed to avoid conversation with Renfro on the ride out and now sat in the lounge of the Explorador de los Océanos with the Argentinian. The coffee was the finest Cuban roast according to Costa and he insisted they have Cortaditos, expresso shots with steamed milk and sweetened with sugar served in tiny mugs. Reg was more of a plain black coffee kinda guy but he rolled with it to appease the man. Costa handed him the Cortadito.

"As you can see by our position we are progressing with our scans, we are making wider sweeps around the Bank to see if there might be a wreck that has been rolled off the top into deeper water." He looked at Reg carefully to gauge his reaction and Reg tried to hide behind sipping his coffee. He'd finished the tiny mug already and hoped Costa couldn't tell that.

"The wreck we are particularly interested in is from the World War Two era Mr. Moore." He watched Reg intently as he spoke. "It's possible you and your young friend Miss Bailey have some knowledge of this?"

Reg is stunned, is this guy just fishing to see if he'll bite or does he really know? He was at a loss how the hell he could know and moreover how to respond. There was no more covering up with an undersized coffee mug now, he knew he had a dumb founded expression on his face. He also noted Costa had reverted to using his surname, not quite as buddy, buddy as their first encounter. "What makes you think either of us would know anything about it? Especially AJ, she's just a kid, she's never done any salvage or treasure work."

Costa looked him firmly in the eye and with a hint of a grin he spoke confidently. "It's especially your young lady I believe has the knowledge, which she undoubtedly shared with you. She is, after all, the granddaughter of Arthur Bailey, the British Navy man that pulled the last surviving member of U-

1026 from the water and spent approximately eight hours with him."

Reg was floored. Apparently he did know, but how? He tried to think it through quickly. There were two ends to the thread of the story, one end from Arthur Bailey, which was how he and AJ knew about it and the other end was from the Germans who put the gold on the submarine in the first place. To their knowledge that end of the thread should have stopped when the U-1026 went AWOL. There were enough reports and speculation from that time to place the U-1026 in the vicinity of Cayman, although the official records state it was lost to unknown causes. The crew of the MTB-67 was public record, as was the report that they pulled the three German submariners aboard, so they could easily have got Bailey's name from that. It still seemed Costa was making assumptions and Reg didn't want to give anything more away.

"So you're looking for a submarine?"

Costa laughed loudly. "Yes Mr. Moore, we're looking for a submarine! You're not seriously still saying you have no knowledge of this are you?"

His tone became more severe. Reg knew this was a turning point and he had to decide. He could either admit he and AJ knew about and had indeed looked for the sub, or keep denying it which clearly they both knew was a lie. If AJ had found the spot then they just needed a few days to dive the mysterious second pinnacle and they'd either find a large German type seven U-boat or they wouldn't. From there they just register the wreck claim if they have one or Costa will keep searching in the deeper water where they couldn't look and he'll find it if it's there. He needed to buy themselves a couple of days and the best way to do that was to keep Costa close.

"Well, sounds like you've done your homework Mr. Costa. If I share what I know, what's in it for me?"

Costa smiled and clearly seemed pleased with himself for talking Reg around. Reg also caught a hint of relief in his face which made him think, maybe Costa is starting to doubt he'll find it and wants all the help he can get. "A generous finder's fee if information you provide helps us locate the submarine. I'm a fair man Mr. Moore, let us say fifty thousand American dollars? Is that satisfactory?"

Hell no it's not satisfactory, Reg thought. If these crooks pulled the gold out of there it was worth millions. But the last piece of the cat and mouse game was the gold. Who knew about the gold and more importantly who thought the other knew? He was sure Costa new about the Nazi gold, he wouldn't be this keen on finding the wreck just to hand it over to the Caymanian government. The fact that he'd hired Renfro was proof of that. The big question was whether Costa thought he and AJ knew about the gold and that would depend on how much Costa truly knew about Arthur Bailey's story.

If Reg knew of the gold he'd want more than fifty K for a fee, if he didn't that was probably a reasonable price. He decided this was a test and he gambled on Costa believing he knew nothing of the treasure. "Sounds fair to me. What about AJ?"

"That's up to you, I'm making an arrangement with you, if you want to split it with her, involve her or leave her out of it, that is not my concern."

"Fair enough. We'll leave her out of it for now." Reg replied assertively.

Costa nodded knowingly like he knew Reg would look after himself all along. "So, Mr. Moore, now we are partners, what can you share with me to aid our search for this elusive submarine?"

Reg took a deep breath, "Let's look at a chart."

AJ and Thomas hurriedly prepared the boat at the dock, filled it full of petrol, loaded fresh dive tanks and headed about five miles offshore towards Herbert's pinnacle. They'd been sitting there waiting for over an hour when AJ's phone finally lights up with a text from Reg.

'Costa knows everything except location. Your Grandfather, everything. I'm leading them to west end of Bank. Will text when there. Wait until then. Time is short. Good luck.'

AJ re-read it aloud to Thomas. She looked at her watch, it was already two thirty in the afternoon and she was anxious to get started.

Thomas looked at her puzzled. "I thought it was just you that knew the story from your Grand Papi?"

"We've always figured that someone from the German side had to know the sub had gone rogue, I don't understand how they'd know about my Grandad though."

She felt bad not telling Thomas the last part of the story, the fact that the missing submarine had a clandestine cargo of Nazi gold aboard. Whoever was behind placing the treasure onboard would certainly have had an interest in where it ended up and there might well have been some record of it that survived the war.

Thomas came from a modest family who'd worked hard their whole lives to scrape by, surrounded by an ever growing display of wealth and extravagance from off-islanders and she wasn't certain how he'd handle the temptation. In his situation who wouldn't want to share in the opulence and grandeur the foreigners enjoyed on the island his family helped build?

AJ wasn't lying to him but she was not including him on all the facts and however she justified it, it didn't feel right. Despite her misgivings something told her now wasn't the right time either.

"Sounds like Reg is steering them as far as he can away

from us so we'll just wait it out until he gives us the green light."

Sitting, just bobbing on the waves waiting, was excruciatingly tedious and frustrating for AJ. She was like a kid at Christmas just itching to get in the water and explore the elusive pinnacle that had almost certainly never been dived by any other human. She just hoped it had been ascended by three other people, seventy two years before.

After what seemed like an eternity her phone lit up again with a text from Reg. 'Go now' was all it said.

Go now was all AJ and Thomas needed to hear and they leapt into action, heading full speed for the coordinates saved in her GPS. It was three forty in the afternoon.

Thomas drove while AJ got into her wetsuit and readied her gear so when they arrived at the location in the RIB boat's GPS fifteen minutes later, she was ready to splash. On the surface a gentle current appeared to be drifting the boat east back toward the island so Thomas eased the boat further west to allow for it.

The moment of truth was here, AJ prepared to back roll off the side of the boat and did her last minute gear checks.

"Okay Thomas, I think I'm ready, just watch my bubbles as best you can. You'll probably have to keep moving the boat to stay above me, I'll see how the current is down below. If you lose my bubbles keep checking three sixty around you, I have my safety marker with me, watch for that."

The safety marker was a bright orange inflatable tube that clipped to her BCD and rolled up to the size of a toilet paper tube when deflated. Once inflated it stuck straight up about five feet so hopefully the user could be spotted amongst the waves.

"I'll keep watching Boss, you be careful now."

With a mix of trepidation and excitement she rolled over

the side of the boat and everything went calm and quiet as she entered the underwater world.

She began descending straight away looking all around to check the open water. Laterally she had visibility for what she presumed was over a hundred feet, there was no way to really tell as all she could see was dark blue open ocean. Below the water disappeared into blackness as the diminishing light reaching deeper gave less clarity. It was an eerie, lonely feeling and she felt like a tiny, insignificant speck in a vast body of water. Which indeed she was.

AJ looked up for the boat and knew she was in trouble immediately. She was only thirty feet below the surface and the boat was well north of her. The current below the surface was running perpendicular to the surface swell and appeared to be quite strong. Without visual markers she couldn't tell how strong until she started finning north and found how hard it was to make any headway. She kept descending but tried to angle down and north to get back under the boat.

As she passed through fifty feet she could finally make out a different texture to the darkness below and at sixty the pinnacle started taking shape and she could make out the coral. A large school of Horse eyed jacks swept passed her seemingly oblivious to the current she was fighting. She heard the sound of the motors start on the boat above her as Thomas presumably was maneuvering to track her.

At seventy feet AJ could make out the steep slope of a coral wall, the top of which seemed to be another fifty feet down, but still north. Kicking as hard as she could, breathing heavily, she knew if she could reach the pinnacle she could stay close to the reef and shelter from the pull of the current.

By ninety feet it became obvious she wasn't going to make the pinnacle. She was descending so the slope below was becoming clearer but barely making any gain towards the top edge as the current kept pulling her away. She thought maybe if she dropped deeper than the ridgeline it would block her from the current but that meant descending to at least one forty and she was sucking down air at an alarming rate finning as hard as she was.

At a hundred and five feet her training and logic overcame her desire and she knew the dive had to be aborted. The longer she struggled around at these depths the more nitrogen loaded she'd be and it would just require a longer surface interval to be able to dive again.

Thomas was to the south of her on the surface as by the time her bubbles reached the top they'd been blown that way by the current. That was good she thought, she was about to drift a long way on her ascent. She headed up promptly but careful not to go too fast. She'd never been in a decompression chamber and planned to keep it that way.

Every dive professional, if they'd been in the industry long enough, knew of someone that had gotten the bends. They ascended too fast and the accumulated nitrogen bubbles in their blood stream expanded rapidly as the surrounding pressure dropped, potentially causing a gas embolism. Incredibly painful, a decompression chamber is the only cure for a severe case. The chamber returns the diver to a surrounding pressure equivalent to being at depth and slowly decreases to atmospheric, allowing the bubbles to be dissipated safely. If there is no chamber nearby the results can be fatal.

At fifteen feet she levelled off and began her safety stop. The three minutes seemed like hours as the current pulled her further away from the pinnacle which was long out of sight again. Occasionally a curious school of fish would wander by but other than that all she could see was ocean all around her. Thomas was dutifully following above which was at least of great comfort as she hung in the vast expanse of water.

Chapter 17
Caribbean Sea, 1945

Andreas groaned and clutched his stomach again, the bouts of cramping and pain were getting closer together. He knew something was terribly wrong. Arthur could do nothing but supply warm wet towels as there was no cold water on the boat. Until they reached Jamaica and the Navy hospital there was nothing more he knew to do than try and keep the man as comfortable as possible. Below deck in a sweaty, confined cabin on a bunk that was nothing more than a thin pad on a wooden board while the boat bounced and jolted its way through the ocean was hardly high on anyone's scale of comfortable but it was the best of circumstances available.

The little German took a few deep breaths as the cramps subsided for a moment and lay still staring at Arthur sitting on the opposite bunk a few feet away. Arthur patted him on the arm and urged him to sleep if he could, rest would help.

Andreas remembered something and fumbled in his pants pocket retrieving a tattered photograph that was barely recognizable from the salt water immersion and sun bleaching. He held it up for Arthur to see. "Mein Frau!"

Arthur studied the small picture which had once been a black and white photograph of a pretty young German girl in a traditional Bavarian dress. It was now a soggy piece of paper with a blurred image that could have been anything, Arthur couldn't tell what it was but he figured once upon a time it was a family photograph of some description and smiled admiringly. Andreas looked at the picture himself. He could clearly see his wife, Ellie, standing in front of their little home in a valley in the German Alps.

Born in the summer of 1922, Andreas Jaeger was the second son of a blacksmith in the small village of Unterjoch in the Bavarian mountains close to the Austrian border. Every family in the village had been there since anyone could remember and every family in the village was poor. Money really didn't matter as the village farmed, worked the land and traded amongst themselves for everything they needed. His father shoed horses and made iron parts for anyone that needed it. In return he accepted vegetables, meats or other goods as forms of payment. His mother kept the house, tended to their small herd of goats and kept their own vegetable garden during the summer months.

In the winter they lived off the stocks stored and preserved from the summer, kept the animals in the barn and fed them from the autumn harvest of hay. The days were short, the nights were long and cold, and sometimes they'd be weathered up in the house for weeks at a time. They were constantly cutting wood for the fire or trading for logs with another family.

This was the life Andreas knew and the life he was content with. The only strangers in their village were occasional trekkers or climbers that passed through on their way to bigger summits deeper in the Alps. They were always happy to put these men up for a night and feed them in return for a few coins and some interesting stories of life outside their own world. He and Ellie went to school together, were friends from age five and in their early teens it was obvious to everyone, including them, that they'd be married when they were old enough.

When he was seventeen, Andreas, his brother, and his father began building a home next to his parent's house for he and his bride to be. They felled each tree, hewed each log, cut every notch and laid every stone. When it was finished it was time for the marriage and the whole village pitched in for the celebration and the furnishing and fixtures for the house.

It was the happiest day of young Andreas' life. At that moment he could wish for nothing more, he had a beautiful wife whom he adored, a home of their own, a loving family and an abundance of friends and relatives. Then Great Britain declared war on Germany.

Tucked away in the mountains they received news weeks, sometimes months later when someone headed to a neighboring town or a hiker with a newspaper came their way. Many of the fathers and grandfathers remembered the First World War and the toll it took on the village. Numerous friends and family had not returned and those that did refused to speak of the horrors they'd witnessed. In the quiet village with its scattering of brightly decorated wooden homes, colourful festivals and gatherings to celebrate the seasons, births, marriages and the deaths, it was hard to fathom the industrial destruction the world was about to unleash on itself again.

When Andreas heard the news and read the stories in the national Nazi controlled paper Völkischer Beobachter of how the British were turning on them on top of the injustices placed on Germany after the Great War, he wanted to sign up right away. His father patiently urged him to wait, if he was needed they would come for him, until then there was much to do in the blacksmith barn and he relied on his two sons to help.

It took almost two years before they finally got around to signing up the young men of the remote mountain villages. They weren't recorded on any government paperwork so a military recruiter hiked to the village and knocked on each door demanding any young man over the age of seventeen report for military service immediately. By this time they were taking any men up to forty five years old, so some fathers were conscripted alongside their sons.

With Ellie and their mother in tears, the two Jaeger boys, along with eleven other villagers, were led away for military training where they were then sent to different branches. The majority of the boys, including Andreas' brother, were sent to the eastern front as foot soldiers in the army. Because of Andreas' diminutive size and high scores on the aptitude test, he was assigned to the submarine division of the Kriegsmarine.

The day after the two brothers were taken from Unterjoch was the last time the boys would ever see each other. Later that year Andreas' brother froze to death, huddled together with two other young men in a foxhole covered in snow in a forest outside Stalingrad.

Chapter 18
Grand Cayman, 2017

Reg had convinced Costa that he and AJ believed the submarine had once rested on the west end of the Twelve Mile Bank and been rolled over in a hurricane at some point. He'd made up a story about seeing damage to the coral in keeping with a large hull. Costa had ordered the current sweep they'd been on to be completed and then they'd concentrate on the west end.

They were now making U shaped sweeps around the far end of the Bank, moving a little deeper each time. The Bank was about three quarters of a mile wide although it narrowed and rounded some at either end. It sloped away steeply so each side scan sonar run added around a hundred feet of depth.

The scanning was tedious work as the ship needed to move slowly enough to capture a clear image. The captain had his work cut out to hold a consistent course with the light swell and current forever trying to move the ship. He couldn't set the ship's navigational computer as they weren't heading straight between any points, they were almost constantly in an arc. All he could do was manually steer the ship on the path they wanted as best he could.

Reg and Costa had spent some time on the bridge with the Captain but now made their way down to the survey room where Renfro was manning the computer receiving the scan images. It was building a large map of the sea floor showing all the bumps, undulations and slopes as they passed over them.

"Anything of interest Mr. Renfro?" Costa asked as they entered the room. Renfro glanced up, giving Reg a nasty look as he followed Costa through the doorway. His tone was dismissive.

"The coral is thinning out as we get deeper on the slope, nothing worth exploring yet, certainly no submarine."

Costa turned to Reg and grinned. "Our friend Mr. Renfro believes you are taking us on, as the Americans say, a wild goose chase, but I think his nature is one of suspicion." He slapped Renfro on the back. "I assured him that we have an understanding Mr. Moore, a business arrangement." He looked back at Reg and the grin was gone. "I feel confident you understand the consequences of wasting our time. Do you Mr. Moore? Understand that there would be significant consequences?"

Reg stiffened and fought back the urge to tell them both to go to hell. He had to buy AJ some time and stomping off or scrapping with these two wouldn't help. "I believe I'm well aware of the seriousness of our deal. I assure you I'm trying to help you locate the sub, this is where we think it is."

Renfro stepped back from the computer screen, glared at Reg and snarled. "You're full of it and when we're done wasting our time chasing our tails here, I'll come see you about those consequences."

Costa raised his voice for the first time Reg had heard. "Renfro!"

"What? I told you I don't trust him!"

Costa pointed at the screen. "Forget him, look!"

They all leaned in to see the scan and Costa reached for the phone to the bridge. "Stop engines! Hold us here."

On the screen was what appeared to be the silhouette outline of a boat and by the scale on the lower part of the screen it was at least sixty feet long.

"That is not a submarine." Renfro mused, studying the image.

Costas smiled, "No, but it looks very much like the hull of a sail boat. Get your gear ready Renfro, it is time to get wet."

Nobody looked more surprised than Reg Moore.

AJ switched her gear to a new tank before digging around in a locker and coming up with a long length of nylon rope they kept for emergency towing. Next she grabbed a small, round marker buoy they kept onboard. As challenging as the dive site was proving to be she decided to be a little more methodical in her approach, which she explained to Thomas.

"The current below the surface is running to the south so we'll start north of the pinnacle for the next dive. That way I'll drift south as I descend and I should be right on top of it when I get down to one twenty."

She picked up the rope and buoy and began tying the buoy about six feet short of the end of the rope.

"I'm going to try and tie off the rope to something on the pinnacle, hopefully a submarine but more likely a dead coral head. There's about a hundred feet of rope so after it's tied and looped this buoy should be floating at around thirty or so feet down."

With the buoy tied on she then started a loop at the end of the six foot portion.

"I'm making a loop we can attach the boat to so from now on we'll be able to tether the boat to the reef on a submerged marker only we know about. I'll use that big stainless carabiner we have to clip the boat line into the loop. We just have to carefully mark the spot over the buoy on our GPS and I have to get the boat's line to the loop at thirty feet without being blown off course by the current. I'll then have a descent and ascent line to use which will save me a lot of air fighting the current."

Thomas found the carabiner and tied it into the line they used every day to tie the boat to the dive site buoys. "That's a pretty trick way of doing things Boss!"

She looked at him and thought for a moment, she had her doubts.

"Well, I still have to carry all this rope with a buoyant float tied to it that wants to pull me to the surface all the way down to a hundred and twenty odd feet, find a place to tie it without hurting any living coral, get it securely tied and then manage to get the boat tied to it next time... I'm not sure how smart that is but maybe it'll work."

It all seemed rather challenging when she sounded it out but it was the best and only plan she had short of taking her chances with the current every time.

She was banking on being able to hide from the worst of the current once she was close to the coral on the pinnacle. It worked like the edge water in a fast running river, right up against the bank the water was barely moving because of the friction against the solid bank but the further away from the edge you got the stronger the river flowed. She would stay as close to the coral as she could without touching it.

AJ glanced at her dive watch, she'd been out of the water for thirty eight minutes, she needed to be out of the water at least an hour between dives, more if she thought a third dive was needed.

"How long 'till we go again?" Thomas enquired.

"Another twenty minutes then I'll gear up and we'll get the boat in position."

"Alright then, let's relax and enjoy this fine weather we're having"

Thomas was far more patient than AJ. The islanders were typical of the Caribbean people, they had no problem putting their feet up, soaking up the sun and letting the clock tick on by. He sat in the shade of the console, leaned his head back and rested his eyes. AJ triple checked her already double checked knots on the rope, scanned the seas through the binoculars, spotting only a fishing boat way east of them and did everything but relax.

On the swim deck of the Explorador de los Océanos, Renfro pulled his five millimetre wetsuit up and secured the rear zipper from the waist to the neck. Next to him was a twin tank rig filled with Trimix to handle the deep dive he was about to embark on. By replacing a portion of the nitrogen content in air with inert helium, the narcotic effect it had at depth was greatly reduced, allowing Renfro to function over thirty stories below the waves.

Three hundred and thirty feet was the depth limit for the gas mix Renfro had filled in his tanks, anything deeper he would be using his hard hat gear fed by an umbilical from the surface. The Trimix set-up would give him only a matter of minutes at the wreck and stage decompression stops of several hours.

The helium, which wicks away more body temperature than the other gases, combined with the extended dive time for decompression meant even in the warm Caribbean Sea he would get quite cold, hence the thicker wetsuit.

The crane on the stern of the ship was swung out over the water with a weighted line running down from it into the depths. They had maneuvered the line over the wreck site using the map from the scans so Renfro could simply descend pulling himself down it. Tanks with various breathing mixtures would be lowered on a second line next to it to be used for his stage decompressions. He could clip onto the line at the prescribed depth and switch his tanks over, it would be tedious hanging in open water for an extended time but at least he would be secured and could relax.

Reg stood with Costa on the main deck watching Renfro put the dive plate holding the two tanks on his back while he was seated on the step with his feet in the water. The rig weighed nearly a hundred pounds so two of his crew he'd brought with him assisted him into his gear.

Reg would have chosen to dive with an umbilical to such a depth but that's also the kit he was most comfortable with. Renfro had said he wanted to be more maneuverable for a quick investigation dive and going to the limit of the gas he was breathing didn't seem to faze him. Although he had a twinge of guilt feeling this way, Reg really didn't care whether this man returned from the dive or not so he kept his opinions to himself.

Costa shouted down from the main deck. "Find some kind of evidence to identify this boat please Mr. Renfro."

Renfro waved his hand half-heartedly in acknowledgement and cursed the Argentinian under his breath. "Fucking Argie thinks I'll be skipping around down there like we're at the shopping mall." His two thugs snickered and helped lower Renfro into the ocean where he reached out and grabbed the line from the crane. Putting the regulator in his mouth he released some air from the inflation wings mounted to his dive plate and disappeared unceremoniously below the surface.

Costa watched his professional diver, henchman, and as far as he was concerned general scumbag, begin what would be a long afternoon underwater. He'd hired Renfro for his diving expertise and his willingness to work outside the rules and laws, which came at a healthy price. Costa didn't mind that, he was willing to pay fairly for the work and the flexibility. What he couldn't abide was the man's lack of any purpose beyond the money. Costa had been raised in a household with firm beliefs and principles which he prided himself on staying true to. Renfro had no principles, no morality, he took no sides. For a man with heavily ingrained Nazi ideologies this was unacceptable.

The price the Costa, nee Neinstadt, family had paid over the course of history was too great to waver from now when he was so close to retrieving what was rightfully his.

Throughout Germany and their occupied territories, the Jewish people were rounded up mercilessly by the Nazis and anything they possessed of value taken. Most of the currency went straight to the war effort and works of art were distributed to high ranking officers or hung on the walls of government and military headquarters. Hitler, an artist himself, was an avid collector of classics and officers gained much favour with the Fuhrer when they delivered him masterpieces.

Considerable gold was also collected in the form of bars, coins, rings and other jewelry and eventually from the eyeglasses and teeth fillings of the victims of the concentration camps. The best quality gold was melted into bars which was secured and stored to be used in the future expansion of the empire. Some was used for covert trading with individuals or countries that required untraceable payment. Only the highest ranking officials knew of and had access to this wealth.

Adolf Eichmann's office in Berlin was responsible for collecting information on the Jews in each area, organising the seizure of their property, and arranging for and scheduling trains to the camps. Carlos Costa's father, Kurt Neinstadt, as one of Eichmann's senior field officers implemented these orders and often travelled to the camps and oversaw the collection and storage of the confiscated goods.

In the winter of 1944 as the Allies pushed forward behind the size and weight of the American Army, many Nazi officers began seeing the writing on the wall. The Fuhrer's decision to pursue the Eastern front along with the European theatre had stretched Germany's resources too thin and the long harsh winters in Russia had decimated the troops from disease and starvation more than the battlefield had.

Neinstadt knew Eichmann was a hard line party man but he also recognized he was a survivor that looked after himself first. He took a huge risk and one evening over drinks he expressed his concern over the direction of the war. To his surprise and relief Eichmann agreed and furthermore made the suggestion they may need to plan for the worst. That single conversation put them firmly in bed together, requiring the ultimate trust from both sides. They knew that any stray word of this would bring down an investigation and in these paranoid times neither would be safe from the repercussions.

The two men began working on plans to syphon off and secure some of the Nazi gold for themselves. They had two big problems to work around and a myriad of smaller hurdles to leap. The main issues were where to move the treasure to and how to get it there. They then had to consider where they could escape to if Germany fell. The gold would be no good to them if it was somewhere they couldn't reach it.

They settled on a split strategy. They'd keep some gold hidden within Germany on the premise they would conceal themselves amongst the population under false identities. The remainder of the gold they'd relocate as far away as possible hoping they could reach it after hostilities ceased.

The first part of the plan turned out to be relatively easy as they controlled all the movements of the seized money and merchandise. By 1945 most of the assets were being directed to Merkers Mine where they were hidden underground and heavily guarded. Merkers was located in central Germany and was an operational salt mine. As sections of the mine were cleared of salt the large vacant rooms were used for storage of the Nazi's gold, art pieces and foreign monies.

Some of the gold was being moved to various banks throughout Europe in an attempt to conceal it for future actions of the Nazi party. The Vatican bank and the Swiss National Bank in particular held under layers of false names and companies much of the stolen treasure which would later disappear. It wasn't hard amongst all the movements he controlled for Eichmann to direct a shipment of gold to a holding area where he and Neinstadt commandeered the truck.

Eichmann's wife and family disliked Berlin and chose to live in Prague, where he visited once a month. He moved his portion of the gold bars to the city on one of his visits using two of his loyal bodyguards for the heavy lifting. Each wooden box contained three bars which were ten inches long by three wide and two tall, weighing forty pounds each; making each box a hundred and twenty pounds. Each bar was worth just over twenty two thousand US Dollars at the time. Eichmann had twelve boxes. His nest egg was worth eight hundred thousand US dollars, a princely sum in 1945.

Unsure exactly where he, his family, and their contraband should end up, he hid it in the basement of their Prague home. As the Russian army approached from the east and the Allied forces from the west he was quickly running short of options. Ultimately, after Prague fell, the gold was presumably commandeered by the Czech rebels or the Russian army, neither confessing to finding it.

Neinstadt's plan was harder to implement, he had a matching stash to Eichmann but he wanted to move it offshore as far from the Allied forces as possible. He had a friend from his early days in Berlin who went onto join the Kriegsmarine and became a submarine captain. He'd stayed in touch with Kapitänleutnant Resch throughout the war and now he gambled on their friendship being as strong as their belief in the continuation of the Nazi party beyond the current conflict.

Kurt Neinstadt loaded his twelve wooden boxes into ammunition crates heading for the submarine docks. The U-boat docks of Saint-Nazaire, France falling to the Allies in late 1944 meant they now had to go to Wilhelmshaven on the Northern coast of Germany. Having sent Resch a telegram telling him he was on his way, he rode the train with his precious cargo across Germany.

From Wolfgang Resch's point of view, he really had no choice. A high ranking SS officer was asking for his assistance so what could he say? He had joined the Nazi party as an idealistic youth before the war but had distanced himself as much as he could since then. He was a patriot who believed in his country but things seemed to have strayed a far cry from the original intention of rebuilding Germany to a proud nation.

U-boat losses had gone up at an alarming rate since late 1942 when unbeknownst to the Germans, the British had cracked their Enigma codes and were deciphering their transmissions, including the position of their submarines. The fitting of snorkels, which began in 1944, allowed the U-boats to stay submerged while running their diesel motors to recharge their batteries. This made them harder to spot by allied aircraft and faster to submerge when spotted which, for a while, slowed their losses somewhat.

As the weather cleared from the winter in 1945 the ships sailed more frequently, the U-boats were deployed to hunt them and the planes could fly more often to chase the submarines. The losses ramped up again and Resch knew his chances of seeing the end of the war were getting slimmer. When he met with Neinstadt in Wilhelmshaven he figured the

Nazi's gold would end up on the sea bed somewhere. He just didn't figure it would be by his own plan to place it there.

Using the GPS Thomas maneuvered the RIB boat about a hundred yards north of the pinnacle and gave AJ a nod. She was already sitting on the side of the boat, ready to roll, the large coil of rope with the buoy clutched in her left arm and with her right she put her regulator in her mouth. With a nod back to Thomas she rolled backwards over the side and hit the water with a splash.

She'd added ballast weight to her BCD to compensate for the buoy that would be trying to pull her towards the surface. Determined not to be blown clear of the pinnacle again, she kicked downwards right away. The buoyancy of the buoy tugged on the rope coil and tried to spin her around making it awkward to fin towards the bottom. In the vastness of the open water it was hard to tell which direction she was heading, but figuring if she couldn't see the surface in her field of vision and pressure in her ears needed clearing, then she must be heading down.

The pinnacle began immerging from the dark blue murkiness below her and seeing coral in all directions told her she was well over it already. AJ turned herself into the current and kicked even harder down hoping to slow her southward path which added to the strain, laboured her breathing and raised her heart rate even further. The deeper she went the smaller the buoy was getting as the increasing water pressure tried to crush the plastic ball. She now began to wonder if the thing would split and leak all the air out rendering it useless and this whole exercise a waste of time.

As AJ finally closed on the reef at a hundred and twenty feet the current's pull began to subside and once she levelled off a few feet from the bottom she could fin lightly against it and remain stationary. She glanced at her dive computer and registered the depth and the fact she'd already used five hundred of her available three thousand pounds per square inch of air just getting down here! She needed to find something to tie the rope to that wouldn't damage the reef and find it fast.

She looked around her. The reef was incredibly healthy with huge Steghorn corals that looked like giant antlers, big sea fans bent over in the current, tube sponges like clusters of bollards and brain corals like massive domes. What she didn't see was any dead coral heads or manmade wreckage she could tie to. As determined as she was to discover her lost submarine she couldn't bring herself to harm the exquisite coral life that was such a significant part of the fragile ecosystem of the oceans.

AJ began swimming in an increasing circle staying close to the bottom sheltered from the current, searching. After five minutes of hunting around she came across a coral overhang with several holes through it. The newer coral had grown over the older and shielded it from the precious sunlight it needed to continue growing. It was this process that formed the island of Grand Cayman and many others with coral growing on top of coral over thousands of years until they reached the surface or the ocean level dropped below them.

AJ threaded the rope through one hole and back through another tying the end in a knot to the line itself. She double checked the security of her knot and released a little more rope out as she swam above the coral head carefully checking where the rope laid against the overhang. Once she was confident it wasn't going to rub against any live rock she released the buoy and watched it shoot up towards the surface expanding back to its former size on the way up. Before it reached the surface it snapped to a stop at the full extent of the rope.

The silhouette of her boat could be seen easily on the

surface as Thomas faithfully tracked her bubble stream. She checked her dive computer. She'd been down for eighteen minutes, burned through fourteen hundred psi and had seven minutes of no deco time left at this depth. Damn she thought, there was no way to get shallower to extend her bottom time as the current would sweep her away so she better make the best of the seven minutes. She gave herself four minutes of search time leaving three minutes to make straight back for the line she could now use for her ascent. That left no margin or she'd go into deco and have to do a series of decompression stops on her way up. That wouldn't be the end of the world if she was done diving for the day but she was sure she would need to get back in again. That would require an extended surface interval to return her body to safe nitrogen levels, especially coming back to this depth.

Disasters rarely happen when one thing goes wrong, it's generally the second problem that turns a difficult circumstance into a tragedy. She was very aware of this from both her extensive dive training and her common sense nature, she knew she was flirting with dangerous waters both figuratively and literally.

AJ kicked away from her line and up a few feet to get a better view of the pinnacle and immediately felt the stronger pull of the current that had not lessoned a bit. She quickly surveyed all she could see to the limit of the lateral visibility which at this depth she guessed to be around eighty feet. The pinnacle was more of a flat topped spine no more than a hundred and fifty feet wide that ran west to east. That made sense as it was a peak of the Cayman Ridge which formed the three islands in the chain and the Twelve Mile Bank about a mile further west. To the east of her position she thought she could see the spine taper off and head deeper so she chose to start the other way.

Staying close to the bottom her view was constantly blocked by outcrops of hard corals and waving arms of colourful soft corals and fans. Every twenty feet or so she'd pop up a little higher to get a better view. The top seemed to widen as she went so both sides were now beyond her visibility and she hadn't reached the end of the ridgeline. It certainly seemed smaller from the surface with twin Yamahas doing the work, down here fighting the ever present current and relying on her legs alone was exhausting.

Reef fish of all shapes, sizes and colours flitted about clearing a path for the strange creature that to them seemed ungainly and very noisy, spewing streams of bubbles every few seconds. Her three minutes were quickly up and she didn't hesitate to turn around. At the rate she was using air doing all this work she had no reserves for multiple decompression stops and she hustled back to her line.

She was tempted to angle up to the line before she reached it to cut the corner off and save time but if the current whisked her away she'd really regret it. Sticking to the plan she stayed deep until the line and then began a swift but safe ascent. With six hundred psi remaining in her tank she came to the buoy at thirty feet below the surface and did an intermediate safety stop for three minutes. Above her Thomas was tracking her bubbles and she saw something splash in the water from the boat and sink quickly down towards her. AJ smiled broadly causing her mask to come unsealed and leak some water in. Thomas had dropped a tank with a regulator attached on a fifteen foot line so she could do her final safety stop with emergency air if she needed it. She loved this kid.

She covered the ground from the submerged buoy to the hanging line and waited out another three minutes before heading up to the ladder and climbing aboard. She had a hundred and fifteen psi left in her tank, about one minute's worth of air at the depth of the pinnacle.

Art Renfro reached the sloping sea floor at just over three hundred feet down, still looped to the weighted guide line from the crane. He landed on an outcrop breaking off a large branch of Black Coral as he did so. He shuffled about, looking at the landscape around him, pieces of decade's old growth splintering under his fins. He neither noticed nor cared.

The other thing he didn't notice was a wreck and for a moment he figured they'd dropped him in the wrong spot. He scanned as far as he could see in both directions along the slope but still nothing. He looked back at the coral hill dropping away to blackness below where he stood and saw nothing. Adjusting his footing to maintain balance with the heavy tanks on his back he looked at his fins and noticed a strange curvature to the coral on the very outcrop he stood upon. Turning he checked the slope behind him and there extending away was the encrusted outline of a mast.

Renfro was standing on the coral growth that had formed over the wooden hull of a sailing boat. The dense, varnished and painted wood had held up long enough for the growth to form over it before it slowly rotted away beneath. All that remained was a shell made up of microorganisms stacked upon themselves in the image of the boat. From that sprouted fans and other corals camouflaging the hull, but sure enough he could make out the distinct shape which had to be over fifty feet long.

The challenge was now to find some kind of evidence that this was indeed the missing sailboat from 1945.

He had only a matter of minutes at this depth so he hurriedly swam towards the edge of the outline of the hull. He went to the shallower side to buy time, he knew most of the debris would have scattered below the wreck of the boat itself but he couldn't risk going deeper. Renfro started pulling at anything that wasn't attached to the rock, stirring up loose particles, broken and crushed coral. He worked his way along the boats outline poking and scraping at anything that appeared man made or covering something man made.

The weight of the tanks and gear was neutralized by the buoyancy of the air in the flotation wings but the mass was still cumbersome and not easy to move about with. He was starting to wish he'd gone to the trouble of using his hard hat suit and umbilical as at least he would have had more bottom time to hunt about. One of the main reasons he didn't was because there would be a radio connection through the umbilical and he didn't want to listen to Costa telling him what to do, where to look, and how to do it. Most people would prefer to have a lifeline to the surface thirty stories above them but not Renfro, he'd rather do it his way without interference and chatter.

Glancing at his dive computer he had two minutes remaining at this depth before he needed to ascend shallower. He franticly dug and rummaged. Most of the coral was alive and attached to the undersea mountain but the gaps and indents were filled with a mishmash of anything heading down that could get caught and stuck. The storms and currents break off pieces of coral that are then ground down into a gravel or sandy consistency and anything from seashells to fish hooks can get mixed up in it.

As he ran his hand through a scoop of crushed coral with the consistency of fine pebbles his fingers felt something smooth. He dug in deeper and pulled out a glass bottle. He shook the debris and sand from inside the tinted green glass and stared at the raised words 'Coca Cola'. There was no telling whether this had been tossed overboard a passing ship or if it was indeed from the sail boat when it sank but he was short on time to wonder. Renfro had no idea if the bottle was distinct enough to be dated but he needed to head up so it would have to do.

Using the weighted line as his guide he began the swim back towards the surface and the long, boring but meticulous process of decompression stops.

Chapter 19
Caribbean Sea, 1945

Kapitänleutnant Wolfgang Resch could barely see his submarine submerge from a hundred yards away in the dark and stormy night. Some white froth was all he could make out and then the silhouette was gone. He and his crew were packed like sardines on the deck of the sailboat that was starting to roll around more and more in the swells.

So far this night had not gone quite how he'd hoped. What appeared to be a British patrol boat, according to the owner of the sailboat, had spotted the Kauri sailing from Grand Cayman towards their rendezvous point over Twelve Mile Bank. Fortunately the gunship had decided not to give chase for whatever reason Wolfgang could only guess, still it concerned him although it didn't appear to be an immediate problem. What was a problem was the approaching storm that seemed to be arriving sooner than the reports had suggested. It had already made navigation very challenging with neither sun nor stars to take bearings from and strong seas moving the U-boat around in the ocean. They had been on a good compass heading during the day when they'd run submerged but by dark when they surfaced the cloud cover had obscured the stars and ruined their chance to get a reading to verify their location.

You can be pointed on a compass heading all day long but if the seas were moving you laterally you still ended up missing your destination. Despite this, Resch and his navigator felt confident they were close to the Bank so they began a search pattern checking the depth to see if they could find it. At four miles long and three quarters of a mile wide they thought they had a good chance and sure enough after only half an hour they got depth readings around thirty metres and held the submarine there while they awaited the Frenchman and his sailboat. The sailboat he now stood at the railing of in the darkness as the seas continued to worsen and the winds seemed to increase by the minute.

He was beginning to question whether they'd even be able to see the three men if and when they surfaced. "Jean Paul?" Resch bellowed over the noise of the wind and seas, "How do we know we're still over the right place? We've been blown all over!"

The man at the helm of the sailboat looked more than nervous and simply shrugged in return. His concerns were starting to shift from the complexities of picking up the men to the overall survival of his vessel and all that currently sailed upon her. When his distant cousin from his German mother's side of the family contacted him, he felt a family obligation to assist the man he'd only met briefly as a child.

Jean Paul Latoir was happily avoiding the whole annoying war in his villa on Grand Cayman, feeling quite pleased with himself for seeing the disaster approaching in 1938 and relocating to the Caribbean with his wealth intact. With a French father, a German mother and no real interest in politics he'd chosen no side and was prepared to bend whichever direction favoured his continued prosperity and safety. The brief communications he'd had with Resch talked about an offshore rendezvous. It wasn't until he met them out here that the extent of the operation was revealed. His plans had definitely not included harbouring a boat full of AWOL German submariners on a small island containing an American Navy outpost. Yet here he was.

Currently, he was hoping he would get to worry about the harbouring the enemy part, for now he had a much bigger problem. Jean Paul hadn't put full sail up all day, he'd motored out here on the small diesel inboard engine that tickled the large sailboat along at a maximum of ten knots. Kick up some heavy seas and she struggled along at six or seven knots. Come to find out, load the boat down with over three tons of Germans in heavy seas and the little diesel was labouring to keep the seventy foot yacht moving. If he couldn't maneuver and keep the bow into the swells they would be in big trouble.

Resch couldn't even see the bow of the yacht anymore as the rain lashed down and the winds whipped both salt and fresh water across the decks stinging the men's faces. Everyone was hanging on to a railing, a guide wire or anything they felt would not come adrift from the boat. He pulled himself along the railing until he stood next to his cousin at the large wheel. He could barely hear the engine churning away below and by the rise and fall of the rpms it was having a very hard time of it.

"Jean Paul, we must find my men! I think we've been blown too far from them!"

Latoir wiped the water from his soaked hair and brow and looked at his cousin as though he were crazy. "We cannot help your men Wolfgang, I don't believe we can even help ourselves anymore!"

The bow rose steeply and the boat swung to the starboard side as a huge wave overpowered the engine and shoved the sailboat backwards and sideways. Several screams could be heard as men were swept over the side, unable to hang on any longer. Jean Paul swung the wheel in an attempt to get the bow back into the path of the waves but without enough power to drive them forward it was useless.

Broadside to the next wave the boat pitched violently

over sideways and several more men were spilled into the water. Jean Paul held a brief hope that if enough men went overboard and relieved the deck of the extra weight he might be able to power back straight again. It was short lived as the next wave, the largest yet, rolled the boat completely over until the keel came out of the ocean and the cabins flooded immediately. The next wave hit the exposed keel like wind catching a sail and turned the boat entirely upside down. It rocked back to its side as the wave rolled past before disappearing rapidly below the surface dragging many of the men with it.

With no life vests and little flotsam of use to keep anyone afloat the remaining men that survived the sinking quickly succumbed to the broiling seas. All were lost.

Chapter 20
Grand Cayman, 2017

AJ once again sat on the inflatable side of the boat and did a round of last minute checks. Thomas handed her the boat tie line with the large carabiner on her end, the other firmly tied to the cleat at the bow. The coil of rope between the two was on the floor next to her, Thomas would toss it in behind once she was ready to submerge. The sun was getting lower in the sky and dipping behind a cloud layer on the horizon. The wind had dropped some and the water was calmer as evening approached, she could only hope the current had lessened as well.

"Here we go Thomas, this time I'll hopefully get to search properly and fingers crossed there's something to find!"

"Alright then, you be careful and all." He replied with a look of concern.

She pulled her mask down in place, popped her reg in her mouth and without further delay rolled backwards into the Caribbean Sea with a splash. They had positioned north of the submerged buoy again so she could drift to it with the current and she looked around as she swam downwards to get oriented. The plan worked perfectly and with minimal effort she met the buoy at thirty feet, clipped the carabiner to the loop she'd made and took hold of the descent line, making sure she got clear of the tie line to the boat.

Head down she began pulling herself to the bottom hand over hand on the line. Gently kicking her fins she marveled at how much time, energy and consequently air, this was saving. About halfway down the line it suddenly wrenched away, almost pulling out of her hands, taking her by surprise. She hung on and looked up realising the boat had taken up the slack in the line and was now being held by the whole tether down to the sea floor. The surface current pulled the line at an angle and she prayed it would hold fast where she'd tied it with the strain of the boat now heaving on it.

AJ hurried the rest of the way down, keen to check her knot, scanning as far as she could see as she went. The rope looked to be holding fine so using her compass she set off on the route she'd planned out during her surface interval. Figuring the flat top was around a hundred and fifty foot wide and getting broader she needed to position herself about twenty five feet south of her line, which she guessed was close to the centre to the ridgeline. From there she'd head straight west until the end of the pinnacle. If she then turned north for fifty feet and returned along an east heading she'd come back twenty five feet north of where she started and would easily see the line. If the flat top got much wider as she went she'd adjust to keep the edge of the pinnacle always in view to her left which would also work for the return and she should cover the whole pinnacle.

The current had died down a bit but was still strong so AJ employed the same rhythm she had figured out on the last dive, popping up and scanning the area about every twenty feet for a wider view and then hugging the coral to minimize the effort in between. She kept reminding herself she was hunting for a submarine so it wasn't like she could miss the damn thing if it was anywhere near her, it was over two hundred feet long after all! Not knowing how far the flat top ridgeline extended she was carefully watched her no-deco time on her computer. The last thing she needed was to get to the west end without enough time for the return to the line. It would mean she'd be doing a safety stop in open water, drifting a long way and Thomas would have no idea as he was now moored and unable to follow her bubbles.

Her other concern was quickly becoming the light. When the sun is overhead it lights up the coral in Cayman's clear water down to five or six hundred feet on most days but as it sinks lower in the sky the undersea world starts dimming quickly. At a hundred and twenty feet everything was becoming gloomier and the surrounding open water appeared darker and more menacing. It struck AJ that she was all alone in fading light on an unexplored pinnacle ten miles from civilization hunting for a wreck that no human has seen in seventy two years. She fought off a momentary case of the heebie-jeebies before scolding herself for not focusing and finning ahead.

At the next twenty foot interval she raised up and this time at the far reach of her visibility she made out something different. Each time before the reef seemed to dissolve into darkness ahead of her but now she could make out a horizon line no more than sixty feet ahead. She was coming to the end of the pinnacle ridge. Glancing at her computer she still had seven minutes of no-deco time and it had taken five to get here. Air wasn't an issue this dive as she hadn't had to struggle against the current the whole time, especially descending, but the nitrogen loading of the deep profile she was diving was the challenge. The good news was the timing of her turn around here was about perfect, the bad news was she still hadn't found the U-boat.

She had allowed her optimism to push out any doubt and leave her mind convinced that U-1026 was resting on this undiscovered pinnacle waiting for Annabelle Jayne Bailey to find it. As she turned the corner at the end of the pinnacle that was only a few hundred yards long it felt like a sucker punch to the gut as the realisation hit her that maybe it wasn't here after all. Reg was right, a hurricane rolled it off Twelve Mile Bank donkeys years ago and now it rested battered and bruised at six hundred feet where Costa was about to find it. She made the second turn once she could see the northwest corner of rugged coral and started the return run to the line.

For a short while AJ hung to the last piece of hope that it could still be perched on the north edge, just out of view of her outbound path. Halfway back she knew a submarine of that size would have been easy for her to see between the earlier dive and this one in the ground she'd covered. She was overwhelmed with disappointment and anger. For years she had felt like it was some preordained destiny for her to find this U-boat, the very same U-boat her Grandfather had seen, the same boat from which he'd rescued and befriended a young German. Her whole path of discovering Grand Cayman, its beautiful waters, moving here and sharing this experience with Reg and Pearl, how could all of this of happened for her not to find it! It felt like her whole world had been tipped upside down, nothing made sense to her anymore.

Familiar movement from off to her left jerked her back to the moment as four Caribbean reef sharks passed by about thirty feet away heading eastwards. Looking around it took her a second to realise she'd overshot her line, she could just make it out over her right shoulder around fifty feet away. The sharks continued ahead where the reef rolled away deeper as she'd noticed in her earlier dive. Checking her computer she had two minutes of no-deco time, she needed to head straight for the line and begin her ascent.

AJ gave a last look at the sharks. She always found it mesmerizing how they moved so gracefully through the water with the unmistakable sway of their muscular torsos. They were just disappearing from visibility when she noticed a huge school of Horse eyed jacks in a swirling circle above the passing sharks.

AJ knew her body was loaded to the brink of disaster with nitrogen and at the end of her third dive, all to well over a hundred feet, there was no room for error. Every ounce of her training and good judgement told her to swim to the line where she would make her ascent inside of safe limits by the narrowest of margins. Yet something stronger made her swim on.

As she followed the direction of the sharks she tried to justify what she was doing in her own mind. Was she so unable to come to terms with her failure that she was willing to risk her life? That was ridiculous. Was the idea that a rich, greedy man would rape an historical wreck of its treasure rather than share its wonderment with the world so unacceptable to her? Yes it was, but not at the price of a trip to the decompression chamber. Who the hell was AJ Bailey to play judge over any of this anyway? Nothing she could think of made any sense as to why she was still swimming away from the safety of the line, chasing sharks towards deeper water, until a distinct, dark outline appeared.

The rest of the pinnacle dropped steeply away on each side but the east end rolled at a gentler angle down to a hundred and forty feet where a large ridge of coral formed a stop before the wall plummeted almost vertically down to the depths. Resting against that ridge was U-1026.

The sight of this massive vessel was breathtaking and AJ hung in the water consumed with awe at the unmistakable profile circled and surrounded by a plethora of large ocean fish. She was still around seventy feet from the submarine at the far reach of visibility but there was no mistaking it. Coral had encrusted most of the structure, especially the deck plating and conning tower but the lower sides of the hull lived mainly in shadow and the smooth steel plate remained growth free.

AJ thought of her Grandfather. How she wished she could tell him how a story he captured her imagination with as a child led to this very moment of rediscovering a lost wreck after more than seventy years on the sea floor. She could picture him now, leaning forward in his chair, so eager to hear the excitement in her voice, wanting to know every detail of what she saw, visualizing the scene through her description the same way she had done with his tales.

The beeping of her dive computer was a stark reminder AJ was now in deep shit. The alarm was telling her she was in deco and needed to ascend immediately, an arrow pointing up and the depth of thirty feet were the directions flashing at her on the screen. Being in deco wasn't a problem in itself, she could carefully follow her computer's commands and she'd be out of it before she surfaced. She had plenty of air left this dive. Breathing it at this depth was now ironically poisoning her but as soon as she ascended she had plenty to do the necessary safety stops. The second issue that threatened to turn her problem into a disaster was the distance she had to cover while ascending to reach the line.

She was now northeast of the line with the current running hard south. As she began to ascend as fast as she dared she also had to kick like crazy to the west hoping she'd catch the line somewhere in mid water. If she missed it she'd be doing several safety stops while drifting and could easily end up a thousand feet from the mooring. That would put her well out of earshot and almost impossible to see in the gently rolling swell and dwindling light. Determined, she finned as hard as she could, using her compass to stay true to her heading while trying to angle upwards at about forty five degrees. She could feel the current dragging her to her left and combined with the fading light seemed to be conspiring against her. The sinister thought that perhaps King Neptune was eager to keep his submarine wreck a secret passed through her mind and made her chuckle. Too many Pirates of the Caribbean movies will put those thoughts in your head.

Ahead, still forty feet out, was the line. As dusk was settling, the light underwater was disappearing at an alarming rate and she only saw the line by a glint of the white rope in the dark blue water. Checking her computer watch she was at thirty eight feet. AJ flattened out her ascent angle and fought with all her might to swim northwest now to cross the gap and slow the effect of the current. She was in full anaerobic exertion, sucking every ounce of air she could through her regulator. When her hand finally grabbed the line she was at thirty five feet where she swiftly pulled herself up the last five feet and hung on tightly.

Panting like an Olympic sprinter she relaxed her body as much as she could and let the current pull her taught on the line like a human flag waving. She rested at thirty feet for three minutes and fifteen feet for five minutes to satisfy her dive computer that she'd processed enough nitrogen through her tissues to return to atmospheric pressure without danger.

Only one problem remained. She still had to disconnect the line from the loop back at thirty feet. To do that the strain from the boat would have to be slackened or she'd never be able to unclip the carabiner. As she pondered the dilemma she heard the motors start on the RIB boat above. Thomas eased the motors into drive and moved forward against the current, slackening the line. AJ quickly pulled herself back down fifteen feet, unclipped the carabiner and shuffled back up the free line to the boat. The boat, line and diver were now drifting together as Thomas cut the motors so she was safe from the props.

As AJ scaled the ladder at the stern of the boat the smile

on her face was all Thomas needed to know she'd found it. He threw his arms around her in a big embrace and babbled excitedly, slipping into his full Caymanian accent that no off-islander could ever understand.

Reg stood anxiously on the rear deck of the Explorador de los Océanos watching the sun sinking on the horizon sapping the light from the sky and turning the waters a deep, dark blue. Renfro had yet to surface and by Reg's rough calculations had another thirty minutes of decompression stops to do. He would reappear in the dark.

Reg had led Costa to this end of the Bank to get him as far away from AJ as he could, now with the discovery of what he was sure was the Frenchman's sailboat, he feared he'd guided them right to the location of the submarine. He kept chewing it over in his mind. There was every chance the sailboat was blown miles from the sub in the storm. The ghosts of forty two Germans and one Frenchman were the only ones who knew, although they almost certainly had no idea exactly where they were when they went down.

His phone vibrated in his pocket and he checked around him, making sure he was alone before reading the text.

'Found it!'

Reg struggled to remain calm and not dance around the deck yelling. He reread it four times before typing 'Atta girl' and hitting send. Screw you he thought. Screw you money grabbing bastards and your fancy boat and fancy gear. Screw you Nazi buggers that took that gold in the first place. All those poor people that did nothing more than be born to a different religion and heritage. Over the years he and AJ had discussed at length how the gold would never be the motivation or the reward for finding the wreck. As far as they cared it could stay locked inside the submarine until the steel finally rotted around it.

There was a good chance from the story told that the interior of the submarine was still air tight and only the conning tower was flooded. If the hatch above the control room had held for all these years the oxygen would have been pulled out of the air inside by the metal rusting and organic materials decaying leaving a rank inert nitrogen filled dry space. In theory a bell could be lowered over the conning tower, fed with pressurized air from the surface and the water in the conning tower pumped out. The hatch to the control room could then be opened, which would take some work after all these years and the sub pumped full of pressurized clean air.

If Costa and his people found U-1026 they could well adopt a method like that to get inside. More likely, they'd gas axe their way in, flood the interior, grab everything of value from the gold and the Enigma encryption machine to each spoon, fork and tea cup. They'd cut the deck gun off the plating and air bag it to the surface so within a day they'd strip the boat bare of all valuable items and leave the carcass to rot.

Reg could feel his temperature rising just thinking about how callous and greedy these men were. Which made him wonder what Costa was up to. He hadn't seen him in a while.

Carlos Costa was standing on the bridge of his boat with his Captain peering down at Reg. He'd watched him take his phone from his pocket, covertly read a message, type something back and return the phone to his pocket. Coincidently this text appeared to arrive at the same time the blip on their radar screen they'd been monitoring all afternoon finally moved and headed back towards Grand Cayman.

Thomas had the throttles pushed forward and the motors singing as they surfed the light swell back towards shore. AJ had slipped out of her wetsuit and dried her hair as best she could with a towel as the boat bounced, swayed and jolted across the water. It was hard for her to contain a mixture of excitement and relief. She'd dreamed, schemed and thought about this moment for so long it didn't seem real somehow.

"I can't believe any of this Thomas." She yelled over the wind and engine noise. "I can't believe we found the wreck, I can't believe I made it to the line!" She laughed in relief at the near miss, shaking her head.

"Meant to be, that's all, meant to be!" Thomas beamed at her.

"First thing tomorrow I have to register the wreck at the Port Authority, I won't sleep until this claim is filed and Costa can't touch it!"

"Legally…" Thomas added not smiling this time.

"Legally… Yeah, I suppose that's true, doesn't stop them going after it anyway does it?"

She thought it through for a moment, the office almost certainly didn't open until eight or nine in the morning and she and Thomas had clients, they'd be at the dock or diving by then. She'd have to go when they came back in. It wasn't like the Port Authority or Coast Guard would rush out there and put up hundred and forty foot stakes and yellow tape around the site! Or twenty four hour guards circling the area. Anyone could dive the site unbeknownst to her or the authorities if they knew where it was. All she had to show the Receiver of Wrecks were the GPS coordinates and a description of the submarine, it's story and vessel number. Which of course she was assuming was U-1026.

"Shit Thomas, I don't have a lick of proof identifying the bloody sub!"

Thomas stared at her confused. "What other submarine is gonna be out here? Not like we got them layin' about the place all over?" He spread his arms across the sea either side of him for emphasis. "Of course it's the one you've been looking for all this time!"

"I know that Thomas but the Receiver doesn't. I was so stupid not taking my camera down with me this time, all I had to do is video the wreck. Video of something on the wreck marked U-1026 would be even better!"

The sun was setting like a fire ball behind them in the western sky and the lights of Seven Mile Beach began to illuminate the shoreline as they approached.

"We have to go back out tomorrow Thomas, I have to get film evidence and a positive ID."

Thomas shook his head. "You're crazy Boss, just get the thing registered after we get done in the morning. Take them the video and such later. They'll be fine with that I'm sure. And remember I can't go out in the afternoon, they're finally putting Uncle Herbert in the ground."

AJ reluctantly conceded. "Okay, okay, I'll go by the office as soon as we're done tomorrow." But she couldn't shake the uneasy feeling that she needed better evidence, irrefutable proof that U-1026 lay at the co-ordinates she had saved.

It was dark when Costa joined Reg on the rear of the main deck as Renfro broke the surface and was helped onto the swim platform below them by his crew. Powerful spot lights lit up the area creating an eerie glow in the water. "What wonders from the deep do you think my diver has retrieved Mr. Moore?"

Reg felt like every question the Argentinian ever asked him had an underlying hidden agenda or intention. He hated these games but he figured it wouldn't hurt to roll Renfro under the bus. "Well, maybe he's got pockets full of artifacts but at a guess I'd say that sailboat started on the top and got rolled down by a storm so anything that spilled out could be scattered over a large area. Seeing as he chose to dive the site with a rig that would give him minimal time down there I'd say he'd be lucky to have found anything much."

Costa chuckled. "That's a fair assessment. I agree it would have been better to dive the site with a hard hat. Renfro is a stubborn man, you may have noticed, sometimes it's too much trouble to fight him on these matters. But maybe he got lucky and will surprise us."

Renfro was free of the bulky tanks and peeled off his wetsuit. Reaching down to his rig on the deck he unzipped a pocket in his BCD and retrieved the bottle, holding it up for Costa to see. "Not much down there, found this though, maybe we can date it, it's certainly not a modern Coke bottle."

Costa turned to Reg and grinned. "Apparently he is a lucky man."

Renfro changed into some dry clothes and joined Costa and Reg in the survey room to debrief from the dive. Costa stood the bottle on the counter top next to a computer and began tapping away at the keyboard.

Renfro began his description of the dive. "It's definitely a sailboat, or what was a sailboat, it's basically reef now, the coral has grown over the hull and the wood is probably all gone underneath. Visually I'd say it's about the right size, single mast, or at least that's all it made it to the bottom with. I didn't see any obvious debris field around the site and had to dig next to the hull to come up with the coke bottle. Not much else to tell really, hard to know whether that's where the boat landed or if it slid down the side, it definitely didn't roll as the mast was still attached."

Costa nodded and tilted the computer screen towards the other two men. "Here's an historical timeline on Coca-Cola bottles, the traditional curved shape was introduced in 1916 and remained the same with the raised lettering until 1957 when they switched to a label."

Reg looked at it carefully. "That's a pretty wide timeframe, is there anything else on here that could narrow it down?" He lifted the bottle and looked more closely at the embossed lettering in the glass. "Here is a patent number, 'Bottle Pat'd 105529', that must be traceable?"

Reg showed the bottle to the other two men and Costa returned to the computer and typed in the information. The Argentinian read to himself for a moment until he found what he was looking for. "Yes, here it is, this bottle was made between 1937 and 1948, that's when the patent was on the front according to this website. I'd say, along with the visual evidence, that's close enough to make an educated assumption that this is the wreck of the Frenchman's sailboat from 1945."

Reg was still stunned that his ploy to get the Explorador de los Océanos as far from AJ's dive site as possible had yielded the wreck of the sailboat. He thought about all the men that went down with her in that storm, it should be considered a war memorial and gravesite.

"The wreck needs to be reported and registered, this could bring some closure to the relatives of the families after all this time. Instead of their loved ones being lost, presumed dead, they'd at least know where they lay."

Renfro snorted and muttered under his breath. "Who gives a shit...?"

Costa took a more diplomatic path. "Indeed, but all in good time, we don't want a lot of fuss and attention about the sailboat before we've located the submarine." He looked Reg squarely in the eyes. "I must insist on your cooperation in this regard Mr. Moore."

Reg figured there was no point fighting over it, one way or another this wreck would get reported either by Costa or Reg would do it himself but not until AJ could file her claim to the sub. He nodded.,"That's fine, at least this gives us an idea we're looking in the right area, the sub can't be too far from here."

Costa looked at Reg and grinned, taking a few moments longer than seemed comfortable to speak. "You would think so wouldn't you? Of course in a storm boats have been known to be blown great distances off course… But, we have a good place to continue our search, we'll concentrate on a wider arc off this end of the pinnacle in the morning."

Something about this man always seemed disarming to Reg. He was incredibly well-mannered and polite, he dressed and carried himself as an educated, sophisticated and wealthy man, yet after any conversation with him Reg never felt like he'd been told the whole truth or maybe any truths at all. Despite that he found himself unintentionally warming to the gentleman and constantly had to remind himself Costa was probably not as he appeared and almost certainly had selfish intentions for U-1026 and the cargo she contained.

Costa continued. "It is late in the day, I assume you are comfortable finding the island in the dark Mr. Moore?"

"Of course," Reg replied.

"Then if you don't mind readying your boat, Mr. Renfro and I need to discuss some items. He'll be down shortly for the trip back."

Reg took his leave and headed to his boat wondering all the way what the conversation he was missing entailed.

Once Reg was beyond earshot Costa turned to Renfro who'd waited with him in the survey room. "Have him bring you back out by eleven am tomorrow, we'll scan more all morning but I believe this is a decoy. He may have known about the sailboat or it may have been a lucky coincidence but we picked up a boat sitting north east of the Bank all afternoon, I believe it to be the girl. We'll send Moore back to the island after he drops you so we can investigate if she comes back out after her morning customer dives."

Renfro sneered. "Why don't we quit messing about with him? We have our own tender I could use, we're paying him for nothing, especially if you think he's lying, which I'm sure he is."

Costa patiently replied. "Because I'd like to keep him busy so he can't help the girl. If we time it right tomorrow he'll get back after she leaves so it'll just be her and her monkey out there."

Renfro chuckled at the man's unguarded racial comment, he didn't consider himself a racist, he hated everyone equally and treated them so. He chuckled again at his own callousness. "Are we finally gonna deal with her properly before she screws this up for all of us?"

Costa nodded absent mindedly. "It might be that time."

Chapter 21
Atlantic Ocean, 1945

Kurt Neinstadt knew the Captain of a freighter sailing under the neutral Spanish flag between Spain and Brazil. The ship was actually supplying the Nazi war effort with goods from South America, moved from the northern Spanish port of Santander through Axis occupied France to Germany. By Neinstadt's calculations, the timing should work for U-1026 to rendezvous with the freighter, appropriately named La Ore Sol or The Golden Sun in English. Both ships should be in the waters off Florida about the same time so if Resch could make contact with Captain Albacete and they could find each other without Allied detection, they could transfer the crates to the southbound ship.

Both Resch and Neinstadt knew it was an imperfect plan fraught with opportunities for things to go wrong. Neinstadt assured the submariner he was aware of the frailty of the operation but it was the best he could come up with. Germany was on its heels, options were not bountiful and the most important thing was that the gold end up somewhere it could be used to keep their ideals alive. Neinstadt would find a way to join the treasure and ensure it was applied to either maintaining or rebuilding the Reich.

As for Albacete, he was in it for the money, he didn't care about the politics either way. He'd sided with the Germans in 1939 when they seemed invincible so he'd made his bed, now he'd like to switch allegiances. Trouble was the Nazis were still paying him and he didn't have the nerve to tell them no.

Resch and his crew left Wilhelmshaven and made the treacherous run out into the Atlantic Ocean. The British planes seemed to know their every move and the Kreigsmarine were losing more and more U-boats before they ever made it to their patrol waters.

They left port at night to try and get as far out as possible under the cover of darkness, running on the surface with the diesels fighting hard in the rough waters of late winter. They had a narrow escape on the first morning when Resch thought they were far enough clear of land to be out of range of the fighters so continued running on the surface. Apparently not so, as they were attacked, strafed and torpedoed by a British De Havilland Mosquito. Diving hastily they got away unscathed, running submerged until midday before continuing at snorkel depth the rest of the day.

The rest of the trip across the Atlantic was uneventful, they received word of a convoy via command too late to intercept, somewhat to Resch's relief. After so many years of fighting he was ready for it to be over. He'd started the war full of German pride and zeal for taking back the land and dignity lost after the first war. By the time he'd been given his own boat in 1942, the heyday of the U-boats, 'Die Glückliche Zeit' or 'The Happy Time' was coming to an end and submarine losses were growing and tonnage sunk lessening. Fortunately for Resch and U-1026, the new offensive in western Atlantic waters off America in 1942 opened up another successful run for the U-boats as American defenses were poor and disorganized. It too had an expiration as the Americans quickly learned from the British and improved their defensive strategies.

For three years now Resch and his crew had been making the trek across the Atlantic, hunting convoys on the way, patrolling the eastern shores of America, and picking off freighters and oil tankers in the Caribbean. The patrols were long and required the submarine to be refueled and supplied from a Type XIV U-boat known as a 'Milk Cow'. These huge submarines were essentially tankers that carried enough diesel fuel, oil and torpedoes to keep multiple Type VII's on long patrols.

In June 1944 the last of the ten active Milk Cows were sunk by the Allies. The Type VII's no longer had the means to make the longer patrols. They could reach the US coast and return but not much more. If forced to make many detours or evasive maneuvers they'd risk running out of diesel fuel before making it home.

Resch's orders sent him to the North East coast off Maine, patrolling south down the coastline to South Carolina and then returning. Kapitänleutnant Wolfgang Resch had the long journey across the Atlantic to ponder his options. He could continue as ordered, figuring his odds of making it back to the pens at Wilhelmshaven were fifty fifty at best. With their rapidly improving radar, sonar buoys and air patrols the Allies were shutting down the U-boats, sending around twenty five boats to the bottom each month.

His next option was to continue into the Caribbean and make the journey a one way trip. He wouldn't have enough fuel to make it back to Europe so it would be a firm commitment to going AWOL. Of course this was not a decision he could make alone. Forty four other men onboard shared whatever fate befell the boat and without their agreement and compliance it would be hard to operate the U-boat. Outside the physical logistics the likelihood of a mutiny or at least a split in opinions was high.

First, Resch decided, he had to decide for himself which direction he preferred and then he could begin work on his officers and crew.

Two things helped him make up his mind. The first was losing a man overboard in heavy seas off the North Carolina coastline. They'd been on the surface charging batteries, running on the diesels throughout the night. The swells were too bad to use the snorkel as the wave action would breach the tube and send salt water down the induction and exhaust. At dawn he pushed on trying to get a full charge before descending for the day. His Oberleutnant zur See, or Executive Officer, and two other men were topside on lookout, hanging on as best they could and scanning the skies for planes.

One of the men sighted a speck on the horizon that appeared to be growing in his binoculars as he struggled to stay trained on it. He yelled to the Exec who tried to pick up what he was looking at but could barely stand, let alone find the plane. The man took his other hand from the rail to point in an effort to guide the officer's view when a wave swept him off the conning tower. One moment he was standing between the two others and the next he was gone, no scream, no flailing arms and legs, it happened so fast he simply vanished.

The Exec immediately ordered the boat to dive and he and the other man lunged for the hatch, tumbling down to the control room after dogging the hatch behind them. Resch desperately wanted to search for their man, he was wearing a life vest and had a chance out there for a short while if he hadn't been injured or dragged under the boat. He drilled his Exec on whether he'd seen the plane or not but the man could not swear to having laid his own eyes upon it. Still, the risk of returning to the surface was too high, it would be gambling the lives of the remaining crew against one man. As they dived to just above the sea floor at one hundred and twenty feet in the broad, relatively shallow coastal waters off the Outer Banks they heard the unmistakable boom of a depth charge. It was well away from them but confirmed they'd been spotted. Resch couldn't feel good after losing a man but at least his conscience was eased that he'd made the right call.

The second element that swayed Resch's thinking was the rendezvous with Albacete and his ship. At great risk of detection Resch had made several attempts to reach the Spaniard over the VHF radio as planned and had been unable to make contact. The one scenario he hadn't given a lot of thought towards was the one he now found himself in. The U-1026 hadn't been sunk or captured and the ship he was supposed to meet and hand over a big pile of Nazi gold to was nowhere to be found.

That night when they returned to the surface to charge batteries under the cover of darkness, Resch and his officers listened to American AM radio as they ate dinner. The news was bleak for the Germans, the Allies had crossed The Rhine. The eight men ate in silence as they absorbed the description of American troops marching across their homeland, their thoughts with their families and friends, most of whom they hadn't seen in over six months.

Finally the Exec spoke up. "Kapitänleutnant, how do we get home?"

Every man at the cramped table, rolling and dipping in the waves of the Western Atlantic, thousands of miles from their homes turned to their Captain. If Wolfgang Resch was ever going to disobey orders and turn rogue, now was the time to make his move. Still torn apart with guilt and apprehension he addressed the table. "Well, my friends, it appears our home is not going to be there when we return. What awaits us, if by a miracle we make it back through the English Channel to Wilhelmshaven, will be a prison camp or a firing squad."

The men muttered and sighed but no one argued or disagreed. Resch pushed on. "As we sit here, we have a healthy boat, a strong crew, enough fuel to travel a long way and a cargo of gold that no longer has a destination."

He now had everyone's attention. "Perhaps the best way to help our families would be to end the war as free men? Surely we would be more effective and have more options to either return to Germany after the conflict or bring our loved ones to us. From a prison camp we will have no options at all."

The men looked at each other in astonishment. Clearly the idea had not crossed any of their minds and they were all nervous to be the first one to speak.

"Come now, we are speaking here as equals, not as men of different ranks, speak freely."

The Exec nervously broke the ice, whispering as though the SS were hiding somewhere waiting to pounce. "Kapitänleutnant, are you suggesting we desert?"

"Please, I am Wolfgang, we are speaking as friends just having a conversation. I'm not sure if we'd be deserting? I don't know that there's anything to desert from at this point? The Reich is collapsing, I expect an order to lay down arms and surrender any day. I am simply suggesting that perhaps we should end this regrettable war on our own terms."

Another voice spoke up. The diminutive navigator Obersteuermann Andreas Jaeger. "Where would we go? We are in a large submarine, we cannot pull into some foreign port? What should we do with the boat?"

Relieved the conversation was starting to gain momentum Resch responded enthusiastically, "I know a man, a relative of mine, he is on Grand Cayman, if we can get close I believe he has a boat with which he could pick us up. There's a small American Navy station on Grand but there are very few people on the two smaller islands, if he could take us to one of those, we could wait out the end and see what happens."

The group appeared to be warming to the idea, Resch carefully surveyed the faces looking for any signs of objection or resentment. He could see none.

Next to speak was the Leitender Ingenieur, or Lead Engineer. He asked the question that was now burning on everyone's mind. "What about the cargo? What happens to that?"

Resch took a moment, sitting up tall in his seat, taking his Captain's stance as he tackled what he figured was the deal maker with the group and more importantly with the crew. "That gold belongs to the people of Germany. It was put aboard this ship to be smuggled to South America by an SS officer. He said it was to finance the Reich after this war ends. I have no idea whether that was true or he was just stealing it for himself, I suspect the latter. But I believe this gold should go back to the people of Germany, to help us all rebuild our homes and our lives. I propose we divide it amongst us, equal shares regardless of rank, each man free to use it as he sees fit."

This set the men into an animated conversation over how much gold for each and how their families would use that money. Finally the Exec got everyone hushed down again and asked, "How do we move the gold? We can't hop from boat to boat with it and surely someone will be looking for it?"

Resch pointed towards his tiny private cabin. "Andreas, get the chart I borrowed from you, it's in my quarters."

As Andreas shimmied out from the table and went to retrieve the chart Resch continued. "No one is looking for this gold except Kurt Neinstadt and he can't tell anyone because he stole it from the Reich's secret reserve. I think he may have bigger problems anyway if the Americans find him."

Andreas returned and sprawled the chart of the Caribbean waters around Cayman across the cluttered table. Resch scoured the map until finding a spot and tapping his finger on it. "Here, right here look, it's called Twelve Mile Bank, that's where we set the U-1026 down gently on the floor at thirty five metres. That's where we leave her until its safe and we're ready to collect the gold."

The group stared at the chart showing the submerged island off the west coast of Grand Cayman. The ocean floor surrounding it was marked over a thousand feet deep all the way to Grand.

Chapter 22
Grand Cayman, 2017

AJ stood under the shower head letting the warm water wash the salt, dried sweat and tension away from the crazy day she'd just had. Normally she took quick showers, aware of the demands placed on the desalination plant on the island to keep up with the population and the growing number of visitors. Today she took the guilty pleasure of an extended bathing.

When she finally stepped from the shower and wrapped a towel around herself she noticed her mobile phone on the bathroom counter showed a new text message. It suddenly dawned on her what she'd forgotten and she cursed herself. The text message read 'it appears I've been stood up. Nice pub you recommended though.'

"Crap!" She checked the time of the text, he'd sent it twenty minutes ago, she quickly typed a reply, 'I'm so sorry! Still there?' She grabbed her hair dryer and started speedily knocking herself into shape for a date. As a girl that didn't wear makeup most days she could get ready in a hurry but for a date with a great looking guy like Mac she would have preferred to make more of an effort. If, she thought, he's even still there and still interested.

AJ didn't feel like she was one of those people that constantly sabotaged their own lives. She'd known friends like that who would find some way of screwing up anything positive in their lives, especially relationships, disaster magnets she called them. She'd come to terms long ago with the fact she may never find her soul mate and unless she did she simply wouldn't settle. Not that she thought of Mac in those terms, she'd just met him and she wasn't one to rush in, but he was rather delicious and seemed quite interested in her... or was until she stood him up!

Her phone finally vibrated on the counter so she ditched the hairdryer and grabbed it, reading the text. 'We're fixing tacos if you're interested?' Reg. Damn it, she thought, that's what she should be doing, celebrating with Reg and Pearl, they'd be dying to know about the sub. Her phone buzzed again. 'Still here, getting hungry...'

Well, she couldn't stand him up twice in the same evening. She shot Mac back a text saying she'd be there in ten minutes then replied to Reg saying she'd be by later for a drink and a chat. That done she put on a touch of eyeliner and lipstick then rummaged around to find an acceptable outfit. She settled on some jean shorts and a short sleeved plaid shirt, mainly because they were clean and not much else was. She thought about some fancy shoes, of which she owned a meager two pairs, but decided that might be too suggestive and stuck with her Rainbow sandals.

Choosing her bicycle over the dive van she peddled the half mile to the Fox and Hare in record time trying not to work too hard and get all sweaty again in the warm humid island air.

The pub was pretty quiet with a handful of regulars around the bar. She spotted Mac sitting at a table off to the side and headed that way, waving to the bartender as she went. Mac stood up and pulled a chair back for her, he looked good cleaned up wearing a pair of jeans and a short sleeved button down shirt.

She blurted out an apology as she sat, "I'm so sorry, my afternoon turned to evening and the day got away from me!"

He gave her a broad smile and she was relieved he

seemed unfazed by her tardiness. "No problem, I've been hanging out watching the locals come and go, I've been entertained."

His Scottish accent was soft, the kind that confused Americans who were already baffled by the various accents of the British Commonwealth.

"You're obviously from Scotland but I'm guessing you didn't spend your whole life there?"

He nodded, impressed she's that perceptive. "Well spotted. Military kid so we moved a bunch. Germany, Japan, all the usual spots, handy for picking up languages but you never really settle anywhere, always feels temporary."

She found herself getting lost in his eyes again, he was certainly easy to be around. He had a relaxed manner, without seeming arrogant or over confident, a trait she found very unattractive and quite common in many men, especially good looking men.

"How about you? How long have you been on the island?"

Talking about herself was probably her least favourite topic but she obliged with the usual background information about family and how she ended up on the island. The bartender saved her when he brought them their drinks and some menus. AJ ordered ceviche with local caught tuna and Mac chose the lionfish tacos which she recommended highly.

He enquired, "You can hunt the lionfish can't you?"

She gave him a cheeky smile. "I can, but you can't... well, actually you can, providing you're with me but you can't just hunt them on your own."

He laughed, "Sounds complicated!"

"It is, the Department of Environment controls the rules and they only issue their DOE approved slings to licensed dive operators. I'm trained to teach the lionfish hunting course and you can get a license taking the course but you can't get a sling, they've stopped issuing them. So basically if you want to hunt, we can tomorrow."

"Sounds fun, I'd like to."

They continued with easy conversation, each probing a little more into the others' lives and interests the way people subconsciously size each other up on first dates. She felt comfortable chatting with him and nothing so far had set off any alarms, which for her was rare. A couple of Stongbow ciders and the manic diving day she'd had, on top of the euphoria of finding the sub were also contributing to her easy going state of mind.

Today she rediscovered a German submarine lost to the world since 1945 on an uncharted pinnacle in the middle of the Caribbean Sea. Every time she thought about it she had a flutter in her stomach and skipped a breath or two. She was dying to talk all about it and couldn't wait to see Reg and Pearl. She considered telling Mac about it, or at least an edited version just to be able to hear the words out loud. He was a fellow diver that would understand the enormity of the difficult dives in addition to the amazing discovery of what she assumed was U-1026. She realized he was asking her something and she'd completely spaced out. "I'm sorry Mac, I was drifting there..."

He chuckled and smiled. "That's okay, seems like you had quite a day? If I'm not being too nosy you've got me really curious what trouble you and Thomas got into all afternoon, something fun?!"

"Well, we did have a bit of an adventure..." She was bubbling over with excitement as she relived the day in her mind. "We..." She paused to think through how she could phrase this without mentioning where exactly or what they had been looking for. He was looking at her expectantly, leaning forward in his seat a little, itching to hear her story. A story she desperately wanted to share with everyone. "It really wasn't anything, Thomas lost his uncle recently, a local fisherman and we've been tidying up loose ends. Clearing out his boat and stuff like that."

Mac sank back into his seat and she felt awful telling a lie, especially as he seemed genuinely interested in anything she did. She checked her watch, it was five past ten. Time had run by swiftly in his company.

He noticed. "It's getting late, you need to go?"

"I do, I'm sorry, I meet Thomas around six to get the boat ready, I had a nice time though and I feel awful about making you wait."

Mac slid some cash into the bill jar on the table. "Don't sweat it, it was well worth the wait, can I drive you home?"

She blushed a little. "I have my own transport actually, but you could walk me to it."

She waved again to the bartender as they walked out and outside the door he looked around trying to identify her car. She laughed and grabbed her bike leaning against the wall.

"Island limousine right here!"

He cracked up and hit the remote for his car. The lights flashed and doors unlocked on a nice rental Jeep in the car park. "Bike would fit in the back if I could save you some peddling?"

She paused. She really liked this guy. They'd just had a lovely dinner together, he seemed sincerely interested in her and she found him more attractive than any man she'd ever met. It had certainly been a while since she'd felt the touch of a man and she missed being held and made love to. She shivered slightly at the thought of Mac's firm, masculine body wrapped around her. Damn her mother she thought, she could hear her warnings in her head. "Thanks, but I have to make a stop on the way, I'll see you in the morning bright and early though!"

He smiled warmly and without hesitation leaned in and

kissed her gently on the lips, brushing his hand across her cheek. It took all the will power she could muster not get in his Jeep.

AJ rang the doorbell and walked in the house having seen the lights were still on. Reg's dog, a standard Cayman brown hound mutt came running up to greet her and she made a big fuss of him. Pearl stepped from the kitchen and gave AJ an enthusiastic hug.

"You did it my girl, you did it! Come and tell us all about it!"

Chapter 23
Bournemouth, 1997

Grandad Bailey returned from the kitchen and eased himself back in his chair. He plucked a digestive from the packet he brought with him and handed it to AJ on the settee. "This a two biscuit story, those women don't get that you see, they think a tale like this can be wrapped up in a single biscuit timeframe. You and I know better."

The young girl giggled and Arthur took a digestive for himself and put the rest of the package on the table next to him.

"That's better." He said, nibbling on the biscuit, savouring each bite.

"Right then, back to it, little Andreas had just showed me the photo of what I presume was his wife. I could hardly make out anything on it but he could see it clearly. I think he had that picture printed on his brain, 'cos it certainly wasn't printed on that piece of paper anymore. He'd drifted off with that picture clutched to his chest and was resting for a while. I ran up top to see how we were doing, I figured we had to be getting close by now. Cap told me less than an hour so I took in some fresh air for a few minutes enjoying the wind cooling me off and had me a smoke.

By the time I went below again we could see Jamaica on the horizon. Jamaica wasn't like Cayman that was dead flat, it had mountains you could see from a ways out so I knew we didn't have too long now. When I got down there he was barely conscious and curled up holding his stomach again, moaning and groaning in terrible pain. I tried to tell him we were close to shore and there'd be help once we got there but I don't think he could understand me.

We were so close to the end of the war, we all knew it from the radio reports, our boys were marching across Germany and it was only a matter of weeks before the Jerrys surrendered. It all seemed so pointless at this stage, the end was inevitable so I couldn't understand why we were still fighting. Of course after the war when all the stories of the terrible concentration camps came out we realized why the Nazi top brass were trying to buy time to get out of Dodge as they knew they'd be up on charges of war crimes."

AJ waved to her Grandad to stop a moment. "What were the concentration camps Grandad? Last time you said you'd tell me when I was older. I'm older now, at least half a whole year older, I think I'm ready."

Arthur smiled at the sweet, innocent girl perched like a pixie on the settee before him. "My girl I don't think anyone is ever ready to hear about such places and the awful things that took place in them, no matter how old."

He thought carefully for a moment. When could you tell a child the horrors that man was capable of? The natural instinct is to hide these things from your children forever, to protect them from the evils and wickedness in the hope their generation will not repeat these terrors. Yet they are being repeated. The Rwandan genocide was only a few years ago in 1994. In the Middle East the complete intolerance of religious diversity continues as it has for thousands of years. Eight years old was still much too young to know the details and the depth of the violence but in the dawn of the internet era and the year of the birth of Google, Arthur knew his granddaughter was a matter of key strokes away from seeing things no child should see.

"Let me explain it this way." He tentatively carried on. "The Nazi Germans, and not all the Germans were Nazis you understand? Most were just regular people like us who found themselves in the middle of a war. But the Nazis, they were the bad ones, they didn't like anyone that was different to them. Different colour, different religion, anything that wasn't the same. They put all those poor people in prisons, took away all their possessions and treated them very badly. Those prisons were called concentration camps."

To Arthur's great relief that seemed to appease AJ and she was ready to get back to the story.

"I kept talking to him in the hope it would help in some way, you know, just having someone there with him. I figured I'd want that if I was in his shoes. I've never got over the irony that one day we were both trying to kill each other and the next we're becoming friends and I'm doing all I can to save the bloke. The further away you get from the face of the man you're fighting the easier it gets to kill him I reckon.

I take his hand and he holds on as tight as he could, whatever it was seemed to be twisting his insides up and he's pouring with sweat again. He's trying to talk but it's just mumbles and moans, nothing I can make out at all. He's shivering all over like he's got the chills but he's burning up on the outside and his eyes got all glazed overlooking and distant. His grip started softening on my hand and the cramping appeared to be letting up again, I remember thinking 'thank God, he can rest a bit and we'll be in port in a few minutes'.

The bouncing in the waves had been settling down like we're in smoother coastal waters and I hear the motors slow down some. One of the lads shouts down that we're pulling into Goat Island so I looked around to see what we needed to take up with us. I was hoping the medic was on the dock waiting for us. 'Andreas' I says, leaning in to wake him, 'we're here, we'll have you to the doctor in no time, get you all fixed up'.

Was then I realized he wasn't stirring at all. I checked for his pulse. But he was gone."

After fifty two years Arthur Bailey still got a lump in his throat and struggled with the words. "Poor little bugger... Died right there, not more than a hundred yards from the dock."

AJ climbed in her Grandad's lap, throwing her skinny arms around his neck and hugging him tightly, making his shoulder wet from her tears.

Chapter 24
Grand Cayman, 2017

Thomas dropped the last of the tanks in the racks on the RIB boat as the Campbells strolled down the dock, excited for another morning of diving. He helped them aboard and stowed their bags and towels in a dry spot. Shortly behind them was Mac. He had a baseball cap pulled down low, sunglasses and wore a loose fitting long sleeved rugby shirt with the collar turned up. AJ stood with Reg by the little storage hut watching the man climb aboard the boat and almost didn't recognize him.

"That your hot date?" Reg teased her.

"That's him... I think..."

"What'd you do to the bloke? He don't look like he's ready for sunlight today, you didn't tell me you got him all liquored up."

AJ punched Reg on the arm playfully as she headed for the boat. "Very funny old man, if he's got a hangover he did it to himself after I left!"

Reg chuckled as he watched AJ cast the lines off and hop aboard.

As Thomas motored away from the dock, AJ asked if anyone had a preference on dive sites for the morning. The kids threw out the names of the sites they'd already been to so they could pick somewhere new. Mac had been pretty quiet since getting on the boat and AJ had wondered if he really was hungover or maybe he felt awkward about their date for some reason but he spoke up and seemed to be chipper. "They're all new to me so I don't mind where we go."

The father asked. "How's north side today?"

AJ responded enthusiastically, "Interesting you ask, I hear it's laid down a bit, we could give it a go if you don't mind risking it getting a bit bumpy?"

The Campbells all agreed it was worth it and Mac was along for the ride so Thomas opened up the throttles and they headed around the west end of the island towards the North Wall. Mac had peeled off the baseball cap and shirt and all seemed normal, he smiled warmly at AJ when she caught his eye.

AJ tried to stay focused on her customers and engage in conversation but as they bounced across the water all she could think about was U-1026. Time seemed to be running at a crawl which wasn't helped by her checking her watch every two minutes. She felt a desperate urgency to get the wreck registered along with the worry that what she could provide for evidence would not be sufficient. Her mind was racing and tormenting her with thoughts of Costa and his men finding and diving the wreck as she, oblivious and helpless, was spending the morning with recreational divers as though it were simply another day in Cayman. Thomas calling her brought her back to the task at hand.

They had rounded the north west corner and the swell didn't seem bad at all so AJ gave Thomas a site to aim for and pretty soon they were easing up to the buoy and tying in. Once secured AJ started her briefing. "This site is a treat we don't often get to do, this is called Ghost Mountain."

The name alone got the kids excited and a slightly nervous look on their mother's face.

"We'll splash in and meet at the bottom of the mooring line as usual, from there I'll lead you straight out towards the deep blue and you'll think I'm crazy. Believe me there's something out there and it's worth it!"

She looked at the two teenagers. "Watch your depth carefully guys, as we head out it's easy to go too deep, make sure you're level with, or above me, okay? We'll spend some time out there at the mountain, max depth a hundred feet, and then we'll work back up to sixty and return to the top of the wall under the boat to finish."

She checked around with everyone and then remembered about the lionfish. "Oh, does anyone mind if we hunt some lionfish on the dives today?"

Ashley looked puzzled. "Why do we need to kill them? They're so pretty and they just hang out under ledges and stuff, they don't do any harm?"

Her mother looked apologetically at AJ who smiled patiently. "That's fine, I'm happy to explain and if anyone is uncomfortable with us hunting we simply won't and that's fine too."

AJ addressed the group while they prepared their gear.

"So the problem with the lionfish starts with the fact they're not supposed to be here. They're a South Pacific fish that have been there for thousands of years and the ecology of the reefs there have evolved in unison with the fish life.

In the Caribbean, where they have appeared and spread prolifically in the last ten years or so, the reefs ecology has no place for them. They multiply very quickly and they have no natural predators. They feed on the smaller reef fish and are seriously affecting those populations, so in short they're turning life on the reef upside down.

For years we've tried to persuade the sharks, eels and groupers to eat the lionfish but because they are venomous the fish won't attack them. If we spear them and feed them to the predators they eat them but all that's done is make the predatory fish follow the divers around hoping for a free meal. Generally, they still won't attack the lionfish themselves.

The only success there's been is to introduce man as the predator and cull the lionfish as best we can. We've got the local restaurants serving lionfish on the menus now, it's a tasty white fish once filleted, so everything we cull we'll eat ourselves or give to a restaurant."

Ashley's mother put her hand on her daughters shoulder. "Perfect explanation AJ, thank you. You okay with it now Ashley?"

"Can we eat the fish you catch?" The girl asked.

AJ laughed. "Yup, I'll strip the venomous spines off for you and they're all yours!"

The mooring was at forty five feet and AJ made sure everyone was okay before finning away from the wall that sloped deeper below them. She slowly descended to sixty feet as they headed towards the deep blue darkness of open water. To the group following her it appeared they were swimming out into the vastness of the Caribbean Sea and away from any reef or land.

As they moved out a little further a dark shape slowly began to materialize in front of them growing larger as they got closer. Ghost Mountain was a large tower of coral about thirty feet in diameter growing from a ledge on the slope of the wall. The base was at a hundred and thirty feet with the pinnacle rising seventy feet above that.

The tower had a mass of beautiful black coral sprouting from the sides, big yellow tube sponges and waving red sea fans. A school of grunts circled the tower, swimming through the diver's bubbles and a large dog snapper followed AJ who carried the sling spear and five gallon container.

They lapped the tower at a hundred feet, marveling at this natural pillar built over thousands of years of coral growing upon coral trying to reach the brighter light closer to the surface.

The dog snapper shot ahead of AJ and circled a small overhang of coral. Keen for a free meal the snappers made great pointers for the lionfish and AJ knew she'd find one tucked under there. She signaled to Mac to follow her and she dropped a few feet to peer in the crevice. Sure enough a good sized lionfish hung there with its colourful fins and spines fluttering gently. AJ showed Mac how she put the rubber loop around her thumb and stretched it forward on the spear to load it, gripping the shaft of the spear with the same hand just behind the three headed spikes. She eased in close to the fish careful not to touch the venomous spines, lined up the spear for a kill shot and released her grip on the shaft. The spear shot forward propelled by the rubber loop pinning the fish against the tower.

It was a clean shot that instantly killed the fish although it seemed to still wriggle around as she shoved it into the plastic bucket. The open end of the container had an upside down funnel shape with slots in it so the fish could be pushed though and the spear pulled out but the fish couldn't come back out. AJ offered Mac the spear and he eagerly took it.

The dog snapper, undaunted by his lack of reward circled another crevice in the coral a little further around. While AJ showed the two kids the lionfish in the container Mac deftly swam to the crevice, inverted to get a better angle and fired the spear for another clean kill. As she kicked over with the container she couldn't help but be impressed with his buoyancy skills and how quickly he mastered the sling. For most it took a few tries to figure out the grip and aim but he was spot on first attempt.

AJ shallowed the group as they wound around the tower and Mac picked off one more lionfish on the way. They perused the top of the mountain that was home to hundreds of juvenile fish and found a green moray eel wrapped inside one of the numerous holes and hollows of the reef.

Back on the boat AJ transferred their catch to a cooler and covered them in ice, carefully avoiding any contact as the spines were still venomous although the fish were dead. The kids were now fascinated by the whole process and begged their parents to let them try it. 'Maybe next year' was not the answer they were hoping for and they kept trying different angles of persuasion throughout the surface interval.

Once they'd moved to the second dive site and tied in, AJ sat down next to Mac who had switched his own gear over to a new tank. "Nice shooting there, didn't take long to pick that up!"

He smiled warmly. "Good teacher I guess and some beginners luck."

"You're pretty good in the water for someone that dives occasionally on holiday." She was simply paying him a complement but he seemed uncomfortable for a moment.

"Oh, I don't know, you make it look like you're one of the fishes down there, I'm just trying not to flap about and touch the reef."

She laughed. "No, you dive like a pro, it's impressive for someone that only dives a few days a year." She thought again how refreshing it felt to be around someone so humble and ill at ease receiving compliments.

Reg pulled up alongside the Explorador de los Océanos at a few minutes before eleven in the morning. A deck hand helped him tie in and he shut down the motor. Renfro had kept to himself again on the ride out, much to Reg's relief, and he hoped they wouldn't keep him out there all day so he could get back and make sure all went well with registering the wreck. He was also relieved to find Costa's boat still scanning the west end of the Bank, true to yesterday's plan. Renfro stepped aboard the big boat and barked at Reg to stay put which he was happy to do.

Renfro met Costa in the survey room and the two huddled around the computer screen showing the morning's sonar scans.

"There's been nothing of interest and we're down to six hundred feet now." Costa summarized.

Renfro shook his head. "It's not here, there's no way that bastard would have directed us this way if he thought for a moment it was. He was as surprised as we were to find the sailboat."

Costa agreed. "The boat we saw on radar yesterday has not returned so far today but if we're correct then we will see it again this afternoon."

Renfro smiled, he could sense the time for more assertive action was approaching, the part he looked forward to. "What do we do with Moore?" He asked.

"Have your man ready at twelve thirty, Moore can bring him out here, that will tie him up for a while and keep him out of our hair. Tell him we'll let him know later about tomorrow but I hope we're done dealing with him at all. I'm tired of his deception."

Renfro nodded and headed back down to the rear deck where Reg's boat was tied up, moving slowly along with the Explorador as it continued to scan the sea floor.

He leaned over the railing and looked down at the Englishman who had the engine hatch up and was performing some routine checks while he had time to kill. "At half past twelve one of my guys will be at the Public Dock by the Lobster Pot restaurant, know where that is?"

Reg squinted his eyes against the bright sunshine looking up at Renfro peering down at him. It struck Reg as a little ironic that the arsehole barking orders at him was positioned above him. He knew Renfro had to be enjoying this. He smiled to himself as he thought of AJ claiming the wreck today. He couldn't wait to tell these two to get stuffed and see the look on their faces when they found out a young girl with nothing more than a story and some perseverance had beaten them to the grand prize. Instead of these greedy thieves raping the wreck, it would be protected as an historical site and preserved intact. The interior would be penetrated carefully and professionally, the torpedoes disarmed and the gold and other artifacts removed to be displayed in a museum. The dive site, the amazing story of the men which was now complete having found the sailboat and anything removed from the sub would be available for everyone to see and admire.

"Of course I know it."

"Bring him out here, you can hang out down there until you need to go get him."

"How about I leave now, I'd like to top up with fuel?"

Renfro had his arrogant smirk as usual. "You've got plenty of fuel, I watched you fill it this morning, stay there like I told you."

Reg wanted to untie and sail away so badly but he talked himself into being patient, a few more hours he thought, I can take this crap for a few more hours. Renfro disappeared from the railing so Reg went back to his engine checklist as he wasn't going anywhere for a while. He pondered why they were so adamant he stay here? Probably just Renfro being a jerk and ordering him about for his own amusement. It all seemed a bit contrived to him though, they were being very specific about the timing of everything, making him run back and forth all day. They were paying for his time and diesel so it's their money they're wasting he reminded himself but why couldn't this other guy come out with them this morning? Bringing these guys the sixteen miles to the far end of the Bank one at a time was expensive and time consuming. He figured that must be the plan, keep him busy. That was fine he thought, it meant they couldn't know it didn't matter anymore, AJ had already found the U-boat.

Thomas skillfully brought the RIB boat alongside the jetty and AJ hopped off and tied the lines in. The second dive had been equally successful hunting and Kelby finally convinced his parents to let him try a shot with the sling. He missed but at least he felt like he'd been involved in bringing home dinner.

AJ heaved the cooler onto the wooden pier and carefully laid the fish out, lifting them by the mouth so the fins and spines hung away from her hands. Mac took a look at the spoils, nine decent sized fish, which should feed a family of four. "Thanks for another fun day AJ, I have to run."

She looked up, she was surprised he had all his gear with him. "You can leave your stuff on the boat, you're going out with us tomorrow right?"

"Yeah, of course, I just wanted to mess with my BCD a bit tonight, move some clips and stuff around."

"Oh, okay." She wasn't sure what to say next. She'd been so focused on getting back to the dock and wrapping up the morning so she could head to the Port Authority offices she hadn't really thought about her and Mac. In the back of her mind she'd assumed they'd meet up again that evening but now she felt awkward and wished she'd thought it through more.

He seemed a little off guard too. "Yeah, okay, well I have to go… but maybe I could call you later?"

AJ was relieved, for a moment she felt a weirdness between them but she figured maybe he was preoccupied too, perhaps he had the interview he'd mentioned. "That would be great, I'll talk to you later then?"

He gave her a big smile and headed up the jetty towards his Jeep. She watched him leave, admiring his broad shoulders and the muscle definition in his long back. Then she realized the Campbells were all watching her watching him and she blushed as she hurried back to sorting the fish for them.

One by one she held them by the mouth and using a sharp pair of medical shears she removed the venomous spines, fins and tails, leaving the rest to fillet. She carefully gathered the clippings and put them securely in a Tupperware container. Pearl had been dabbling in making jewelry from the colourful fins and spines, so welcomed any they could bring her. Several boutiques on the island were now selling her creations and they were becoming quite popular.

The Campbells promised to bring the cooler back in the morning so AJ put the fish back on ice and they left excited to make dinner that evening from the catch.

By the time she was done with the lionfish Thomas had all the tanks loaded in the van to take to get filled and had topped the boat off with petrol ready to go again. "Thomas, I know you have to go, I'll take the tanks when I go to the Port Authority, I can reload them when I get back and take the boat out to the mooring. Go get cleaned up, you have to give your uncle a grand send off."

Thomas was sweating, he'd been hustling getting the tanks loaded in a hurry. "Thank you Boss, I can load the tanks in the morning if you leave them in the van?"

She waved him off. "Get outa here, I got it, tell your mum and dad how sorry I am and I hope it's a nice service."

Thomas thanked her profusely as he ran up the dock to grab his bicycle.

Finally, she thought, time to head to the Port Authority

and see the Receiver of Wrecks. AJ felt slightly overwhelmed by the prospect, it wasn't everyday someone waltzed into the office and announced they'd found a U-boat that had been missing since 1945. Especially a young woman with purple streaks in her hair and tattoos up both arms. She believed with all her heart that that shouldn't make a difference and she knew with all her good sense that it still did. Taking every precaution, she grabbed her long sleeved windbreaker and threw it on before firing up the van and heading for town.

As she drove down West Bay Road behind all the hotels on Seven Mile Beach she caught a glimpse of the cruise ships anchored off George Town. Grand Cayman's tiny port was the same place the cruise ship tenders loaded and unloaded the passengers. Many proposals had been made to build giant docks and dredge the ocean floor to accommodate the huge ships but so far all had been rejected. So the behemoths anchored in the sand flats in deeper water and tendered the folks to shore.

With nothing but a narrow two lane road running through George Town's waterfront, cruise ship passengers everywhere, along with the shuttles and taxis ferrying the people to beaches and excursions, the town would be a mess. Sure enough, shortly after the light where West Bay Road became North Church Road and continued into town the traffic slowed to a crawl.

The closer she got the more nervous she became. She had the GPS coordinates and that was basically it. She had her word that she'd seen the U-boat, her Grandfather's story, which again was her word and she had some photo copies of the original reports filed that the sub was missing presumed lost. If only she'd thought to shoot some video, it would at least be something more concrete to show them. She kept wondering if they could reject her claim without further proof.

She impatiently shuffled along past The Lobster Pot, Rackham's and Casanova restaurants before the line of vehicles was reduced to stop-and-go backed up from the next light in the centre of downtown.

Reg glanced up from the deck of his Newton and noticed AJ's van edging along in traffic on North Church Road. He was tied on to Public Dock waiting for his passenger and happened to see her between the buildings. He'd just been thinking about calling her to check in and see if she'd made it to the Port Authority but clearly she was on her way. He reached for his phone to call anyway when he heard someone step down onto his boat from the dock.

He turned to see a tall man standing in front of him with wrap around shades, a wide brimmed sun hat shielding his face and a thin sweatshirt.

"Let's go." Was all the man said in a gruff tone.

Perfect, Reg thought. Another arsehole like Renfro. He put his phone back in his pocket and started the motor, letting it idle while he untied from the dock. The man pushed the boat away from the dock with his foot so Reg could go up top to the console and start easing away. Reg shouted down thanks which the man ignored or didn't hear. Reg decided he didn't care either way and settled into his chair for the ride back out to Costa's boat.

He allowed himself a wry smile knowing AJ was about to walk into the Receiver of Wrecks and give them the biggest news they'd had in a long time.

AJ gave up with the traffic and pulled around the back of the Greenhouse Restaurant, a little café tucked one building back of the main drag through town, hidden from the tourists. The place was spilling over with customers from the office buildings, banks and businesses that populated downtown. She parked there, waved to Jen the owner, and walked the rest of the way into town, weaving between the cruise shippers strolling around the shops.

Finally she reached the office building for the Port Authority and stepped into the reception area where there were a couple of people waiting in line. She looked around to see if there was a sign directing her to the Receiver of Wrecks, maybe it was in a different building? There weren't any signs directing anyone anywhere she realized as the dock could only fit one freighter at a time so it wasn't like they needed rows of customs officers. In fact how often would someone come in reporting a wreck she asked herself? Hardly a full time position.

She made it to the desk and the large Caymanian woman wearing a Cayman Port Authority shirt, which was stretched to what had to be close to bursting point of the buttons, asked how she could help.

AJ spoke quietly. "I need the Receiver of Wrecks please."

"What's that honey?" The woman bellowed back, she was as jolly as she was substantial and clearly did not possess an inside voice.

AJ tried again a little louder. "The Receiver of Wrecks please."

"You done wrecked your boat or you find someone else's boat been wrecked?"

AJ was completely taken off guard and stared back at her blankly for a moment while she thought about it. "Uhh, I guess it would be someone else's... but I'm claiming it now."

The woman laughed loudly. "Well good for you honey! Where's this wreck at then?"

This was not how AJ had imagined this playing out at all. "Ma'am, are you the Receiver of Wrecks?"

The woman threw her arms up and laughed again. The

couple of co-workers milling around in the office were staring and chuckling now. "No honey! That's funny right there, I'm the receiver of anyone coming through that door!" She pointed at the front door. "Mister Edwin Neville is who you'd be looking for, but he ain't here at this time. He's on the Brac today on account of him being the Port Manager as well as the Receiver of Wrecks, he's at the office there once every month or so. He'll be back in the mornin' I believe. I can take down the details and hand it right to him in the mornin' honey."

AJ felt like she'd been punched in the gut. Once a bloody month the guy goes to The Brac and it has to be the only day she's ever likely to need him. She couldn't believe it. This lady seemed lovely and quite the hoot but there was no way she was leaving the details of the biggest discovery in these waters for decades with her. "I'll come back in tomorrow, thank you for your help."

The woman was obviously a little disappointed to miss out on the scoop of a drifting boat somewhere which would have been great gossip material. As AJ left she could hear she'd quickly recovered and was greeting her next customer with loud enthusiasm.

Despondent, AJ drove to Island Air and got the tanks filled before continuing back to West Bay Dock. The whole way she mulled over her options. By the time she pulled in and parked she'd made her decision. She would go back out and shoot the video.

With that she reached behind her seat and grabbed a small case containing her GoPro camera.

Pearl was at the dock supervising the turnaround for their afternoon dives and shared AJ's disappointment in not being able to claim the wreck. AJ quizzed her. "Have you seen Reg?"

Pearl shook her head. "Last he texted me they had him

picking up a guy at Public Dock and running him back out there, that was about an hour ago."

"Did he have any idea when they'd be done with him?"

"He didn't say. He was pretty fed up with all the running back and forth. I can ask him? His phone doesn't have great reception out there but seems to get my texts eventually."

"If you don't mind asking, I need to load the rest of these tanks for tomorrow and get the boat off your dock out the way." AJ finished ferrying the tanks down to her boat and loading them in the racks, by the time she was ready to move the boat Pearl came back over.

"He's back out there on the Bank, says they've got him tied alongside just waiting. He figures he'll have to run the two guys back at the end of the day."

Damn it, AJ thought, she was counting on Reg going out there with her as Thomas was busy. She thanked Pearl and pushed away from the jetty, motoring slowly towards her overnight mooring. What should she do now? There was a good chance that one of Reg's divemasters would be free as they rarely have as many customers in the afternoons as mornings. She knew them all pretty well but it made her nervous to include anyone else in the secret, especially after being unable to register the wreck.

The thought crossed her mind to do it alone. She'd have to dive down with the line and get tied in quickly before the boat drifted away too far. If she missed she'd have to pull herself back up the line to the boat and drive it over the mooring and try again. Providing she didn't drop the line. If that happened the boat would be adrift in the surface current and she'd be left trying to swim on the surface with all her gear on to catch the boat… or not, and be adrift as well. That was a scary prospect.

She'd reached her mooring and shut the motors down.

She floated there thinking. What if she secured the line to herself so no matter what she couldn't lose the line before getting it tied in? The line already had a carabiner on the end to clip to the loop underwater, if she clipped it to her BCD on the descent then the only risk would be when she unclipped it from her to secure it to the loop!

She fired the motors back up and pushed the throttles forward, aiming the RIB boat west. She knew this was the craziest thing she'd ever done but she was determined to get video proof so tomorrow Mr. Edwin Neville wouldn't have any reason to deny her claim. If she could find some evidence that the sub was indeed U-1026 that would seal the deal. She glanced back over her shoulder, in the distance she could see Pearl fussing around the dock sorting out the crews and customers for their afternoon dives. She looked at her phone and contemplated calling her and explaining what she was doing. She knew Pearl would tell her to turn around and she'd have to defy her. She'd also tell Reg who would immediately abandon Costa and come straight over, which Costa would then see where they were.

She decided to skip permission and beg for forgiveness, which she would do with video in hand. As she cleared the west wall and the sea floor dropped away to six hundred feet she opened the throttles up further and the RIB boat skimmed across the surf at nearly thirty knots.

Chapter 25
Bournemouth, 1997

Annabelle Jayne always ended up in Grandads lap in tears even though she knew Andreas died. The very first time she heard the story she was inconsolable for hours and when she asked to hear it another time Arthur was reluctant to put her through that again. Since then she'd managed to have a good sniffle at that point in the tale and recover so Grandad could finish the final part.

She was settled back on the couch again and ready to hear more. "Okay Grandad, I'm fine now, I'd like to hear the rest."

He smiled at his granddaughter. He didn't like to see her cry but loved to hold the little girl in his arms. It reminded him of telling her mother the same account, except Beryl hated crying and would fight the tears until she couldn't anymore and end up in his arms anyway.

"Back to it then. So there was a big fuss at the dock and all the Navy brass wants to know what happened and where these Germans came from. They take me and the Cap into the field offices and we have to explain over and over to this British Intelligence Officer, name was Lieutenant Brody, what we knew, which of course wasn't much. I tell 'em what Andreas said to me and he gets real interested then about this gold. He asked me each way to Sunday anything about where the sub might be and I keep telling him I have no idea but it must be in fairly shallow water as the three of 'em swam out of it.

He always talked to us separately and kept switching back and forth, I guess to make sure our stories matched, and we both ended up feeling like we were being interrogated more than debriefed. Anyway, Brody tells me not to say a word about any of this to anyone, the Cap, me mates on the boat, nobody, he's right uppity about it, says it's national security and all that. I told him fine, I won't say a word and finally about ten o'clock that night he lets me go. That was the last time I ever saw the man and it wasn't until months later, war was over and I got shipped back home, I heard what happened after that.

The Lieutenant was scheduled to fly out of Jamaica the next day, he'd been the intelligence officer at the base for a year or so and he was due a trip back to England. Apparently, Mr. Brody and a young lady from the island had taken a liking to each other while he was stationed there and after he left the base that night he took off in a hurry to see her one more time. As best anyone could figure out, this young Jamaican girl must have done some snooping and finally learned that Brody had a wife and two little kids back in Blighty. Don't know what he'd been telling her or promising would happen but sounds like she was a bit surprised and none too happy about it.

Next morning the base is all a panic as the Home Office realized they were shipping Brody home within what appeared to be weeks of the end of the war and the base commander is trying to find him to tell him he'll have to wait a bit longer. Finally someone was dispatched over to the house he was billeted in and discovers the unlucky Lieutenant lying dead in his bedroom with a kitchen knife in his chest. Their romantic last night must have taken a bad turn and the young lady took the news of his wife and family rather poorly and let him have it.

They looked for that girl all over the place but never found her. Shortly after the war ended most of the Navy people cleared out and I doubt the local police cared too much to pursue it. Best I know she was never brought to trial, probably an olden like me telling stories to her grandkids sitting on her porch in Jamaica still.

Other part of this saga was just a rumour but I always wondered if it was true. Military Police does a search of Brody's house looking for any clues to find the girl. Turned up nothing on her but supposedly they found a German radio transmitter and a Swiss passport under a different name for our man Brody. Looks like he may have been a spy for the bloody Krauts.

That same day they turned us around on MTB-67, and back out on patrol we went so that's why I didn't hear about all this kerfuffle until much later. He swore me to secrecy and I didn't think anything of it as I was too busy being transported back to your Gran who I was pretty excited to see. A Navy mate of mine told me what happened when we was having a beer down the pub back home a few months later. I assumed Brody must have done some kind of report or sent a message to his intelligence people or something but as the years rolled by and nothing ever came up about a U-boat off Grand Cayman I realized maybe he hadn't. Don't know if he was in too big of a hurry to see his girlfriend and planned on doing the paperwork in the morning or if he had thoughts of finding the gold for himself. Maybe he really was a German spy and told the Nazis instead. Either way it appears Andreas' story never made it back to the Allies.

Only people I've ever told the tale to is Lily, your mum and you. I always thought it would be a great adventure to try and find the sub one day, carry out Andreas' wishes and get his portion of the gold to his family. For a while I tried to reach his wife in Germany but it took me years of writing letters all over the place just to find out his last name. I finally did, Jaeger,

Andreas Jaeger was it, but the trail stopped there. The three bodies were buried on Jamaica as the Navy couldn't figure out where to send them as Germany collapsed under the Allied attacks. No idea if his wife was ever informed, but eventually I'm sure she would have seen the records that say the sub and crew were missing in action.

Needless to say, I've never managed to get back out there to try and find his U-boat, wouldn't know where to start quite honestly but I keep expecting to see a headline in the paper one day, 'U-boat full of Nazi gold found off coast of Grand Cayman'!"

Arthur chuckled and smiled at the little girl beaming back at him from across the room. "Maybe one day you can find it, what do you think to that?"

The smile dissolved into an intense and determined glare. "I will Grandad, I'll find it and then you and me will bring it up and get the gold and we'll give it to all the people that are supposed to have it!"

"We have a good plan then," he finished with a warm smile.

Chapter 26
Grand Cayman, 2017

Pearl had texted Reg again on his run back out to Costa's boat and explained the situation at the Port Authority. By the time Reg was tied alongside and his passenger delivered he was more than ready to get the hell out of there and get back to Grand. He couldn't think of anything he could do to help the situation but he'd rather be back with AJ and Pearl than stuck out here with these crooks.

Renfro had told him to hang out and wait after he'd greeted the man Reg had brought out. The two seemed pretty friendly so he presumed the guy was just another one of Renfro's crew. Reg figured he'd give them an hour before he left whether they were ready or not. If AJ had clients the following morning he'd go to the Port Authority for her and claim it under her name. One thing he knew for sure was today was the last day he was working for Costa and Renfro.

On the bridge Carlos Costa studied the radar screen. He'd been watching the blip of a small craft heading west from the island, it had now stopped four miles short of his current position at the far end of the Bank. He went down to the survey room where he joined Renfro and his man. Costa wasted no time with introductions. "The boat from yesterday is back."

Renfro grinned. "It has to be her."

Costa agreed. "I believe so. We need to get rid of Moore, now. Send him back and tell him we'll contact him about tomorrow later."

Renfro didn't move. "What if he goes straight over to join her?"

Costa looked at him impatiently. "Then we'll deal with both of them. Now get him out of here!"

Renfro left the survey room smiling.

Reg had kept himself busy arranging the rental BCD's and regulators they kept below deck in the cramped cabin. He emerged when he heard Renfro's voice at the railing.

"What's that?" He shouted up to him.

Renfro sneered down. "You can get outta here, we'll call you about tomorrow."

Reg nodded, more than happy to leave. Then he paused, figuring this was his last day he'd be dealing with him he wanted to get his money. "I need to get paid through today, I've used a bunch of diesel running taxi service for you and your thugs."

Renfro glared at him. "Your wife has a card on file, bill that."

He waggled a finger down at Reg. "Don't try and screw me over either, I know exactly how many runs you've done, I'm not funding your fat tourist fishy watching business."

Reg laughed at the man without humour in his voice as he threw the lines off and started the motor. "I'm an honest man Renfro, but you wouldn't understand that."

Renfro gave him the middle finger as Reg motored away, bringing up West Bay Dock as his destination on his marine GPS.

It had been an easier ride out, the winds were down and the waves were long, gentle one to two foot swells, a lot calmer than the last few days AJ had been out near the Bank. She prayed the current had also lessened, it would make the task ahead much less challenging. The whole ride out she'd been vacillating between turning around and being sensible or pushing on and getting the job done. She never really made a conscious decision either way but she was still heading west so figured her stubborn streak must have won out.

She was back at the GPS spot they'd marked for the buoy. The surface current was light so she was allowing herself to be optimistic below would be the same. She motored a little north of the mark to allow some drift while she prepared and began gearing up. It had been a long time since she'd been this nervous before a dive, her alarm bells were ringing loudly and she knew full well she was breaking a ton of diving safety rules.

She double checked all her gear and made sure she had the little GoPro video camera in her BCD pocket. She checked the red filter lens was on the camera so the picture would be colour corrected for the loss of red spectrum light at depth under water. Finally she secured the boat's line to her BCD with the carabiner and gathered the coils of line up in her hand. A last glance at her GPS position showed the RIB boat was still slightly north of where the buoy should be, so without further opportunity to second guess herself, she back rolled over the side.

Reg felt like a weight had lifted off his shoulders. He'd wanted to ditch the whole deal when Renfro showed up and he'd only stuck it out the past few days to distract them from AJ's search. Now, with the cool wind rushing over him as his boat skimmed the soft rollers back to home he could finally breathe a sigh of relief and relax. He sent Pearl a text saying he was on his way and how much to charge the credit card Renfro had left her, he didn't want to wait and give him a chance to cancel the card.

From the Bank the only thing you could see on Grand

Cayman was the very top of the two tallest buildings and the goliath cruise ships if they were in town. Reg could pick out two ships in port and a third that had already left anchor heading west towards Cozumel. It was passing him on his port side. He instinctively looked over to his left as he cleared the south east corner of the Bank. About a mile or so to his north lay a World War Two German submarine he thought, how amazing is that? And there are only four people on the planet that currently know that fact. He smiled despite being annoyed that the cruise ship was obscuring his view as they passed about half a mile apart.

Reg, like most, felt the number of cruise ships coming into the little island had gotten way out of control and was adamantly against the proposals of dredging and building big docks. He would be fine if they limited it to a couple of the smaller vessels so the place didn't get completely swamped with passengers, but seven of them on some days, he agreed with most of the residents, was ridiculous.

He stopped looking that way and focused ahead so he could enjoy the ride home. If the cruise ship had not been in the way, he may well have seen AJ's unmistakable RIB boat bobbing on the water.

AJ had seen the cruise ship approaching before she rolled in and now could hear the huge propellers crushing the water even though the massive ship was more than half a mile from her. Ignoring the deep drone resonating through the ocean she stayed laser focused on the buoy below her and kicked hard down towards it, releasing the coils of line to free up both hands. At thirty feet she reached the buoy and fumbled for the short line and loop that floated from it. Her heart was pounding with a mixture of adrenaline and exertion as she clutched the loop in her left hand and reached to unclip the carabiner with her right. She glanced up to see how much slack she had and quickly realized the boat was well south of her and the line was about to run out. She thrust her right hand forward and swiped the carabiner at the loop knowing if she missed the boat would try and wrench the line from her grip and would be separated from her and the mooring. The slack immediately ran out and the line yanked violently out of her hand throwing her backwards in the water, flailing to catch the line. For a moment she was terrified she'd lost the boat until she realized the boat line had pulled tight on the buoy line and the whole length to the sea floor was now pulled taught. She'd just clipped it in time.

AJ took a few deep breaths through her regulator to regain her composure and let her heart rate settle back down. The next thing she noticed was that she was gently moving away from the line. The current was far less than it had been on the previous days when she would have been swimming like crazy to hold position, now a few solid fin kicks and she was holding the line again. She looked at the carabiner held tight against the line, pulled by the weight of the boat in the light but still present surface current. She wondered how she'd be able to create any slack to undo the carabiner. Oh well, she thought, maybe she'd just cut the line above the carabiner. It would leave her with only the severed end of the rope to hang onto but it was that or release the line from the boat. She figured she'd have time to decide on her safety stop and right now she was burning precious air so it was time to get to the sub.

Visibility was outstanding and she was amazed how quickly the U-boat came into view. She scolded herself over that first dive when she'd ruled out this end of the pinnacle after only a quick look having not seen anything. A few yards further or better visibility and she would have found the sub right away. With the current so much lighter she was comfortable making a diagonal path down instead of following the rope and then the sea floor. This gained her no deco time as she reached her maximum depth at the same moment she arrived at the submarine rather than all the way on the approach along the bottom.

As the boat came into full view she was struck again by the magnificence of it. There was a whole ecosystem enveloping the sub from coral growth to shoaling fish colonies to the larger predatory fish that patrolled above. The sight was breathtaking and she shot some video to capture bow to stern before arriving at the conning tower.

There was a lot of coral growth around the top of the tower and much of the sheet metal and railing had rusted away. A huge tube sponge grew from the back of the platform and AJ was careful of not damaging the growth as she examined the top area of the boat where she pictured three or four men scouring the seas on lookout. In the base of where they would have stood was the hatch into the sub and sure enough it was open just as Andreas, Lars and Wilhelm left it as they escaped in 1945. Upside down in the water she reached out and tried moving the hatch. It was heavily encrusted with coral growth and didn't budge at all.

She unclipped her torch from her BCD and shone it inside the conning tower. Between the tilted angle at which the sub had landed and the shadow of the hatch cover, less than half the interior had received sunlight, allowing coral to grow. The rest of the interior appeared relatively clear of growth but covered in silt and other particulate from decades at rest.

The hatch was only about three feet in diameter and the conning tower looked cramped inside with the ladder and various controls and gauges packed around its interior. To find the evidence she needed AJ knew she had to go in there but the idea of squeezing into the tiny space a hundred and twenty feet below the surface with all her gear on was terrifying.

Pearl stood on the jetty to greet Reg as he backed the Newton alongside and she tied his lines to the cleats on the dock. Stepping onto the jetty he threw his arms around his wife and kissed the top of her head. He was easily a foot taller than her and Pearl always felt like no one could ever harm her with the broad shouldered man's arms wrapped around her. "I'm glad that's all over with," she whispered to him.

"Me too love, me too." He let her go and looked out across the azure water as flat as a lake. "I didn't think AJ had clients this afternoon?"

Pearl looked over at the empty mooring spot AJ used. "Oh? I didn't think she did either. She couldn't, Thomas is at his uncle's funeral."

They both pondered a moment, trying to recall if AJ had mentioned about going anywhere else. Reg retrieved his phone from his pocket and dialed AJ's number. It rang until her voicemail picked up and her cheery voice relayed her greeting.

"Hi you've reached AJ Bailey and Mermaid Divers, sorry I missed you, please leave a message and I'll call you back on our next surface interval!"

Reg waited for the tone. "Hey girl, give me a call, me and Pearl were wondering what you're up to?" He hung up and stared out across the ocean in the direction of the Bank. He couldn't imagine she'd gone back out there. Alone.

"None of the lads went with her did they?"

Pearl was perplexed. "I didn't notice she went anywhere. Last I saw her she was idling over to her mooring, I went back to the hut after that. No one said anything about going anywhere, besides I'm sure she was on her own last I saw her. You think she went back out to the wreck?"

Reg shook his head. He reran his trip back from

Explorador de los Océanos in his mind, trying to recall if he saw any boats or any sign of AJ. Her RIB boat was instantly recognizable, there's no way he thought he could miss it. Only thing he remembered seeing was the cruise ship. "I'm sure I would have seen her," he answered, but something still nagged at the back of his mind. She's smart and she's cautious he thought to himself, attempting self-reassurance, but she's bloody stubborn and determined too, there's no telling what she might try. He couldn't shake his anxious feeling.

The interior of the conning tower appeared to be oval shaped, about six feet across by eight feet long to the steel walls. Mounted to that were all kinds of equipment and sticking up through the compartment were two periscopes and the ladder. With the addition of coral growth on the starboard side there was very little room down there.

AJ couldn't afford to waste any time, at this depth she was burning through her bottom time quickly and needed to get moving. She carefully unbuckled her BCD and laid it down next to her by the hatch opening. Her spare regulator, the octopus, had an extra-long line for emergencies and training if she needed to share her tank with another diver. She switched from her normal reg to the octopus to give her more reach and slid her fins off, wedging them under the weight of the BCD and tank.

She now had much more freedom and less bulk to maneuver and just had to hope that nothing pulled the BCD and her air supply off the conning tower! AJ carefully started down the ladder, placing her feet daintily on each rung trying to avoid the coral growth on the side of it. She clutched her underwater torch in one hand and the light splashed around the pitch black interior reflecting off the glass lenses of the gauges. Around her other wrist she'd wrapped the tether for the little camera which clanked against the ladder as she descended. She felt something brush her leg and about spat the regulator from her mouth in fright. The two foot Grouper she'd apparently disturbed wriggled up past her and swam away leaving AJ to calm herself down again.

Two more steps and her foot reached the floor causing a wave of fine silt to billow up all around her obscuring all visibility. She froze motionless and waited for the particulate to slowly settle back down which seemed to take forever. Once she could finally see again she tried to keep her feet still and rotated her body around shining the light all over the interior. She couldn't believe the submariners operated their submerged attacks from this claustrophobic space. The Captain and the Torpedo Data Computer operator, or TDC operator, would both be in the tower with the lower hatch open to yell at the helmsman and navigator below in the control room.

She shone her light at the floor to find the hatch below but there had to be at least six inches of silt and debris covering everything. She dare not start brushing it away, it would fill the space with a brown cloud that would take forever to clear. Somewhere below her in that mess was a hatch that led to the main interior of the submarine, an interior that in theory was as it was left in 1945. Including twelve crates of gold bars.

AJ shone the light on her dive computer, she had three minutes of no deco time left and she needed to find some kind of evidence. She pulled out the GoPro and filmed a three hundred and sixty degree sweep using her torch to light the interior, finishing by filming herself briefly to show she was the one there. Switching off the camera and letting it hang from her wrist again she started a more detailed search for anything removable she could take with her.

She knew any articles made with rubber or fabrics would have rotted away long ago, what she needed was something metallic that had weathered the salt water over all this time. She shined the torch in all the nooks and crannies she could reach but short of small Shrimp and a few Blennies scooting away from the beam she found nothing. She considered trying to unscrew a gauge but that required tools which she'd have to bring back down from the boat and they were probably rusted on so tight anyway.

With only a minute left of bottom time she figured her last chance to find something was to rummage in the silt below her. She stepped the other foot to the floor which felt like stepping into a bowl of flour and crouched down lower so she could touch the deck. The brown silt wafted up all around her completely filling the interior and for a moment she was overcome with fear as all vision was lost and even her torch was just a faint glow at the end of her arm. AJ calmed herself enough to reach down and start dragging her hand through the silt and debris hoping to scoop up something useful. Her hand came across something smooth, circular and unmoving. After running her hand around it she realized it was the dogging ring for the interior hatch. She stretched further and felt a few odd shaped things that she guessed was broken coral.

AJ knew her time was up so she stretched as far as she could and made a final sweep through the soft sediment. Her fingers brushed something that moved. It had some weight to it, felt smooth which suggested it was man made and wasn't fixed down. She stretched out her arm as far as she could and brushed it again which only moved it further away. She was at the full extent of the octopus hose which was pulling at the side of her mouth as she reached out, she needed more slack. With her other hand she tugged on the hose, trying to drag the BCD and tank a bit closer over the hatch above, but it wouldn't budge. She wriggled around in the silted out blackness, trying to get more extension but it was no use.

With one final effort she lurched around the side of the ladder and as her fingers wrapped around the object the regulator was pulled from the side of her mouth. Well, she thought, at least Thomas knows where the wreck is so Reg can come and retrieve my body. They'll take a look at the BCD and tank outside and find my body in here being picked apart by the fishes and crabs and realize what an idiot I'd been. She thought of the article in the diving magazine using her as an example of how ignoring the rules and procedures leads to disaster, a perfect example of how the second thing that goes bad causes the tragedy. The first in this case being a series of poor decisions by her.

Gathering her wits and holding her breath, she stood up still clutching the object in her left hand. She managed to wrap a finger around the torch which she passed from her right hand. Reaching up she was then able to grab a rung of the ladder and began climbing up. Fighting off the urge to panic she kept going up the ladder and feeling the octopus and hose brushing against her calmed her considerably, at least she knew it was there. Once her head poked out into the light through the hatch she reached up and placed the object and torch on the conning tower deck and used her left hand to sweep around her for the hose. Finding it she chased it to the end and grabbing the regulator stuffed it in her mouth and purged it to flush the water out. The first inhale was a mixture of silty water that tasted disgusting and a hint of the precious air she craved. The second was a lungful of beautiful, clean, life preserving air.

Without wasting time to check her bottom time she threw her BCD back on, switched back to her normal reg and pulled her fins on. At this point she needed to ascend as fast as she could, so knowing how deep in the shit she was really didn't matter or change anything until she was shallower. The silt had blown out of the hatch and made a murky cloud around the conning tower but at least she could see something now. With fins on she scooped up her torch and what she could now see was a pair of binoculars she'd retrieved from the conning tower. A wave of excitement rushed over her as she pushed off of the tower and kicked back in the direction of the buoy and her boat.

Halfway up, once she cleared the silty water and could see her boat on the surface, she allowed herself to look at her computer. The word 'Deco' flashed with an arrow pointing up to the depth of '30ft'. She had eight hundred psi of air left so she should be fine to do the deco stops and she finned her way to the buoy with great relief. Once there she looped her arm around the line to secure herself in place and examined the binoculars.

The leather eye pieces and lens protectors had rotted away and the strap had succumbed too over time but the body and glass looked perfect. She gently rubbed the remaining silt from them and could clearly see the engraving by the eyepiece '7x50'. AJ turned them around in her hands, she'd seen pictures of these beautiful Carl Zeiss binoculars on the internet but to be holding a pair straight from the conning tower of a U-boat was remarkable. She looked more carefully along the side of the body and rubbed away some more dirt and staining. Hand etched on the body it read 'Wolfgang Resch'.

She had found the Captain's very own binoculars.

The droning of a boat's engine and propeller grew louder pulling her back into the moment. She looked up curiously towards the surface. Her first thought was either an inquisitive fisherman had seen the RIB boat bobbing stationary and had come to check it out, or more likely it was Reg. He may have seen her out here when he left Costa's ship or guessed she'd come back out. Boy, Reg was going to be furious at her. She shuddered at the tongue lashing she had coming from him and Pearl both.

She glanced at her computer, she had another minute at thirty feet before she had to do five more minutes at fifteen feet to put her in the clear. She tucked the binoculars away in a drop down pocket in her BCD to free up both hands. Above, the mystery boat coasted up alongside hers and she studied the hull from below. It definitely wasn't Reg, it was smaller than a Newton and had twin outboards. It was hard to make out exactly looking through thirty feet of water and a moving surface but it looked like a slightly shorter version of her boat, she could see the inflatable upper above the surface. No one else on the island had a rigid-inflatable boat?

As she pondered who it could possibly be she noted her time was up at thirty and moved further up the boat's line to fifteen feet. Many Coast Guards and Marine Police used RIB boats but the Cayman branches didn't to her knowledge, unless it was new to them? She figured she would have seen something about that in the paper though, that might not be big news in Florida or North Carolina but a new marine patrol boat on this little island was front page worthy. She was worried they'd think her boat was abandoned but surely they had to see the mooring line? They'd be confused what the hell it was attached to way out here but if they had a depth gauge they'd see it was shallow enough for an anchorage with a long lead.

The line pulled and tugged a little with the strain of the boat in the swell above, and then she noticed it didn't anymore. Confused, she looked up to see the end of the line floating down towards her from her boat, someone had untied it from the cleat and released the line. The visitor's boat had remained running the whole time but now she distinctly heard two more motors starting and with that the propellers spun into life and both boats started to leave. Stunned, she stared up at the two hulls moving away leaving a turbulent wash behind them.

Instinctively she started for the surface. She knew she was risking decompression sickness but she was about to be abandoned in the middle of the Caribbean Sea which was almost certainly a death sentence. As fast as she could ascend without risking the bends she finally broke the surface and punched some air into her BCD to hold her up. They were already fifty yards away and she couldn't recognize the second boat or the man at the helm, but the tall, athletic man driving her boat she knew instantly was Mac.

Confused and devastated she had enough wits about her to retrieve the GoPro from her BCD pocket, pull the red filter off and press record. As the boats roared away she caught a glimpse of Mac looking back at her. I knew something didn't add up with him, she berated herself, thank God I didn't sleep with that piece of shit, I'd really die disappointed in myself. She hit the button again to stop the recording and put the camera away. At least, she thought, there's video evidence of how stupid I've been, what I found, who stole my boat and abandoned me out here. If they ever find my body that is...

AJ quickly deflated her BCD and descended back to fifteen feet, surfacing before the decompression stops were complete was incredibly risky but it could be somewhat offset by at least finishing it. She knew there was safety margin built into the algorithms of the dive computer, she just hoped that combined with her youth and physical conditioning it was enough to keep her from decompression sickness.

Renfro throttled back and coasted to a stop in the middle of the sea well south of the Bank. He waited while Mac pulled up alongside in AJ's RIB boat and they hooked the two together. Whatever combination of genes and learned behavior it takes for a human to take pleasure in harming others, Renfro had it in spades. As Mac hopped over to join him on Costa's tender even he couldn't believe how happy the Canadian seemed.

Mac didn't have anything against AJ, he'd been pretty keen to sleep with her last night, after all he thought she was quite a knockout, but he cared more about the money than any girl he'd ever met. He was actually a little surprised she didn't succumb to his charm, usually he had no problem getting women to do whatever he wanted them to. Historically the problem was getting them to leave him alone once he was done with them. She'd actually resisted giving him any useful information which Renfro had pointed out to him in no uncertain terms.

Pieces of what he'd told AJ were true, he was indeed the son of a military father and had moved around the world which was how he met Renfro many years ago. James Mackenzie was eight years younger than Art Renfro but their fathers had both been assigned to their respective consulates in Japan, one as a diplomat and one as the military police chief. The two fathers happened to frequent the same squash club and eventually enjoyed weekly games. Over the year their postings coincided they and their wives had become friends so the boys had known each other from a young age. Renfro had always been impressed how the eight year old had stood up for himself when he'd picked on him and when their paths crossed again twenty years later in a bar in Houston, Texas, Mac impressed him again taking on three of Art's crew. Once he realized who he was he pulled his men off and bought the bloodied man a drink.

Mac had spent the prior ten years bouncing around between jobs from construction to divemaster on a boat in the Red Sea, but nothing seem to last. Renfro offered him a job on the spot and Mac had finally found a home with his crew of hard living ruffians.

Over the years Mac had helped Renfro beat the crap out of countless people. Men, women, young, old, he'd broken bones, he'd left them unconscious, he'd kidnapped, he'd done everything except take a life, until now. He'd known for years that this day would come and he'd be expected to do his part but he was still shocked how his boss appeared to be savouring and celebrating the moment. That aside, this was going to be a huge payday and a fun project cutting that gold out of the submarine. Any pangs of conscience he had evaporated quickly when he reminded himself of that.

AJ's GPS was removable so Mac had grabbed that and her cell phone before leaving her boat. He had wiped the wheel and controls down to clear his finger prints, anywhere else on the boat they were found would be fine, he'd been a customer onboard for several days with plenty of witnesses. He gave Renfro the GPS which he immediately threw overboard, the cell phone he tried to unlock but it was password protected so he tossed it as well. They loosened the lines holding the two boats together and let AJ's drift away.

It would most likely be found, or at least seen at some point, but with the direction of the surface current it would certainly miss the island. She'd be missing with the boat found adrift and the only conclusion would be she was out alone and went overboard. Wouldn't be any proof otherwise. By the time the search bore fruit they'd be long gone with twelve crates of gold bullion. Renfro fired up the tender and made a heading for Grand Cayman, only thing left to do on the island was to gather his and Mac's stuff from the hotel. Tonight they'd be back on the Explorador de los Océanos and at daybreak they'd be cutting holes in a submarine.

Reg's other two boats were both back to the dock about the same time. He and Pearl met them as they pulled alongside the jetty, helped tie them in and unload their divers and empty tanks. Reg asked all his crew if they'd seen or heard from AJ but none of them had seen her since lunchtime.

He'd already taken his boat out to its mooring so he asked one of his captains to leave his boat at the dock and checked it had plenty of diesel. Reg didn't know what was going on but he felt something wasn't right and he wanted to be prepared.

Pearl joined him at the end of the jetty having wrapped up her paperwork. They watched as their third boat motored out to its mooring. He tried AJ's cell phone again, this time it went straight to voicemail without ringing. He shook his head. "Something's not right, this isn't like her to just disappear and not answer her phone."

Pearl was getting more and more anxious but was trying to stay calm and clear headed. She kept reliving the last time she saw AJ, she'd asked where Reg was and then took her boat out to the mooring. Pearl distinctly remembered watching her leave the dock and she was idling in the direction of the mooring when she'd turned and walked back towards the hut. She must have changed her mind and gone somewhere in her boat. She tried to stay positive despite feeling as worried as Reg did.

"She probably got her phone wet and it's dead, that's why she's not answering." Happened to everyone on the boats about once a year, they'd donate a phone to the ocean, jump in the water with it still in a shorts pocket or get it so wet on the boat it would fry the electronics.

"It was about this time last year she dropped her phone off the dock and was running around in a panic as no one could get a hold of her. She's probably lionfish hunting somewhere and doesn't know her phone's dead." Pearl put her arm around the big man as he continued to stare out to sea.

"Maybe," he said quietly, "I hope that's it. Just seems odd while we have so much going on."

They stood in silence for a while, a gentle breeze cooling their faces from the warm sun that was starting to make its way down the sky towards the horizon. There was a scattering of boats milling about off Seven Mile Beach as far as the eye could see but none was the distinct RIB boat they were looking for.

Reg struggled with the guilt of not being able to father children with Pearl who he knew had desperately wanted to have a family. Now, with the fear creeping in of what might have happened to AJ, the girl that felt like a daughter to them, a deeper guilt plagued his mind. What if he couldn't protect her? What if he couldn't stop Pearl from losing her? Any other time he'd be concerned about her whereabouts but not unduly worried. The presence of Renfro and Costa changed all that, he knew what these men were capable of and how badly they wanted to find the wreck. They would stop at nothing.

Pearl pointed to the horizon and nudged him. "What's that?"

She turned and ran up the pier to the hut, leaving Reg squinting trying to make out what kind of boat he was seeing coming in from deep water. Pearl returned out of breath with a pair of binoculars which she thrust into his hands. Reg picked up the boat in the lenses and dialed in the focus. "That bastard…" He muttered.

"Is it her? It's a RIB boat ain't it?" Her London accent getting stronger under duress.

"Yeah, but it's not hers, it's the tender off Costa's ship." He handed the binoculars back to Pearl and turned away, striding up the dock.

"Where you going?" She asked after him as he dashed away.

"Have a chat with that piece of shit Renfro," he barked

over his shoulder as he strode towards his Land Rover.

AJ bobbed in the water and took stock of her situation. While on her makeshift safety stop she'd realized she had a line that reached the surface she could use as a tether, the one her boat had recently been attached to. She tied the end off to a D-ring on her BCD so once she surfaced and inflated her BCD she was a human buoy moored to the reef below.

She had about a hundred and seventy PSI left in her tank which was very little to dive with but would last a few minutes if she had to dive shallow for any reason. Her computer freaked out on her first ascent to the surface and told her she was in deco again. It had then given up and locked her out so it couldn't be used for diving for the next twenty hour hours. That didn't matter, she didn't plan anymore dives in the near future and as for decompression sickness she'd know soon enough. If her joints started aching really badly and she felt like crap, she needed a decompression chamber. Seeing as that wasn't an option right now it would be what it would be.

Golden rule of search and rescue, if possible stay put. Searching for a moving target is much harder than a stationary one, if what you're looking for could have moved to where you've already looked it's exponentially harder. Tethering to the line meant her position was set so it was just a matter of time before a boat came by close enough for her to signal. That could be a cruise ship that blindly mows right over her of course, but if that scenario played out she'd use that last bit of air to head down and hope for the best.

All things considered she felt she was in decent shape for someone who'd been abandoned in the open ocean. AJ felt fortunate that the seas had laid down today, it would make her easier to see and a lot better than being tossed around in bigger waves. She slowly turned all the way around three hundred and sixty degrees and then unwound again so the line wasn't twisted. It was certainly a creepy feeling looking out at nothing but open ocean and she fought back a rush of anxiety. She tried to put the fear aside by focusing on her assets.

She didn't have a life raft but she had her BCD that acted as a life vest so she didn't have to expend energy staying afloat. She was anchored in place within signaling distance of any fishermen coming out to the Bank which she felt should happen over the next few days. She had her inflatable safety marker which was a bright orange tube about five feet long when unrolled and inflated that made her easier to spot. It lived rolled up tightly in a BCD pocket.

She'd already decided she had to be prepared to spend several days afloat. She figured if she wasn't spotted by a passing fisherman then Reg and Thomas would come out searching. As long as she stayed over the submarine, although they didn't have the GPS coordinates, Thomas knew the approximate location close enough to find her. The key was staying put. On the flip side, the bad guys presumably assumed they'd found her at the sub and would be back to dive it. They must have planned on her being taken away by the current never to be found again, which saved them from actually pulling a trigger or finding some other nasty way of finishing her off. How sensitive of them she thought.

It was hard for AJ to process how a man she'd been so attracted to and even kissed last night could leave her to die today. Mac had to be an Oscar winning actor and a first class douche bag. She felt the anger boiling inside, mixed with embarrassment of having misjudged someone so badly it spilled over and tears welled in her eyes. Crying made her even madder and she slapped the water and screamed as loudly as she could, wiping the tears away and cussing up a storm.

Calming herself down she considered the problem of

Renfro returning. It was five thirty so there was about two hours of daylight left, plenty to do a reconnaissance dive, she just hoped they'd wait until tomorrow. She really didn't know what option she had when they did come back, she was sure they'd be surprised to find her still there instead of floating off miles away as they'd intended. If she saw them soon enough maybe she could duck under using the last of her air and come up under their swim step and hide? She ran a bunch of scenarios through her mind but none seemed very appetizing.

She moved on to other challenges she faced. It would be uncomfortable without food and fresh water but not life threatening for several days. If it rained she needed to capture some drinking water somehow but short of tipping her head back and opening her mouth she didn't have much to save the drops in. A bigger problem was going to be hypothermia. As balmy as the Caribbean water felt she knew it was still around eighty two degrees Fahrenheit which was well below the body's normal average core temperature of ninety eight point six. Extended immersion in the water would drag her body temperature down and once it got below ninety five hypothermia sets in. She would begin feeling the effects starting with severe shivering and mental confusion. Again, it wouldn't be life threatening in the next twenty four hours but she knew she was in for a rough time of it tonight. Still, she thought, I'd rather be cold and thirsty than running into Mac and Renfro.

Reg sped along West Bay Road behind Seven Mile Beach towards George Town. There were no piers, jetties or docks allowed along Seven Mile Beach so he guessed they were coming into Public Dock where he'd picked Renfro's man up that morning. Traffic wasn't heavy but what there was moved along at a familiar leisurely pace. Unfortunately Reg was in a hurry so he received some disgruntled honks as he passed people using the shared centre turning lane.

Reg had no idea what role Renfro currently played in AJ's whereabouts but he had an overwhelming feeling he was involved in some way. What he could accomplish by confronting him he didn't know either but he couldn't stand on the end of the pier staring at the ocean any longer, he had to do something.

The Land Rover swerved into the small gravel parking area by Public Dock and slid to a halt at the jetty. Costa's tender was the only boat at the dock and Reg spotted the man he'd taken out that morning tying the lines to the cleats on the dock. He bolted from the Land Rover and strode down the pier. The man stood up and now seeing him without the hat and sunglasses Reg recognized him as the guy that had been diving with AJ. The same guy she'd gone out on a date with and told he and Pearl about. She'd been excited about this guy, told them how nice he was, first date she'd been interested in for ages and here he was with Renfro. Reg was even more confused about what was going on and definitely more pissed off about it.

As Reg approached the boat Mac walked forward to block his path and he saw Renfro stepping onto the jetty with a grin like a Cheshire cat. Mac was a strong athletic man but didn't expect Reg to make a move so quickly and decisively. Without hesitation Reg swung with his right fist and caught Mac in the jaw knocking him off his feet and over the side of the jetty. He landed awkwardly on the bow of the boat, which being the inflatable edge, bounced him on his way into the water with a huge splash. Reg didn't even pause, the big man was in front of Renfro in four more steps and reached for his throat. He figured he had a minute at most before Mac would be back to help and he'd be a lot tougher to take on without the element of surprise.

Before Reg could reach the smaller man's throat Renfro swung with something in his hand that knocked Reg aside and felt like a truck had just hit his left shoulder. He reeled back a few steps and saw he'd been hit with a steel pry bar and Renfro was stepping in again for another go. Reg used to be pretty nimble for a big fellow but it had been years since he'd thrown a punch or had one come his way and he felt sluggish as he tried to dodge the blow. It caught him on the arm and hurt like hell but as Renfro recoiled for a third strike he took his opportunity to step in closer, blocking the pry bar with his left arm he swung for his stomach with all his might.

Reg heard all the air leave Renfro's lungs and the man staggered back gasping and doubling over. Reg pounced, grabbing his right arm that was clutching the pry bar he slammed it against Renfro's body and drove him backwards off the jetty into the RIB boat where he landed hard on his back. Reg jumped down into the boat and ripped the bar from his hand holding it aloft ready to swing.

Mac had extricated himself from the water onto the pier and hesitated as he arrived by the boat when he saw Reg poised over Renfro. "Stay right there!" Reg barked.

Mac looked down at Renfro who was groaning on the deck of the boat and raised his arms to signal he was complying. "Where's AJ?" Reg roared. Renfro made a gurgling sound that Reg realized was a pained laugh. He really wanted to kick him as hard as he could but he managed to hold back. "You piece of shit, where is she?!"

Renfro looked up at him with that same arrogant expression despite being laid out on the floor trying to catch his breath. "Ask her boyfriend over there, maybe he knows," he spluttered out.

"One of you better start talking or I'm gonna be breaking

bones until you do!" Reg looked back and forth between the two of them hoping one would say something, neither did but Renfro was getting his breath back and continued to grin at Reg, baiting him. "You don't have the balls Moore, besides what makes you think we know anything about your little bitch?" Renfro propped himself up against the console as he spoke. "Mac was hoping to get in her pants tonight, weren't you Mac? He'll be upset if she's gone mi..."

Reg swung the pry bar before Renfro could finish the sentence and struck him across the forearm as he raised his arm to protect himself. He screamed in pain as his radius bone broke with a hideous cracking sound. Mac started towards the boat from the jetty until Reg raised the pry bar again while looking at Mac, clearly signaling he'd strike again if he didn't back off. Unsure, he halted and stayed on the pier. Reg would still have to deal with him to leave the boat but for now he realized his boss would take another hit before he could reach Reg.

Renfro's sneer had finally vanished and was replaced with pain infused rage, he spat the words out, clutching his broken arm. "Fuck you Moore! I'll kill you for this you son of a bitch! You'll never find that little whore of yours! Never, you fucking fool, never find her!"

Mac started to panic, Renfro was mouthing off and saying too much in his fury. "Shut up Art! He doesn't know what he's yapping about Moore, he's just trying to rile you, we have no idea where AJ is! We've been on Costa's boat all day, you know that, you took us both out there. We came straight here with the tender."

Renfro continued cussing under his breath at Reg but had gotten control of himself. Mac carried on, trying to diffuse the situation. "If you hadn't beat the shit out of him we could have helped you look for her. I really like AJ she's a cool chick, seriously we've got no idea where she is."

Mac was working on his best sympathetic look but Reg was no fool, he knew he was full of shit. Renfro had confirmed in Reg's mind that they had been involved but Mac had accomplished what he'd hoped and got the situation calmed down, now Reg had to make a decision. He could keep beating on Renfro in an attempt to get more information that he was sure he had but was unlikely to give up or he could start the search now as he was certain AJ was somewhere out there on the water or on Costa's boat. Reg had had his fair share of fights over the years but he wasn't a violent man. He took no pleasure in causing Renfro pain despite loathing the man and knowing he had something to do with AJ's disappearance. He also knew all he had was a pry bar and if he went back to hitting Renfro Mac had no reason to hold off and he'd be contending with him too. "This ain't over Renfro, believe me."

Reg could see the contempt in his eyes and knew Renfro thought he was weak for not continuing the beating. For a second he almost changed his mind and at least got one more shot in but the urgency to start searching was greater. He looked up at Mac. "Get in the bow of the boat and stay there, you can have a broken arm too if you try anything."

Mac raised his arms again and walked to the front of the boat, jumping in from the jetty. The boat rocked as he landed and Renfro groaned in pain. Reg wanted some maneuvering room to get out of there and figured it would be harder for Mac to ambush him from the boat. He stepped to the dock, never taking his eyes off Mac and once he was clear of the boat ran up the pier to the Land Rover.

The sunset was turning into a gorgeous one with bright oranges and yellows filling the horizon outlining the wispy clouds. AJ was already getting cold and occasionally an involuntary shiver would run through her as her body sensed its temperature dropping and tried to warm itself. She hadn't seen a single boat, not even a dot on the horizon. From her perspective about eighteen inches above the waterline she guessed she could see for maybe a mile or so when the rolling waves picked her up. From the troughs she couldn't see anything.

The wind seemed to be staying a steady breeze so she didn't expect any bad weather to blow in. She tried to prepare herself for a very long night. Shortly after daybreak the fishermen would be out and as calm as the ocean was at least a few would head for the bank. The restaurants up and down Seven Mile Beach and in George Town would want fresh catch ready for lunch so she was optimistic someone would spot her then.

She knew Reg and Pearl would have noticed her boat missing by now but they had no way of knowing where she was. She cursed herself for not giving them the GPS coordinates of the wreck. Of course that would only have helped if someone knew she'd been stupid enough to come out here alone and dive. Thomas knew roughly where it was but the only record of the exact coordinates were in her marine GPS and written on the paperwork she'd had ready for the Port Authority. Assuming they'd sunk or set adrift her boat the only accessible copy was locked in her van, the keys for which were on the same keyring as the boat keys, on the boat. She'd even hidden the paperwork under the seat of the van so if they looked in the window for any useful clues they wouldn't see it.

AJ pondered the series of mistakes that had led her to her current predicament. She really didn't consider herself to be reckless or illogical but nothing she'd done this afternoon held any water in that argument. It was just plain stupid to come out here alone she decided. She'd been so concerned about the challenges of making the solo dive without losing the boat, she hadn't given a thought to how other people might play into this. Of course Costa and Renfro would play dirty, everything Reg had told her about Renfro spelled out the man was capable of anything without conscience.

As nightfall descended the darkness seemed to cloak her and she was hit with a strange mixture of claustrophobia and awareness of being a speck in an immense ocean. It made no sense how she could feel so enclosed yet conscious of the massive space she was lost in. She was intent on reassuring herself that things were the same at night as they were in the day, just dark, when something bumped her leg.

AJ jumped and her heart leapt into her throat. Instinctively she drew her legs and feet up tightly underneath her and fumbled for her torch. Slipping her mask back over her face she dipped her head down in the water and shone the light around. It illuminated a narrow beam maybe twenty or thirty feet down into the inky blackness and she moved it around in a sweeping motion to see what was down there. The light flashed across the rope and startled her, she could barely make out the buoy when she followed the line down so that told her she could only light up about thirty feet. She cursed herself for not charging the torch batteries more often.

She lifted her head up and took another breath, she didn't dare use her regulator and suck on the precious little air in the tank. She knew she might also need what battery was left so she dipped her head for a last check around her and that's when she caught a glimpse of the powerful grey body circling beneath her.

AJ loved diving with sharks and had spent countless hours underwater in close proximity to them. She'd never been bothered by one or felt seriously threatened by one. This was different.

AJ knew all about the sharks keen senses, not only the

five that humans have but also electrosensors and two forms of pressure sensors that allow them to identify and hunt prey extremely effectively. SCUBA divers in the water appear nothing like food to a shark, they're noisy, covered in rubber, neoprene and metal parts, but a human on the surface is more curious to them. They can appear like a wounded creature flapping around when they're swimming or playing and in certain waters humans are confused for seals that sharks do hunt.

She imagined she'd be fine if she didn't flounder around, especially if there was only one but if more showed up they might get competitive and more aggressive. Her hope that the bump had cured the shark of his curiosity was dashed when she was bumped again, a little firmer this time and a dorsal fin briefly broke the surface about six feet from her. The clear night was now alive with stars but no moon yet so the light was faint but at least it wasn't pitch black. She made out another dorsal fin a little further away about the same time a shark rubbed along her leg under water. There was definitely more than one but she couldn't make out what kind they were.

Most common near the island are the Caribbean reef sharks which as their name suggests spend most of their time in shallower water and are smaller and less aggressive. Offshore in the open water could be bull or tiger sharks which are larger and a lot more hostile. She prayed they were reef sharks that would be less likely to attack. A bull shark might take a bite just to figure out what she was, a taste test. Even if he decided he didn't like it, she'd still be left with a fatal wound. She felt herself being lifted in the water as the shark glided underneath her for what seemed like ages, this was not a small shark, this was not a reef shark. She had to do something, she couldn't just bob here trying to hold her legs up, her stomach and quads were already burning from the effort, but she didn't have a lot of options.

AJ racked her brain to think of anything she had that could be used as a deterrent, she certainly didn't have any weapons, her dive knife would cause a superficial wound and blood in the water was the last thing she needed. What she did need was some way of getting herself out of the water or at least elevated so she wasn't suspended vertically as she was now. Her SCUBA tank and BCD would be of the least interest to a shark, they didn't smell good, vibrate or move like a fish. The thought occurred to her maybe she could balance on top of them.

To do that she had to slip out of the BCD, try and perch on it and use it as a mini raft which meant quite a bit of movement in the water. The BCD was inflated so with the tank hanging down acting like a keel it was actually fairly stable but not very big. She tried tipping over on her back and then unclipping the waist strap of the BCD and shuffling herself backwards until her backside was on the BCD. Slowly and carefully she started sitting up. The tank immediately began sinking under water with her weight directly over it and the wings of the BCD started folding around her either side as they tried to stay afloat filled with air. The result wasn't as stable as she'd hoped and she, the tank and most of the BCD were submerged but the assembly levelled itself out there and she had her feet drawn up out of the water.

The BCD was still tethered to her submerged line so it tugged and rocked in the swell requiring her to constantly focus on staying balanced. More than anything it made her nervous not being directly connected to the line anymore, if she fell off and lost contact with the BCD she'd be screwed.

She felt another few bumps and saw a couple more fins but the sharks appeared to be losing interest and AJ allowed herself to breathe a little easier again. She took a moment to scan the horizon. As the swell raised her up she could make out a slight glow in the sky straight east which had to be the lights of Grand Cayman. Just that tiny connection with civilization was a huge relief and a surprising comfort to her. For a few seconds each time she was raised up she felt like safety was within reach.

She slowly spun her makeshift raft around to check out all around her. The western sky was now black like the rest with any sign of the sun long gone. Something way out there just caught her eye, she strained to pick up two separate twinkling lights. A red light that appeared to be blinking was slightly south of the other that appeared more yellowy white. Damn, she thought, the red light is the mast light on Costa's boat at the other end of the Bank! She couldn't pick out the mast top in daylight but the red light was clear to see against the black night.

She hadn't thought about Costa for several hours or the prospect of them returning tonight as other perils had consumed her attention, now at least she knew where they were. What was the other light though? It seemed to be further away which meant it had to be bigger if she could see it. Whatever it was it was a long way away and she couldn't tell whether it was coming, going or running parallel to her position so she resolved to keep an eye on its progress while she settled in for an uncomfortable night.

Chapter 27
Grand Cayman, 2017

Illuminated by the hotels, condos and street lights Reg raced back up West Bay Road in the Land Rover and dialed Inspector Roy Whittaker of the Royal Cayman Islands Police Service. The two men had known each other for years and Reg had often been called upon to help in underwater search and rescues around the island with the Police Marine Unit. Roy was also a big fan of Pearl's and would often stop by the Fox and Hare of a Friday evening after his shift. Reg knew they needed to act fast if there was still a chance to find AJ, and his friend was the best place to start.

The voice on the end of the phone was slow, relaxed and deliberate with a light Caymanian accent. "Evening Reg, how's that lovely wife of yours?"

"Hey Roy, she's great but AJ's in trouble, I need your help." Whittaker immediately picked up the urgency in Reg's tone and switched into official police mode. "That's not good man, what's the problem?"

Reg launched into the briefest version of the story he could put together that made any sense, including the submarine, Costa and even his scuffle with Renfro. Whittaker let him spill everything before he came back with questions. As incredulous as the story was the policeman had never seen reason to doubt Reg's integrity and honesty over the years and took him at his word now.

"Not been seen since around one o'clock you say?" Reg

affirmed and Whittaker continued. "You're confident she's not just had trouble with the boat?"

"She has a cell phone and a VHF radio on the boat and she kept a battery booster on there in case of a battery or alternator problem, she would have been able to communicate from the boat. I really feel she's been separated from her boat Roy."

There was a pause on the phone. Whittaker was a man who worked from the evidence and followed a bread crumb trail, he liked to process information and formulate a logical plan in his investigations. "You know that's too soon for us to launch a missing persons search man? Based on her not been seen for five or six hours." It was a rhetorical statement and Reg let him continue. "But there's some suspicious circumstances that's for sure. I need something more to send out the cavalry though Reg, let me get a man to the hospital and see if this Art Renfro fellow has showed up there, maybe he'll slip something useful.

Of course the only crime that is clearly apparent so far is you assaulting a fella. Pretty sure Renfro's buddy will back him up on the assault, so you know I'll be forced to at least investigate that, right?"

Reg hadn't thought that part of it through, he knew what a scumbag Renfro was but he was still the one with a broken arm and a witness that would say it was unprovoked. "Jeez Roy, pull up the man's record, it has to be a file about as long as War and Peace! You know I wouldn't do that unless he came at me first."

"I'm sure that's the case Reg but you can see I don't have so much to work with this end. As far as sending the Marine Unit out to this guy Costa's boat it's the same situation, there's nothing except your story to say this man is involved in anything illicit. My boss is not gonna let me launch a search on a wealthy visitors boat based on that. Word gets out we do that and every fancy yacht owner will be up in arms, you know that, those folks have a lot of influence on the island."

Incredibly frustrated, Reg knew the man was right but they had to get to Costa's boat, if they'd snatched AJ that was the place she'd be. Only reason they'd do that would be to get the subs location from her and it terrified him to think what they'd do to get that information. One thing that gave him hope was the fact that Renfro almost certainly was at the hospital right now getting a bone set and he presumed he'd be the one to handle an interrogation.

He dreaded to think of the other scenarios that seemed plausible. First would be if she tried to dive the sub alone and something went wrong. AJ was an incredibly skilled and experienced diver but a solo open ocean dive to that depth with only a submerged mooring she'd described to him was perilous and damn right foolhardy. Second would be if Costa and Renfro had found her at the sub. In that case she was nothing but a witness they needed out of the way.

He shuddered at the thought. "I get it Roy but we have to start looking, you know the drill, every passing minute reduces the chance of finding her, best chance she has is if she's on that boat! If you can't send someone then I'm going out there myself."

"Please don't do that Reg, don't make this worse, you'll be forcing me to end up chasing you 'stead of trying to find our girl here. I know we need to move quickly and all but I need to work on it from my end so we do this correctly, if there's foul play involved we must go by the book. I'll start by seeing if there's any Marine Unit boats on the water right now, if there is I can make them aware of Mr. Costa's boat and we can start watching it. Promise me you won't go out to the boat Reg?"

Reg sighed, he felt confident his friend would do all he

could but the strings attached to proceeding by the book would slow things down so much. Of course the police after him wouldn't help things either and he understood the Inspector's predicament. "Alright Roy, for now I'll not, but we've already lost daylight, I need to get out on the water and at least start looking for her boat. Once I find Thomas I'm heading out."

He promised to update Whittaker once he had anything more. Hanging up, he arrived at the Bodden family house in West Bay. It was a typical single level concrete house with a stucco exterior and a clean, sparse but well kept garden surrounding it. Cars were packed in the driveway and parked all along both sides of the narrow street, there was no mistaking an event was going on at the house.

Reg didn't have time to park courteously and pulled in tight to the cars in the driveway leaving just enough room for a car to still get by on the road. He ran towards the house where he could hear the commotion of a gathering out back with music playing. He went around the dimly lit side to the brightly floodlit back yard full of people dressed up in their best church going outfits, most were Caymanian locals. He quickly scanned the party searching for Thomas and several people close by turned in curiosity at the stranger in shorts and a polo shirt crashing the family service.

Thomas spotted Reg before he could pick him out, Reg wasn't used to seeing the lad in a suit and tie, he'd only ever seen him in board shorts and a tee shirt before. Seeing Reg show up at the house immediately told Thomas something was up.

"Hi there Mr. Moore, is there a problem, is AJ okay?"

Reg put his hand on Thomas' shoulder, his tone confirmed all was not well. "Have you seen or heard from AJ since lunchtime or did she tell you where she was going this afternoon?"

Thomas looked around, people were staring and close

enough to hear, he guided Reg back around the side of the house out of earshot and lowered his voice. "I've not seen her or talked to her, last I heard she was going to the Port Authority to... you know... register the wreck and all, she never said nothing about anything else."

"I hate to ask you Thomas, I know it's your uncle's funeral but AJ's missing and I suspect those guys with the salvage boat out at the Bank have something to do with it, can you come and help me search for her?"

Thomas didn't hesitate. "I'll be out the front in two minutes, I gotta change outta this suit and tell my Mama real fast."

Pearl was waiting on the boat at their dock with the motor idling. She'd already loaded torches, the big waterproof metal kind, some sandwiches, Clif bars and a large thermos of coffee. Reg hurtled into the car park in the Land Rover and he and Thomas ran down the jetty glancing at the dark and foreboding ocean beyond. Thomas cleared the lines and jumped aboard as Pearl eased the Newton away and Reg spread a navigational chart out on the table below.

He heard Pearl yell down from the console upstairs. "Got a heading Reg?"

"Straight west to start, I'll have something better in a moment."

"Straight west," she affirmed, "I called the boys, they'll be a few minutes behind us but they're on their way, we'll have all the boats out."

"Thanks love" Reg shouted back and nodded for Thomas to join him. Pearl opened up the motor wasting no time getting to full speed.

"Narrow it down for me Thomas, what's your best guess where you were?" Although Thomas was young Reg was aware he'd spent his whole life in these waters and knew them as well as any man. The kid was pretty switched on and could read a map and use a GPS which few Caymanians chose to do, preferring to rely on their experience and sense of direction. Thomas slid his finger over the chart picking up the Bank and the pinnacle that was incorrectly depth marked, the deeper of the two. "Right there."

Reg felt his phone vibrating in his pocket and fished it out, the caller ID read 'Roy Whittaker'.

Reg shouted to Thomas. "Go up and tell Pearl two hundred and eighty degrees, just ten north of straight west, you watch the GPS okay?" Thomas leapt up the ladder to the fly bridge and Reg yelled into the phone over the noise of the motor and wind.

"Anything new Roy?" He strained to hear what the man replied.

"Have you had your VHF on?"

"No, we just left the dock, what's going on?"

"Old Robert Ebanks found AJ's RIB boat, it was drifting about four or five miles off the southwest corner of the island. Lucky he was heading back towards Bodden Town from being out west. If he'd not seen it Lord knows where it would've ended up. He's towing it in to George Town for us. No sign of AJ I'm afraid though Reg."

Reg was devastated. He'd played it all out in his mind and figured she had to have been separated from her boat or they would have heard from her, but the reality was still like a bolt of lightning. His blood began to boil. "I'm going to Costa's boat! That bastard must have her!"

The Inspector actually raised his voice, Reg had never heard him do that before and sensed the urgency from him. "Do not go out there! I have the Marine Unit dispatched, they're on their way now Reg. You need to be figuring out where she may have been if she was diving and got separated from the boat."

Reg calmed and focused on a search plan. He looked at the chart and picked out the spot where the boat was picked up. "If I take a point about four miles off the southwest corner of Grand and follow that back reverse of the surface current which is south south east right now it takes me straight to the wreck site Roy. I'll start there or as close as Thomas and I can figure it to be and then we'll follow the current."

"And Reg?"

"Yeah?"

"You're right, that Renfro guy's a real arsehole. We've detained his buddy Mac and we'll do the same with him once he's out of surgery. You did a pretty good number on his arm, they're putting it back together with plates now."

"I was aiming for his head."

"Well, I'm glad your aim isn't better then..."

Roy said he'd update them when he knew more and hung up.

Chapter 28
Grand Cayman, 2017

AJ was floating on her BCD still safely tethered to the reef near the wreck of the U-1026, but she had a serious problem.

The other set of lights she'd noticed were now a lot closer and she could clearly see they belonged to a cruise ship heading towards George Town. The unnerving part was she could only see the broad bow which meant it was heading directly towards her. At over a hundred feet wide and quite a bit taller than that above the water it was a daunting sight. She pictured all the happy people onboard having their evening meal, enjoying some drinks, maybe soaking up some live entertainment while they unknowingly plowed right over her.

The cruise ships usually arrived early in the morning having travelled overnight, this one must have been delayed somewhere in its itinerary to be coming to port in the evening. Just her luck she thought.

She wondered if anyone way up there on the bridge would even notice her torch if she tried signaling? Deciding that the only way they might would be when they were too close to perform a turn to miss her anyway she moved to another plan.

As the massive ship continued approaching, AJ did some math. From what she could recall these ships were almost a thousand feet long and had a draft of around thirty feet. She figured her only avoidance option was down as by the time it was close enough to tell its exact path she wouldn't be able to swim clear either side of it. The pull of the water displaced around the hull would drag her in from probably fifty feet or more either side and she felt she couldn't get further than that away. With a draft of thirty feet she'd have to get well below that to not get pulled back up into the colossal propellers, she estimated sixty feet down to be sure.

These ships made about twenty to twenty two knots which was around twenty four miles an hour. She calculated that into feet per minute which took a few tries and had her racking her brain to recall how many feet were in a mile. When she was done AJ decided the ship would take about thirty seconds to pass over her if she was stationary. She'd turned the valve off on her tank to make sure no air could escape accidently but last she'd checked before that she had a hundred and seventy PSI left. On a normal, calm dive she used about 50PSI every minute at sixty feet down.

This would not be a calm dive. She'd need to go under around thirty seconds before the ship reached her to get down to sixty feet, stay there for another thirty seconds before taking a further thirty seconds to safely ascend well clear of the thrashing propellers and broiling wake behind the ship. That's a hundred and fifty PSI in calm conditions, leaving twenty PSI of life sustaining air… in calm conditions. She would be plunging into blackness with a hundred and ten thousand ton vessel steaming over her, hardly a calm environment.

Next problem was she had no way of knowing her depth or time below as her dive computer had locked her out after going into deco. A safety measure on the computer's part was now an additional hazard for her current predicament. She would be in the dark while diving in the dark. Only thing she could do was count in her head and hope she swam down rather than laterally. Then she remembered she had the line to the reef. She could use the line as a guide, at least for direction, but still wouldn't know her depth.

The cruise ship appeared like it was bearing down on her but she knew it was still maybe half a mile away. Dive too early and she'd run out of air, dive too late and it would hit her or drag her into the turbulent flow being fed to the propellers. She had a lump in her throat and felt like she could throw up at any time. This monolith would most likely crush, thrash and obliterate her into fish food and no one would ever know what happened to her. She slid off her makeshift perch on the BCD and put her arms back through the straps again, hoping the bull sharks had gone hunting somewhere else.

The BCD was still tied to the line which AJ realized was thirty feet long, if she swam down the line towards the reef until the boat line she was tied to became taught against the submerged buoy she'd be at sixty feet. Now she had depth and direction taken care of, all she had to do was count. And breathe very little. But she'd also still be attached to the reef if she survived this escapade and would remain in place near the wreck where she had the best chance of being found. She reached over her shoulder and turned the tank back on. Next she unclipped her torch from her BCD and turned that on so it was ready and finally she dumped all the air from her BCD so she was prepared to dive.

Judging the ships distance from her in the black of night with it coming straight at her was almost impossible and she was fighting back panic the closer it came. The bow wake was visible and she tried counting until it reached a point she estimated was halfway to her but with the rise and fall of the swell she'd lose her reference point. At twenty seconds counting in her head she realized it was more than halfway to her and it felt like it was towering over her like a booming elephant over an ant, she was too late.

With a big gulp of air from the surface she plunged under and kicked as hard as she could with the torch illuminating the way in front of her. She made her gulp of air last until she could see the buoy and then popped the regulator in her mouth to start breathing off the tank. The first pull on the reg was mostly water as she daren't purge it and waste any air. Choking and spitting it finally gave her air and she grabbed the line below the buoy and pulled with her left hand while lighting the way with the torch in her right.

The noise of the massive engines were amplified under water and combined with the rushing and swirling of water for a deafening, terrifying roar. She felt a tug on the BCD as she reached the extent of the line from the buoy and clung to the line there at what she hoped was sixty feet and safety. She tried to take easy breaths on the regulator but she was winded from the manic swim down and almost paralyzed in fear. The noise took on a different, more enclosed tone even louder than before and she shone the torch up to see streaks through the water above her which she knew was the hull of the ocean hotel and the water being displaced violently around it.

The line to the reef began whipping and bucking as though a monster above was shaking it and she clung as tightly as she could while the water around her became more turbulent. The racket was so intense she wondered how the fish could ever survive one of these ships passing over and the waters around her kept swirling and pulling her more and more in the direction the ship was travelling.

Somehow in the middle of this complete chaos a thought dawned on her. She was tied to a buoy line hanging at thirty feet, which was the draft of the cruise ship. The buoy would rub along the bottom of the ship until it was sucked into the propellers where it would likely wrap itself around and be wrenched from the reef with her attached.

AJ grabbed at the knot on the BCD D-ring that tethered her to the line. In doing so she let go of the line to the reef which allowed the churning water to immediately drag her away from it. The knot was pulled tight from hours of tugging against the tether and she couldn't budge it, though she tore at it with her fingers. The cacophony was overwhelming and she was sure she was being pulled up closer to the ship but she fought to stay focused on the line. Grabbing her knife from its sheath on her BCD she hacked and sawed at the line but it was slack and writhing as she tumbled around in the water making it hard to cut.

The line suddenly went tight, her spinning stopped, and the direction she was pulled reversed. Not that she could tell up from down but it definitely yanked her the opposite way with a great deal of force. All the breath was knocked out of her and she gasped into the regulator to recover and get her wits about her. With the line tight she made a last hack with her knife and it finally gave, releasing her back to spinning and rolling in the washing machine under the hull. It was then she got the awful clunk in her regulator. The inhalation that ends with a diaphragm closing shut when there's no more air to deliver, the tank was finally empty.

AJ surprised herself. She actually relaxed and gave in to the will of the churning water gyrating her around. This is it she thought. 'There'll be a violent crash as I hit one of the massive propellers and it'll be lights out'. Somehow she was sure she was about to be crushed before the half lungful of air ran out and she drowned. A calm had washed over her as she accepted her death was imminent and unavoidable. It was almost comforting in some way, she didn't feel scared or panicked. As she was tossed and beaten by the ocean being forced around the colossal hull a sereneness enveloped her with a mixture of happiness at the life she'd experienced and a sadness to leave the ones she loved. What a shame she thought, to have never found the soulmate she believed was out there somewhere. She'd been fortunate to experience love but never the complete rapture of knowing you were with the one other human that made you both complete.

The ear splitting roar increased as the ferocity of the whirling grew even greater and compressed the last bit of spent air from her lungs. All she could feel was a disappointment that the ocean water she cherished would be the death of her as consciousness faded and a darkness enclosed her.

A moment later, spluttering and choking, she realized she'd broken the surface and was gasping for air. The towering mass of the cruise ship was moving away from her and she was being lifted up on a soaring wave that was the wake behind the 'Pleasure of the Seas' according to the illuminated letters she read across the stern. AJ coughed some more until she cleared the water from her throat and had enough breath to inflate her BCD to float her. Incredible she thought, 'I just dived under a speeding cruise ship and lived! Reg will never believe this!' Her next thought was the realization she was back in her initial predicament… except she was no longer tethered to the one spot they would know to look for her, she was adrift in the Caribbean Sea.

A beam of light flashed across the water in front of AJ and startled her. It took a moment for her to realize it was a search light moving across the waves. She twirled around in the water to see the source of the light was a boat about a hundred yards away. Instinctively she reached for her trusty torch on her BCD and realized it was gone. Of course, she'd had it in her hand when she dived down and somewhere in the chaos she must have dropped it. The light beam was moving further away from her. She remembered the whistle attached to her inflator line and blew into it. A muffled spitting sound emanated as the water blew out of it and she gasped to catch her breath again. The second time the whistle let out a shrill blast that sounded ear piecing to AJ but she had no idea if it could be heard a hundred yards away above the noise of the boat's motors. She blasted the whistle again.

AJ heard the boats motors shut off and the light beam scanned across the water, she blew as hard as she could. The light beam flashed across her and she franticly waved both arms in the air. The boat's motor purred back to life.

Reg and Thomas hauled AJ onto the swim step of the Newton and she collapsed in a heap, smiling up at them.

"You alright my girl?" Reg managed in a choked up voice.

AJ pulled the velcroed flap back on her BCD pocket and rummaged inside. Producing the binoculars, she held them up to Reg with a big smile.

"I know I'm an idiot… But it's definitely U-1026!"

Chapter 30
Epilogue

With the video evidence AJ provided from her camera, the case against Art Renfro and James Mackenzie for attempted murder was a slam-dunk. The Cayman courts didn't take kindly to this kind of behavior and were keen to show the world the island wouldn't tolerate such crime, or the bad press stemming from it. Both men were convicted for fifteen years.

Although each of them were happy to throw Costa under the bus it was to no avail. The Argentinian sensed things were going awry when Mac called him to report he was taking Renfro to the hospital after Reg took a pry bar to him. Costa pulled anchor and motored well clear of the twelve mile mark that put him out of Cayman Police jurisdiction. Once it was clear the whole operation was a bust he turned the Explorador de los Océanos for home. With no launch to return them to shore, Renfro's other two men took the ride with him as far as Aruba where they were unceremoniously deposited on the pier as they refueled the ship. Short of a warrant for his arrest in the Cayman Islands, Costa got away a free man and returned to his vineyard to regroup.

The financial hit the Argentinian took, having spent a good sum on the operation with no return, left him angry and in need of replenishing his savings. The fact that what he considered to be his father's gold still lay on the floor of the ocean and not funding his anti-Semitic projects, made his blood boil. As long as the treasure remained incased in U-1026, Carlos

Costa was determined and committed to retrieving it, in the name of his father.

AJ and Reg claimed and registered the wreck of the U-1026 with the Receiver of Wrecks the following day. After a long string of meetings and discussions with the Caymanian government and the officials from Germany it was decided the wreck would remain intact where it lay at least for the foreseeable future. A committee of experts was formed to investigate the feasibility, options and cost of removing the cargo with the least harm to the war wreck. The goal being to one day return the funds to families of victims of the holocaust. That was fine with AJ and Reg, it was never about the money for them.

In the meantime the U-1026 was considered an historical wreck, protected by the Cayman government and dived by permit only. A strict limit of twenty permits a month were issued and Mermaid Divers and Pearl Divers held the exclusive rights to take permit holders to the wreck.

The permit list, which upon initial release covered the first two years, sold out within forty eight hours of being announced.

The world's media descended upon the little island as soon as the news broke and for weeks AJ and Reg were inundated with interviews and requests for appearances from national newspapers to dive publications and even Time magazine. They were interviewed live via satellite for morning news shows in both the UK and America and Thomas was elevated to celebrity status on the island after AJ made him join them for CNN's feature. The buzz and attention slowed down after a few weeks and things were gradually returning to normal when the BBC contacted AJ about making a documentary about U-1026 and the discovery of the wreck. She was overwhelmed when they offered a good amount of money to have the exclusive film rights to her part in the story. Two days later while she was eagerly waiting for the formal proposal to arrive America's Discovery Channel tracked her down asking for the same thing with a better offer.

AJ had no idea what to say or how to handle any of it and was more than happy to turn it all over to her mother to act as her agent. After several months of negotiation the two channels agreed to work together on the project and AJ's fee was three times the original offer. Beryl Bailey didn't take shit from anyone.

Things soon returned to normal and apart from a new wreck to dive once a month, their routine fell back into the rhythm of island life they enjoyed before their adventure. After paying Reg and her father off for the RIB boat, AJ took the rest of the TV money and was able to make a large down payment on a small two bedroom condo on the water in West Bay. She continued to live in her little beachfront apartment and rented the condo out to a couple of Reg's crew. Choosing the income over the extra space was typical of her frugal nature and besides, the Atlanta couple were distraught when she mentioned she may move out.

Thomas passed all his divemaster course requirements so the two of them now split the diving duties which was working out well as AJ had a lot more bookings to organize with their new found fame. Pretty soon she was sending her overflow clients to Reg and filling his boats to the point they were having to turn customers away through the summer. An additional boat seemed inevitable and Reg, Pearl and AJ worked together on ordering a new Newton, this time under Mermaid Divers.

The wreck of the sail boat was also registered and marked as a war grave. The German authorities took great interest and diligently tracked down descendants of the U-1026 crew to inform the families of their loved ones final resting place. AJ and Reg received a multitude of letters and emails over the following months from members of the families. Many had questions, some enquired about visiting the island but all sent their heartfelt appreciation and thanks for closing the book on the mystery of what befell their beloved family members.

Acknowledgements

This book would not exist without the unwavering support and encouragement from my amazing wife Cheryl and great friend James Guthrie. The influence of your encouragement and input should not be underestimated.

My wonderful Mum and Dad always encouraged my creative adventures and for that and much, much more I'm forever grateful and in their debt.

A big thank you to Michael & Jo Harvey, Craig Lobo, Chase Campen, Rich Rutherford, Markus Niemela and Michael Zimicki for their friendship, honesty and support. All of your input was welcomed and appreciated whether utilized or not. Casey and Keith Keller of Neptune's Divers, Grand Cayman for their inspiration, training and friendship. Finally, Nick whose last name escapes me but he was the young instructor at the Grand Caymanian in 2001 that gave me my first dive experience which was clearly unforgettable.

About the Author

Nicholas Harvey was born and raised in England before emigrating to America in the late eighties. Writing is a second calling alongside a successful career in professional motorsports in both Europe and the States. He and his wife Cheryl live in North Carolina and have been certified divers since 2001, Nicholas is trained as a PADI Divemaster.

Made in the USA
Columbia, SC
27 March 2019